TANNING SOME HIDE

Still busy butchering, Barlow had worked his way around to the other side of the buffalo, leaving his back toward his two companions. Crunkleton, seeing an opportunity, suddenly charged at Barlow, his knife raised. Barlow spun when his dog began barking and brought an arm up instinctively as he did. The arm partially blocked Crunkleton's knife thrust, though the blade sank into Barlow's shoulder just below that collarbone on the right side.

As Crunkleton tried to jerk the knife free to stab him again, Barlow kneed him in the stomach, the power of it doubling Crunkleton over and lifting him a foot off the ground. Barlow caught hold of Crunkleton's neck. At the same time, he jerked his knee up, and it smashed into Crunkleton's chin. Crunkleton groaned and fell, but Barlow was too enraged now to let him lie there.

"You dumb piece of crap," he muttered, as he grabbed Crunkleton by the hair and hauled him up. With his left hand, he smashed the man's face.

Stavely ran over, yelling, "Stop, Barlow! You're gonna kill him." But he was too afraid to try and stop him . . .

Wildgun
Oregon Trail

Jack Hanson

JOVE BOOKS, NEW YORK

This is a work of fiction. Names, characters, places, and incidents either are the product of the author's imagination or are used fictitiously, and any resemblance to actual persons, living or dead, business establishments, events, or locales is entirely coincidental.

OREGON TRAIL

A Jove Book / published by arrangement with
the author

PRINTING HISTORY
Jove edition / February 2003

Copyright © 2003 by Penguin Putnam, Inc.

All rights reserved.
This book, or parts thereof, may not be reproduced in any form
without permission.
For information address: The Berkley Publishing Group,
a division of Penguin Putnam Inc.,
375 Hudson Street, New York, New York 10014.

Visit our website at
www.penguinputnam.com

ISBN: 0-515-13470-8

A JOVE BOOK®
Jove Books are published by The Berkley Publishing Group,
a division of Penguin Putnam Inc.
375 Hudson Street, New York, New York 10014.
JOVE and the "J" design
are trademarks belonging to Penguin Putnam Inc.

PRINTED IN THE UNITED STATES OF AMERICA

10 9 8 7 6 5 4 3 2 1

1

FROM THE OUTSIDE, a short distance away, the ramshackle house looked pretty much the same as when Will Barlow left just a couple of weeks earlier. It still sagged in all the same places, and leafless trees remained, starkly surrounding it. A thin stream of smoke curled out of the poorly constructed rock chimney, whisked away by the cold winter breeze. Though it sat on the riverbank, the marshy ground was frozen.

Yet there was something different, something that Barlow sensed more than saw. "I know, Buffler," he said quietly to the big Newfoundland standing beside the black mule on which Barlow sat. The dog's whole body was tense, almost quivering, as his nose sniffed frantically, plumes of vapor blowing out from nose and mouth.

Then Barlow heard a whinny that apparently came from the rickety lean-to stable behind the old house. "These doin's don't shine, Buffler," he muttered, shifting his bulky weight in the saddle. There was not supposed to be a horse here. Unless Dulcy Polzin, the woman he had put up here, had gotten one while he was gone. Which was highly unlikely, considering her financial situation.

"Well, boy," he said, "no use in sittin' here wonderin'

just what doin's are goin' on down there. Best to find out."

He gently prodded his mule, Beelzebub, into motion and covered the dozen or so yards in seconds. He stopped and dismounted. Leaving the mule ground-staked, he hefted his Henry rifle and, with Buffalo 2 at his side, strode up to the house and quietly pushed open the door. He stepped into the cabin and stopped, looking around. Where there had been simply one room, now there were two, of a sort. Dulcy had partitioned off an area in the left rear corner for a bedroom, leaving the rest of the house to continue serving as kitchen, eating area, and sitting area.

The sounds of rough lovemaking came from the "room" in back. Barlow's stomach recoiled when he heard the sounds, but within seconds he realized that something was different about that, too. The sexual sounds were not very joyous. It sounded more like someone was forcing himself on a woman.

Barlow headed soundlessly across the room, gently setting his rifle on the table as he went. He grabbed the cloth that partitioned off the room, jerked the whole thing loose, and tossed it aside.

One man was holding Dulcy down on the bed—which was a new addition—while another pumped in and out of her, grunting like a hog. The latter was oblivious to Barlow's sudden presence, but the former looked up in surprise and shock—just in time to catch Barlow's massive fist in the forehead. The man let out a muffled groan and fell off the rickety bed, landing with a thump on the rough wood floor.

The other popped himself out of Dulcy and stepped back. One hand grabbed his pants, which had been lowered only far enough for the business at hand; the other whipped out a long knife with a wide blade that tapered to a slightly curved point.

Buffalo 2 growled and leaned back on his haunches, ready to charge, but Barlow said, "No, Buffler. This chile's mine." Barlow looked at the man and snarled, "I don't know who you are, hoss, but you're in the wrong place takin' part in the wrong doin's."

"Piss on you, boy," the man growled back. He advanced on Barlow, still holding his pants up with one hand.

Barlow was hard-pressed not to laugh at the sight. Still, the man held that knife, and he looked like he both knew what to do with it and would enjoy using it.

Barlow risked a quick glance at Dulcy. She half sat, eyes wide with fear, watching. She had managed to yank the shabby blankets up to her chin, covering her nudity.

Seeing his momentary distraction, the man charged, his wicked blade furiously slicing the air between him and his intended target. Suddenly he stopped, feinted to his right, and when Barlow moved to block the thrust, shifted toward the other side.

The point of the blade punctured Barlow's chest just below the right pectoral muscle, but it did not sink very deep. Barlow's thick blanket coat kept it from doing much damage, even though the blade point chinked against a rib right away and slid raggedly upward. It tore a rough, bloody line up Barlow's chest, but it was pretty much all on the surface. Though the coat was now ripped, the slight wound couldn't even be seen.

Barlow jerked back reflexively, and almost unthinkingly lashed out with his left hand. The punch barely grazed the man's shoulder as he slid back out of the way.

"How do you like that, boy?" the man said with a sneer.

"I've been stung worse by skeeters, hoss," Barlow countered with a humorless smile.

"Well, there's more where that come from." The man took the respite to slide first one arm, then the other through the suspenders that had been dangling. His pants were still open at the front, but his flaccidness was now mostly hidden.

"Let's see what you got, hoss," Barlow growled. He would not underestimate the man again. Barlow eased out his tomahawk. The worn wood handle felt comfortable in his hand.

The man edged forward more slowly. He had time now to take in Barlow's thick, powerful body and hard, glittering eyes. And the sight gave him pause.

Barlow observed his opponent, too, and while he did not plan to underestimate him again, he was not very impressed. The man was shabbily dressed, had a scruffy beard, and was filthy. His dark brown eyes had a wild look in them. He was a big fellow, taller than Barlow, and while not as thick of body, was still a substantial size.

The man suddenly darted forward, knife raised over his head, ready to slash downward.

With no more room for backing up, Barlow simply swept the tomahawk out. Though the man had shifted the direction of his stab again, Barlow's tomahawk clanged off the knife blade, sending it flying across the room. It hit the wall and clattered to the floor near the other man, who still lay there unconscious.

The first man did not hesitate, however. He swung his knife hand back hard, and his fist thumped into Barlow's midsection, partially knocking the air out of him. Barlow banged back up against the wall, and he dropped his tomahawk.

Barlow's foe charged in, his fist delivering a quick, short series of powerful blows to Barlow's torso, each eliciting a grunt of pain—and annoyance. Barlow suddenly reached out and grabbed the man in a bear hug. He lifted the man's feet off the floor as he squeezed. When several of the man's ribs cracked, Barlow let him go.

The man fell to the floor; wheezing and groaning.

Barlow knelt next to the man. He was breathing hard himself, but regaining his wind rapidly. "You are one dumb ol' chile," Barlow said. "It ain't a bad enough thing that you're havin' intimate doin's with the woman I'm involved with, but then you go and try'n carve me up. Dumb, hoss. Plain, plumb dumb."

"Eat shit, boy," the man gasped.

Barlow shook his head. The man's attitude simply made finishing this off all the easier. "You got any last words before I put you under, hoss?" he asked.

"Yeah, piss off, you dumb bastard." He suddenly started to jerk upward, a small knife in his hand, pulled from his boot.

Barlow was ready for him, though, and grabbed the knife arm. With slow deliberation, he broke the man's arm, then took the knife and plunged it into the man's heart. Within seconds, the man was dead.

Barlow pushed himself slowly up and walked to the bed. He plopped down, sitting next to a still-cowering Dulcy Polzin. He glanced at the man he had hit. The man was still out, his breathing ragged. "So, woman, what's these here doin's all about?" he asked quietly.

Dulcy tried to burrow even deeper into the crackling straw mattress, her eyes welling with fear and shame.

"Ain't no cause for concern about me hurtin' you, woman. From what I seen here, you weren't much of a willin' participant in these doin's." He shrugged. "Even if you was, and you was still to want some other fellers, I ain't one to stand in your way." He paused. "But it don't seem to me that you did such a thing."

Dulcy's jaw and lips worked, but no words were forthcoming.

"Did you think I might've gone off forever and weren't comin' back so you invited them boys in here?" Barlow asked. "That what happened?" He reached out and with the upper side of a thick forefinger, gently stroked the hair that hung down along one of her cheeks.

"No," Dulcy finally squeaked. "I never asked them in here. They . . . They . . ."

"Did they force their way in?"

"Yes. No. Well, sort of." She sighed, and inched the covers down just a fraction, believing in Barlow's warm eyes and gentle smile. "The old lady who owned the boardin' home I was stayin' in when I met you was sellin' this old bed—my own from my time there. So I bought it for a dollar."

Shé glanced at Barlow, concerned that he might think her frivolous, but he just nodded in understanding and smiled.

"Mrs. Waggenhalls sent the two"—she nodded at the men lying on the floor—"to bring the bed here. Right after that, I put up the curtain to make a room. . . ."

"I'm sorry I tore it down, Dulcy," Barlow said quietly, with feeling. "We'll get it put back up."

Dulcy nodded. "That'd be nice." She paused. "Anyway, they just come walkin' back in a couple days later. I had no way to stop them, of course. They knew, after havin' been here with the bed, that I was a lone woman livin' in this house. If there had been a man around—I guess they never saw you before you left—he wasn't around now. And since I had this house, even if it ain't the most fanciest place around, they figured I must have some money, too. There was always at least one of 'em here with me all the time."

Barlow nodded. That made sense of a sort, if one considered what kind of men these were. "So they just come on in and made theirselves to home?"

"That's the way of it." Dulcy pushed herself a little way up the wall behind the bed, some life returning to her face and eyes. Then she grew a bit defiant. "There was nothin' I could do, Will," she said in a trembling voice. "You gotta believe me."

"I reckon there weren't," Barlow said honestly.

"I mean, I couldn't even run nowhere. I didn't have nowhere to go anyways, but with one of 'em always here watchin' me . . ."

"I understand, and I believe you." Barlow cupped Dulcy's chin in a big hand. He smiled at her. "It don't matter none now," he added after a short pause. "These two boys ain't gonna be botherin' you no more. It's done with."

"No, no, it ain't," Dulcy exclaimed, the worry sparking back into her eyes.

Barlow looked at her, puzzled.

"There's two more of 'em. Claude and Bob. I don't know where they've gone off to, but they'll be back sure as anything."

Anger grew in Barlow. He held no jealousy, really. After all, he had no real claim to Dulcy, and he had been truthful when he had said she could have other men if she wanted. He could always go find someone else. But he believed her when she said she did not want that. What really made him angry, more so than those men taking Dulcy against her will, was the thought that these thugs had just waltzed into a house he had paid for and taken it over—and taken over the woman he was involved with at the moment. That was something he simply could not bear to accept.

"Well, woman, them other two boys ain't gonna bother you no more neither," he stated matter-of-factly. "If that's what you want?" He had to make sure she still did want him around. He would leave her on her own if she didn't, without too much concern. There were any number of willing women in St. Louis. He didn't need to waste his time or emotion on one who didn't want him around.

"Yes," Dulcy said, almost whimpering, but with certitude.

Barlow nodded. He rose, adjusted the thick leather belt around his waist, then got the tomahawk and slipped it into the belt at the small of his back. He grabbed the dead man by the scruff of the neck in one hand, and the unconscious one in the other. "Get the door, woman," he ordered.

Dulcy rose, and holding the blanket around her both to ward off the chill and in a sudden bout of shyness, hustled across the room. She pulled open the front —the only— door, letting in a blast of cold air. She shivered a little as she stood behind the door, holding it wide.

Barlow dragged the bodies outside and around the back, then to the riverbank not far away. He dropped them on the ground, then lifted first one, then the other, and tossed them into the icy water, where they were swiftly swept away by the current.

Without remorse, Barlow turned and headed back to the front of the house. He got Beelzebub, the mule, and tugged him around to the rickety lean-to, putting him inside next to the horse that belonged to one or both of the dead men. He unloaded and unsaddled the mule, then gave him a good currying. He made sure both animals had fodder and water, then headed back into the house. He stripped off his belt and laid it on the table next to his rifle.

"You hungry, Will?" Dulcy asked as he pulled off the heavy coat. She had dressed while he had been outside, and she looked demure, desirable, and considerably more relaxed.

"I can always use something," Barlow said with a small smile. "You should know that by now." He poured some water that had been heating on the stove into a basin, and washed his hands off with strong lye soap, getting rid of the blood from the man he had knifed. He dried himself off on an old piece of blanket cloth and then sat at the table.

Dulcy set a plate of too-done buffalo steak and some yams in front of him, then a tin mug, which she filled with coffee. She placed the coffeepot on the table and then sat across from Barlow. She looked at him a little warily. "You sure you ain't put out none by what happened?"

"Cain't say as I'm particularly fond of them doin's," he said as he stuck a piece of meat in his mouth and gnawed on it. Dulcy never was much of a cook, and she had not improved any in the time he had been gone. "But they weren't your doin'." He shrugged. "So I ain't put out none with you, if that's what's concernin' you."

"It weren't," she said.

Barlow smiled. He could tell by the look of relief on her face that she was lying. He didn't mind. She was embarrassed, he knew, and was allowed to tell a fib in such an instance.

"How was your . . . business . . . in Westport?" Dulcy asked after some minutes of silence.

"Finished," Barlow said bluntly. He tossed a piece of gristle to the dog, who gulped it down. "At least the important part is," he added while taking a sip of coffee — the one thing Dulcy made well. "Once I took care of them two bastards who kilt Seamus and the others, I spent a few days lookin' to see if Seamus had any kin in the area." He shoved another chunk of burnt steak into his mouth, followed by a bite of yam.

"And?" Dulcy asked.

"Couldn't find none, but a couple of folks there said they thought he had some kinfolk in this area. Once things are settled here, I'll go around askin' some questions, see what I can find out."

"You're making a mighty big effort to find them folk just to tell them he's gone," Dulcy commented. "I mean, it ain't like you was lifelong friends with the feller."

Barlow shrugged. "He was a good man. And I have some personal effects of his that his family might want." What he didn't say was that he had several thousand dollars he had taken from Enos Priddy and Robert Dunsmore—ill-gotten gains they had collected by taking the Mexican silver and selling the goods Seamus Muldoon had been bringing back to the States with him. Barlow figured their ill-gotten gains belonged with Muldoon's family, if he could ever find them. He had to at least try. While it was true that Muldoon was a new friend, he had proved to be a good man, and Barlow thought he deserved the extra effort.

Dulcy nodded. She wondered how such a good man had come into her life. But she also fretted in knowing that he would soon enough be out of it. She had no illusions that he would be willing to spend the rest of his life with her, though she couldn't help harboring such a desire.

2

BUFFALO 2'S HEAD suddenly perked up and then cocked, as if listening for something. The big Newfoundland rose seconds later and snuffled a soft warning look at Barlow and then toward the door.

"Somebody comin', boy?" Barlow asked.

The dog looked back at the door and growled softly.

"Reckon it's them fellers Claude and Bob," Barlow said, glancing at Dulcy. In the hour since he had finished eating, he and the woman had sat at the table—a heavily scarred, whiskey-stained one, with two chairs he had bought for pennies from a saloon before he had left—sipping coffee and talking. Barlow had been eager to take the woman to the bed, but without knowing when the two other invaders would return, he would not chance it. Plus he was keenly aware that Dulcy was not ready. Not yet anyway. He more than half hoped it was only because she was anxious about the return of the two men, and that once that problem was removed, she would be more amenable to lovemaking. If not, he supposed he could wait a day, two at most.

The more he thought about looming events, however, the more concerned he had gotten, so he had left for a short while. He had saddled Beelzebub and taken the mule out behind a knot of trees a quarter of a mile upriver. The animal would not be seen there by anyone approaching the house or even going around the back. Barlow had become concerned that Claude and Bob might stop at the lean-to to unsaddle their horses before coming into the house. When he had returned, he had strapped the belt around his waist, comforted by the weight of the two Colt Walkers in the simple leather holsters.

Barlow rose, looked at Dulcy, and jerked his head toward the bed, which now sat out in the open. Barlow had not been of a mood to rehang the cloth partition.

She nodded and quickly swept across the small kitchen.

Barlow swiftly gathered his belongings from the table and tossed them into the corner. Then he positioned himself to one side of the front door, where he would be hidden when the door swung open. A wary, almost quivering Buffalo 2 stood, tail swishing slowly, next to him. Dulcy perched nervously on the bed, trying to paste on an inviting smile.

They waited.

And waited, the tension growing rapidly.

Then two men clomped into the house, talking and laughing in crude voices. They stopped, door still open, and one said, "Well, there's our little strumpet." They headed toward the bed.

They got two steps when Bob stopped, grabbing his companion by the arm. "Hey, Claude, where the hell're Frank and Bart?"

"Who the hell cares."

"One of 'em was supposed to be here with her all the time," Bob snapped. "Yet there she sits all alone."

"Yeah, she's alone," Claude countered, unconcerned, "sittin' there waitin' for us."

"And why would she do that all to a sudden after she's been fightin' us all the way, you damn fool?" Bob snapped.

"You think she maybe killed them both?" Claude

asked, more amusement in his voice than fear.

"Maybe, goddammit. Maybe not. All I know is that this ain't right somehow. And where the hell's that curtain thing that made a sort of room?" Bob was perplexed and beginning to sweat.

"You're just bein' yeller, Bob."

"No he ain't, hoss," Barlow said as he stepped forward and kicked the front door shut behind him.

Bob and Claude spun, shocked. Claude recovered first. "Who the flyin' hell're you, boy?" he demanded.

"I'm your executioner, hoss," Barlow said flatly.

Claude laughed, while Bob blanched. "You're as mad as a hatter, boy," the former said.

"There's some might agree with you, hoss," Barlow said with a shrug. "But that don't matter none as far as the veracity of my statement. You fractious shits're dead sure as hell and it'll be by my hand." He took a step forward.

Before either Claude or Bob could respond, Buffalo 2 slid out from behind Barlow and moved up to stand next to his master, low rumbles of warning issuing from his throat.

"You keep that goddamn beast away from me, boy," Bob warned, backing up a bit.

Claude stood his ground, glaring from dog to man. "What's your interest in this, mister?" he asked. "Besides killin' us, I mean," he added with a sneer.

"This is my house, hoss," Barlow said evenly. "And it's my woman you and the other scum have been molestin'." He didn't see it as necessary to say that she was his woman of the moment.

"Well, how was we to know?" Claude said in what he presumably thought was a reasonable—and reasoned—tone.

"And because you didn't know, you figured it was fine just to walk in here and take over a house and molest the woman at regular intervals at your leisure?" Barlow countered with barely concealed incredulity at the man's audaciousness.

Claude shrugged. "It kind of seemed she was just waitin' here to be plucked. What's a man to do?" His shoulders rose, as did his hands, palms upward, all innocence.

Barlow had had enough of the man's boorishness and insufferable arrogance. He simply took another step forward and slammed the heel of his right hand into Claude's nose, mashing it.

Claude staggered backward, banging into Bob, who drew his pistol as he started to fall. He cocked it as he landed and brought it to bear.

But Barlow already had one of the Walkers in his hand, and he fired once, punching a quarter-sized hole in Bob's forehead, just above the right eye.

A dazed Claude was frantically trying to pull the pistol from the piece of rope he used as a belt, but was having trouble. Before he could complete the task, he received the same treatment as Bob had.

Barlow removed the guns and what few dollars were available from the bodies and tossed it all on the table. His only thought was that he should have done that with the first two bodies. The guns could be sold for a few more dollars, and Dulcy could always use the money for some food or maybe some frilly nicety. She deserved at least that much after what these four men had put her through.

He rose and pulled on his coat over his belt, then grabbed Claude and Bob as he had Frank and Bart. Dulcy had already opened the door, and Barlow hauled the two fresh corpses out.

He was back before long, having disposed of the two in the same manner as the first pair. Then he had returned Beelzebub to the lean-to stable, after which he brought Claude's and Bob's horses there and quickly cared for them. He wondered why there was only one horse in there when he had first arrived, but he decided the men might not have been able to afford a horse for each of them.

• • •

When Barlow reentered the house, Dulcy was pouring a bucket of steaming water into the tiny round bathing tub next to the stove. She set the bucket down and glanced at him. Color had returned to her face, and she looked almost serene. "Done?" she asked, suppressing a shiver.

Barlow nodded. He leaned his rifle against the corner to the left of the door and tugged off his coat, then hung it on a peg.

Without shame, Dulcy let her simple, now-shabby dress drop to the floor. She gave him an impish smile as she lifted one stick-thin leg and dipped a toe into the water, testing the temperature. She deemed it fine and stepped into the tub. As skinny as she was, she still had to scrunch up considerably to get most of her body in the wood tub. She sighed as the warm water enveloped her.

"Want some help?" Barlow asked with a lecherous grin.

"From you, yes," Dulcy answered truthfully. She suppressed another shudder at the thought of such "help" if it had been offered by her recent jailers.

Barlow knelt beside the tub and shoved up the sleeves of his colorful cloth shirt. He took a little of the lye soap from the bowl next to him and applied it gently to Dulcy's back as she hunched forward as best she could. He tugged her gently backward, then worked his way around to her front, where he paid soft, soapy attention to her thin breasts. The nipples puckered in his hands, though they did not grow or darken much.

Dulcy sighed deeply with enjoyment. But moans were soon forthcoming as Barlow's hands worked down her belly and to the warm entrance to her womanhood. His stubby middle finger eased its way inside, where it maneuvered with gentle insistence. At the same time, Barlow's thumb played with her ripe love button.

Dulcy soon shuddered again, but this time it was in pleasure. She squealed in delight in a mild climax.

Barlow grabbed the back of Dulcy's neck and pulled her head around. Then he kissed her hard, lips mashing hers. She moaned into his mouth and flung a wet arm around his neck, clinging to him tightly. His fingers continued to work their magic on her femininity, making her squirm, which was tough in the tight confines of the tub.

Twice more Barlow brought Dulcy to new heights, leaving her quivering with aftershocks. Barlow hurriedly finished bathing her, then hauled her up in his arms and carried her, soaking, to the bed he had not yet used. He set her down and covered her thin, shivering body. Swiftly undressing and sliding into the bedcovers, he enveloped the slender, almost bony woman in his vast bulk, his front to her back, spoon style.

She shivered with cold and pleasure as she relished the warmth of his body, and his hardness pressing against her buttocks. They lay that way awhile, letting Barlow's heat flow into Dulcy, first warming her, then stoking the fire inside her anew.

She finally turned to face him, her soft lips searching hungrily for his. And found them. Their tongues played and danced, while Barlow's big hand explored Dulcy's gaunt body, stroking the smooth flesh, toying with her pert breasts, his thumbs circling her pale nipples.

He gasped when her scrawny hand softly encircled his erect manhood and slowly slid up and down its length.

Barlow bought his fingers into play again, teasing her womanhood until she fairly exploded with pleasure. Her hand holding his erection spasmed with it, tightening and jerking hard on it in a not-unpleasant way for him.

When Dulcy had returned to earth somewhat, she suddenly pushed Barlow over onto his back and swiftly, expertly mounted him, easing onto his large length and girth easily and joyfully, until she had absorbed him. The position, they had learned early on, was beneficial to them both, but especially to Dulcy, who did not have to have his weight atop her this way.

She reached behind her and pulled one of the blankets up around her to keep the cold air off her back. Then she began a slow rise and fall, alternating the action with a back-and-forth rocking that soon had her squealing in a rapidly building series of climaxes, each taking her to ever-increasing heights of pleasure. Her gray eyes, when they were open, sparkled brightly.

As he felt his own lust beginning to storm toward a peak, Barlow grabbed ahold of Dulcy's bony hips and held on, guiding her, helping her. He gazed at her, thinking again about how quickly and completely she'd changed from a mousy, overly thin, plain-looking woman into one whose passion increased her attractiveness.

Dulcy's string of climaxes continued, and now Barlow was racing toward his own pinnacle. Still holding her hips, he bounced her on his midsection, as their breath became faster and faster, matching Barlow's wildly increasing thrusts. The bed creaked and rattled, threatening to collapse with a crash under the ever-increasing wildness of their consuming passion.

Then he bellowed and grunted. His back arched and he strained as he emptied himself into her, gasping.

They finally slumped together, nestled in the blankets, and soon fell asleep.

Barlow placed the two revolvers on the General Store's counter late the next morning. "How much you give me for these, hoss?" he asked.

The proprietor—a tall, scrawny, grizzled man with scraggly strings of thin white hair—picked one of the single-shot weapons up and looked at it. "That's Claude Weams's piece, ain't it?" he questioned, giving Barlow a baleful glare.

"Reckon it is at that," Barlow said. He had no idea that Weams was Claude's last name, but it seemed likely under the circumstances.

"How'd you come by it?" Again the glittering, accusatory look.

"Just where'd you get the notion that'd be any of your concern, hoss?" Barlow countered.

It took only a glance at Barlow's face to make the man

decide that arguing was not in his best interest. He looked at the gun, then the other. If he thought he knew who that one had belonged to, he did not let on. "Give you a buck for the two of 'em," the man finally said.

"You can do better'n that, you goddamn thief."

"Them ol' one-shots don't sell much anymore. Not worn-out ones like these." He paused. "A dollar each."

"Five each."

"I might's well jist give you over my whole store was I to make a trade like that, boy. One dollar and a half each. No more."

"That plus a dollar each in goods," Barlow countered.

The shop owner considered that for some seconds, then nodded. It was more than he usually would give in such a deal, but he wanted to be shed of Barlow, considering him nothing but trouble.

Barlow took the cash and then gave the man Dulcy's name, saying that she would be in soon to pick out two dollars' worth of supplies. Before turning to leave, he asked, "You know a family in these parts named Muldoon?"

"Nope."

Since he had not expected a positive response, Barlow was not too disappointed. He had just figured that since he was there he might as well ask. He really didn't think Seamus Muldoon would frequent such a store. He left and headed toward the heart of the city. He spent the rest of the day—and the next several days—wandering from saloon to general store to blacksmith shop to whatever other place caught his attention—asking about Seamus Muldoon. After almost a week of searching, he was beginning to think that he would never find any of his late employer's family.

Then, as he was leaving a saddler's one afternoon, a man stopped him, saying, "I couldn't help but overhear you in there, mister. You're lookin' for Seamus Muldoon's family?"

"I am," Barlow said, giving the man a looking over.

He was decently dressed, and Barlow took him for a modestly successful businessman of some kind.

"My name's Sean O'Malley." He held out his hand. When they had shaken hands, he continued. "Do you know Seamus, if I might ask?"

"I did," Barlow responded flatly.

O'Malley's eyes rose at the use of the past tense. "He was a good man," he said sadly.

"He was that," Barlow agreed. "Chile plumb shined, he did."

"Then I take it you have news for his family?"

Barlow nodded. "You know where I can find them?"

"He has a wife, brother, and sister in Bellefontaine, a town perhaps ten miles north of here. Ask anyone around there, and they'll be able to direct you."

"I'm obliged, Mr. O'Malley," Barlow said. "Did you know Seamus well?"

"Not real well, no," O'Malley said with a shake of the head. "But I did business with him at times and found him to be an honorable and decent feller."

"I saw the same things in that ol' chile. A good ol' hoss all around."

"You mind tellin' what you know of his demise?" O'Malley asked.

Barlow hesitated a moment, but then realized it could do no harm. He explained it quickly.

O'Malley nodded in sad understanding. He held out his hand again.

Barlow shook it, then said, "Obliged for the information." He turned and headed off to the sagging house on a marshy stretch of riverbank just south of the docks.

3

WILL BARLOW COULDN'T help but stand there and stare for a few moments when the Widow Muldoon opened the door of her small, neat home. She was a gently beautiful woman, almost as tall as Barlow, yet willowy despite the vocal evidence of more than one child in the house. Her long flowing mane of golden-red hair was tied with a yellow ribbon at the nape of her neck. Liquid blue eyes looked evenly out at Barlow from under softly arching eyebrows. Beneath, a slightly pudgy nose, thin crimson lips, and a strong jaw did little to mar her loveliness.

"Yes?" she questioned, eyes not leaving his once she had given him a quick looking over and taken in the big black Newfoundland dog at his side.

"Mrs. Muldoon?"

She nodded, but answered, "My husband isn't here." Her voice was full of Irish lilt.

"I know," Barlow said quietly, his bulky form tense with unease. He swallowed hard. He did not look forward to what he had to do. "That's why I'm here, ma'am."

Those delightful blue eyes clouded in worry, but Bridie Muldoon, née O'Donnell, just nodded curtly. She stepped back a little, pulling the door open wider. "Come in, then, Mr. . . . ?"

"Will Barlow, ma'am," he said as he stepped inside, removing his hat. Awkwardness and worry rose up in him.

Bridie held the door open long enough for Buffalo 2 to enter, then closed it. She eyed the dog a bit warily, but with no fear. "Please, be seated, Mr. Barlow," she said, leading the way into the room. "Would you like some coffee? Or tea perhaps?"

"Whichever's less troublesome for you, ma'am," Barlow said as he settled his bulk into a chair at the clear, unscarred table. The inside of the trim little home reflected the exterior—simple, though comfortable. There was no ostentation, but everything was as neat as a pin. While it was not the home of someone wealthy, it was far removed from the cramped cabins his brothers and their families occupied.

"You children hush now," Bridie called as she turned toward the stove. She pulled her apron up, used it to grasp the hot coffeepot from its spot on the stove, and carried it to the table, where she set it down. She got two cups and placed them there. "Do you take sugar, Mr. Barlow?"

"When I can get it, yes."

Bridie set a small bowl of it on the table. "Are you hungry?"

Barlow managed a slight grin. "Man like me can always use some feedin', ma'am," he said. "But don't make no fuss." He paused. "Looks like a piece of that there pie would set in this ol' chile's meatbag plumb fine, though." He pointed to a peach pie sitting on a table next to the stove.

"You sound like my Seamus did sometimes," she said with the barest hint of a smile.

"He said he was a mountaineer. I were, too, for a good many years."

Before he could add to that, two children—a boy of about eight and a girl two or three years younger—ventured just past the doorway to a bedroom at the rear of the house. They were too frightened of Buffalo 2 to advance any farther.

Barlow saw them. "Ol' Buffler won't hurt you children none," he said. "C'mon and see."

The girl was the first to move, easing forward, blue eyes bright and saucer-sized as she gingerly approached the big black canine. A moment later, the boy followed.

"This here is Mr. Barlow," Bridie announced to her children. "He's a . . ." She hesitated a second, then said, "Friend of your pa's." She had no idea if that was true, but it was the easiest way to explain the situation to the children right now. She would worry about the truth of it later, if need be.

The little girl squealed in fright, then delight as Buffalo 2 lapped her face a few times. She giggled. The boy moved in to pet the dog, and received the same welcome from the Newfoundland.

Bridie set a dish of pie in front of Barlow, then a mug of coffee. Ill at ease, Barlow dug in right away. Bridie fussed around the kitchen for a few more minutes, then sat at the table in the chair at right angles to Barlow. She poured herself some coffee and sipped quietly.

Barlow glanced at her out of the corner of his eye. Her outward appearance of serenity was belied by the haunted look in her soft blue eyes and the throbbing of the vein at the side of her pale forehead.

Barlow quickly finished off the pie and pushed the plate away. He gulped some coffee, then pulled out his pipe. He needed it to be able to do what he was facing. Once it was fired up, he said, "Seamus hired me to hunt for him on the Santa Fe Trail, ma'am. We hadn't ever met before, but a mutual acquaintance arranged my employ for him. I took to Seamus right away. He was a fine man, your husband."

"There's no need for you to extol my husband's virtues, Mr. Barlow," Bridie said softly. "I'm well aware of them."

"Yes'm." Barlow cleared his throat but hesitated, trying to come up with a way to couch what he had to say in terms that would not be so painful for the new widow. But there were no such terms. "Seamus was killed, ma'am. Almost three months ago . . ."

Bridie's gasp of despair was cut short by a knock on the door. She rose and hurried to answer it. As soon as she pulled it open, a man's gruff voice demanded, "I have heard that you are entertaining an unknown man."

"Come in, Liam," Bridie said resignedly.

A short, plumpish man stormed in, his jowls virtually aquiver. He stopped across the table from Barlow. "Who are you, sir, and what is your business here?" he demanded, glaring at Barlow.

"He's a friend who has news of Seamus," Bridie said, somehow managing to force down her grief momentarily and present a show of strength.

"Then give me your news and get out," the man snapped. He was beside himself with anger.

Barlow offered him a small smile full of derision, then looked at Bridie. "Who's this fractious chile, ma'am?" he asked.

"Seamus's brother, Liam," the widow said. "Liam, Mr. Will Barlow."

"I said," Muldoon snapped in high dudgeon, "that you should state your business and then leave. It's not right that a man should be visiting a married woman unaccompanied."

Barlow fought back the urge to shoot the man down. "Have a seat, hoss," he said instead, keeping his tone even. "Mrs. Muldoon here makes a right fine peach pie, and I'm sure she'd let even a pompous, pushy critter like you have a taste."

"Why you arrogant, insufferable . . ." Muldoon started.

"Sit down!" Barlow said sharply in a voice soaked in warning. "And watch your manners, hoss," he added when a livid Liam Muldoon plunked himself into a chair, "lest I have to administer some corrective measures in front of the children."

"What're you doing here?" Muldoon asked through clenched teeth.

"Mrs. Muldoon already told you, hoss." He looked up at Bridie and smiled. "Get him a piece of your fine pie, ma'am," he said in a gentle tone. "Might help him get hisself under control."

Bridie managed a wan smile. But before she went to the sideboard for the pie, she turned to her children. "Tommy, go and fetch your aunt Kathleen. Tell her it's very important she come here right away."

The boy, a bit confused at all the activity and the harsh words, pulled on a coat and cloth cap before running outside.

In the uneasy silence that followed, Bridie served her brother-in-law a piece of pie and a cup of coffee. It was some minutes before Muldoon actually partook of either, since he was trying to stare Barlow down. It didn't work, though Barlow was almost amused at the attempt.

Finally the door swung open again, allowing in another blast of frigid air. Tommy Muldoon burst in, flinging off his coat and cap and hurrying over to Buffalo 2 again. A woman followed the boy in. She stopped and closed the door behind her, then turned and smiled tentatively at Bridie, then looked around at Muldoon and Barlow.

"Kathleen," Bridie said, hurrying over to take the woman's coat, "thank you for coming."

Barlow gave her a quick appraisal, and was favorably impressed. The woman was short and somewhat round, at least compared with the taller, willowy Bridie Muldoon. Her face held a vivaciousness that was evident even across the room. Her green eyes were bright despite their concern, and her full lips were compressed tightly at the moment.

"What's going on, Bridie?" the woman asked.

Bridie nodded at Barlow. "Mr. Barlow here is—was—a friend of Seamus's. He has news." Her voice faltered.

"Oh, Bridie," Kathleen said, embracing the other woman. "I'm so sorry."

"Will someone tell me what in heaven's name is going on here?" Muldoon demanded, his voice cracking with anger.

The two women ignored him. Bridie indicated that Kathleen should sit. When she did, Bridie said, "Kathleen, this is Mr. Will Barlow. Mr. Barlow, this is Kathleen Byrne, Seamus's sister. She's . . . she's a widow," she added with a hitch in her voice. She sat once she had made sure they all had coffee. "Please, Mr. Barlow, begin where you left off when Liam arrived." Her voice was steady, but Barlow could see her inner pain reflected in her eyes.

Barlow relit his pipe, and through a cloud of acrid smoke, said bluntly, "Seamus was put under by several of the men he had hired to handle the wagons he was bringin' back from Santa Fe."

The two women hung their heads, the better to hide their tears, while Muldoon glowered. "How'd it happen?" the man demanded.

"I don't think the ladies need to hear the particulars, hoss," Barlow said flatly.

"Do you know who did it?"

Barlow nodded, puffing casually at his pipe. He sipped coffee.

"And what are you planning to do about it?" Muldoon demanded.

Barlow stared evenly at Muldoon for a few moments. He looked enough like his brother to show that they were related, but that was about it. Where Seamus had been weathered by a life outside, and his clothing reflected a life involved in hard work, Liam looked like a businessman with his silk suit and tie. His pudgy face was pale and pasty from a life of never being outdoors more than traveling from his house to whatever business it was he ran. Though he was, apparently, a few years younger than Seamus, his pate was every bit as hairless as his brother's. He appeared to Barlow to be a man accustomed to getting what he wanted through financial intimidation rather than through presenting a good example, as his brother had.

"I ain't plannin' to do a thing about it, hoss," Barlow said flatly.

"Afraid?" Muldoon asked with a sneer.

Barlow laughed in a mocking way. "Does your stupidity know no limits, hoss?" he countered.

"Why you . . ."

"Shush, Liam," Kathleen snapped. She dabbed at her eyes with a small handkerchief. She looked at Barlow. "Excuse Liam, Mr. Barlow," she said in a mellifluous voice. "He has no manners at times. Or sense." She eyed Barlow shrewdly. "I expect there's more here than what you're telling us about this whole matter. Is that true?"

Barlow nodded, impressed again with Kathleen Byrne. "Yes, ma'am, that's true." He paused. "The critters who perpetrated this horrible deed won't be doin' so to any other decent men."

"You've seen that they were jailed?" Muldoon asked smugly.

Barlow laughed again. "Such men don't belong in jail, hoss," he said harshly.

"You killed them?" Kathleen asked, her voice strong despite her grief.

"Yes'm," Barlow said with a nod, not taking his eyes off the handsome, intriguing woman across from him.

"All of them?"

Another nod.

"How many?" Kathleen inquired.

"Seven." It was said without pride or boasting.

"Hah!" Muldoon snapped sarcastically. "You expect us to believe you killed seven men all by yourself?" He was smug, thinking he had caught Barlow in a bald-faced lie.

"I would think Mr. Barlow could certainly do such a thing should he put his mind to it," Kathleen said, staring appreciatively at Barlow.

"Thank you for your confidence, ma'am," Barlow said. "In this particular case, though, I didn't rub 'em all out at once." He hesitated, not sure whether he should bother them with the details.

"Tell us about it, Mr. Barlow," Kathleen said. She was sad, and mourned her brother, but she was in control of herself. And not only was she truly interested in all of what Barlow had to say, but by keeping him talking, she gave her sister-in-law Bridie time to grieve for a bit without being bothered by having to talk.

"Not much to tell, ma'am," Barlow said modestly. "I was off on a hunt when it happened. I kilt three of 'em once I caught up to 'em, but one of the others creased my skull with a pistol ball, knocking me out. They left me for dead out on the Plains. Some Comanches found me instead and hauled me off to their village, where they aimed to make wolf bait out of me. Fortunately, old Buffler here"—he patted the great dog's head—"had gotten away. He come and saved me. Once I got back to the States, I hunted down the rest of those miscreant bastards—beggin' your pardon."

"Then you came looking for my brother's family?" Kathleen questioned.

"Yes'm. Took a while, though."

"Well, Mr. Barlow," Kathleen said, "as hard as it has been to hear this news, we do appreciate you coming here to tell us. At least now we know what happened, and we won't have to sit here wonderin'."

"I thought I owed it to him to let his family know," Barlow said with a shrug. "Plus there's a bit of specie from the sale of the goods he was bringin' back that I recovered from the men who brought about his untimely demise."

The two women nodded, though Bridie was still crying, and Kathleen was trying to stifle sobs. But Liam suddenly got a gleam of interest in his eyes. "How much?" he asked.

"It ain't gonna make any of you rich, hoss," Barlow said, his dislike for the man growing rapidly. He forced himself to calm down, and looked at Kathleen, who smiled wanly, then at Bridie. "I'm truly sorry, ma'am," he said quietly. "I didn't know Seamus for very long, but I found him to be a man of honor." He looked pointedly at Muldoon, who squirmed. "He deserved a far better fate than the one he got at the hands of those evil critters. I wish I could've prevented it from . . ."

"If you hadn't been off huntin' or whatever you said you were doing at the time, you might have prevented it," Muldoon said self-righteously.

"I was hired as a hunter, hoss," Barlow said, his anger beginning to spiral upward at an alarming rate. "I was doin' what your brother had paid me to do."

"But if you . . ."

"Shut up, Liam," Kathleen snapped, surprising them all a little. "What's done is done," she continued, her voice more modulated, "and we can't do anything about that. Mr. Barlow did all that he could do, and we should thank him for it all. He could have just kept the money for himself. He didn't have to come lookin' for us to tell us what happened to poor Seamus. Now stop trying to make trouble with your words and be grateful we know what happened to Seamus." She looked back at Barlow again. "Did you bury him?" she asked, voice catching.

"As best I could under the circumstances out there, ma'am," Barlow responded sadly. "There ain't no marker at all, let alone a proper one, but there wasn't much else could be done at the time."

Kathleen nodded. Muldoon glowered. Bridie went to tend the infant in the cradle, who had started squawking moments before.

4

BARLOW GRIMACED IN displeasure when he saw Liam Muldoon enter the saloon. He was in no mood to deal with the insufferable horse's ass at the moment. He disliked Seamus's brother so much that he was certain that if Muldoon bothered him any more today, he would kill him. And that, Barlow figured, would not sit well with either Bridie Muldoon or Kathleen Byrne. His heart went out to Bridie in her grief, and he would not want to add to her pain. And while he did not want to hurt Kathleen either, with her it was more personal. Because she was a widow, and because she had shown some interest in him, he could not help but consider the possibilities held by her slightly plump body. He intended to see if those possibilities were real, too.

Muldoon stopped just inside the doors and surveyed the saloon. When he spotted Barlow, he headed purposefully toward him. He nodded greetings at several men as he made the short journey. Without a word, he plopped down in a seat across the table from Barlow, then waved his hand absently toward the bartender, indicating not only that he wanted a drink delivered to him, but that he wanted it brought to the table immediately.

Barlow, who had just taken a sip of beer, set his mug down on the table. "You know, hoss," he said flatly, "you really do need some lessons in mannerly behavior."

"What do you mean?" Muldoon asked, apparently genuinely surprised.

"Is it your custom to just walk up to someone's table and plunk your fat ass down without so much as a how-de-do?"

"I must talk to you," Muldoon said, as if that explained everything. He barely acknowledged the waiter who set a mug of beer down in front of him.

"Ain't a damn thing I want to hear from you, hoss," Barlow said directly. "And I got nothin' to really say to you either. Leastways nothing you'd be eager to hear. So just mosey on off and annoy someone else for a spell."

Buffalo 2, who had been lying with his head on his paws beside Barlow's chair, lifted the great cranium and released a very low, very short, but still very ominous growl to add emphasis to his master's words.

"This has to do with my brother's estate," Muldoon said hastily, turning a frightened eye toward the dog. When the animal made no move toward him, he turned his doleful gaze back on Barlow. "And I think that would concern you," he added.

Barlow shrugged. "Doesn't concern me much, comin' from you, whatever it is. However, since you apparently aim to be a pain in my ass until you say what it is you got to say, get it over with and then take your miserable carcass somewhere else."

Muldoon stiffened. He was not used to being insulted. In fact, he was used to being treated with deference around the town. On the other hand, he wasn't used to dealing with men like Will Barlow either. Barlow, it was plain to see, was half savage, and seemed to be the type of man who would raise a physical ruckus at the least provocation. Or with no incitement at all. Muldoon had begun to realize that he couldn't deal arrogantly with Barlow as he did with most of the people of Bellefontaine.

However, he didn't know quite how to treat him. It was perplexing, and that made it annoying, which in turn angered him.

"Well, then," Muldoon finally said tautly, "I'll get right down to business." He paused for a sip of beer, then wiped foam off his thick mustache. "After you left my sister-in-law's, she and Kathleen and I talked awhile."

"I'm sure you did, hoss," Barlow said dryly. He sipped beer, then began filling his pipe.

Muldoon ignored the insult, at least outwardly. "What we decided was that I will take charge of the money of Seamus's you recovered from his killers." He paused. "Just how much did you say it was?" he asked diffidently, as if it was of little importance and he just needed to refresh his memory. But the gleam of avarice in his eyes betrayed his real emotions.

"I didn't," Barlow responded flatly. He struck a lucifer against the rough wood table and held the flame to the pipe bowl, until a stream of smoke curled up out of it.

"I probably should know," Barlow pressed. "Just so I can start makin' plans for where best to invest it to help m—Bridie, Kathleen, and me."

"I ain't rightly sure how much there is," Barlow said with a straight face. He had counted it, and knew to the dollar how much there was, but he didn't trust Muldoon one little bit, and he was not about to let the weasel-like brother of the slain Seamus Muldoon know anything about it. At least not yet.

"That's rather odd," Muldoon said, trying with little success to hide his disappointment.

Barlow shrugged again. "I never got around to countin' it."

Muldoon battled down his annoyance. "Well, then, I guess it doesn't matter any. Just give it on over to me, and I'll see to it that it's put to good use for the three of us."

"Can't do that, hoss," Barlow said with a touch of humor at Muldoon's growing irritation.

"Why not?" Muldoon was almost apoplectic. "I'm perfectly willin' to wait here a bit while you go to your room to get it. Or, if you prefer, I'll even go with you."

"I wager you would, hoss," Barlow muttered around his pipe stem. "But the thing is, I ain't got that money with me. I ain't so foolish to travel around with money on me like that, hoss. Not when I didn't know who or what I'd find once I got here. That cash's sittin' in a St. Louis bank for safekeepin'."

Judging by the look on Muldoon's face, Barlow thought the man might have a stroke, and he was almost sorry when it didn't happen. It took more than two minutes for Muldoon to regain his composure enough to speak, which he did in strangled tones. "Well, when can you have it here?" he asked.

"In due time, hoss," Barlow responded enigmatically. "In due time." He polished off his beer and called for another. When it arrived, he paid the man, and nodded his thanks. He looked back at Muldoon. "That all you wanted to talk about, hoss?" he asked.

"Yes," Muldoon gargled. Embarrassed, annoyed, and angry, he pushed himself up, the chair legs scraping across the floor. "Good day to you, sir," he managed to squawk before he turned and walked stiff-legged away from the table.

"Lord A'mighty, what a blustering insolent blowhard," Barlow muttered as he watched Muldoon stride off. "Right, Buffler?" Then he laughed, petted the dog's head, and went back to concentrating on his pipe and beer.

After two more beers, Barlow partook of a supper of ham and fried potatoes, a meal that rivaled Dulcy Polzin's in lack of quality. Finished, he had a pipe, and then strolled over to the small, inexpensive hotel where he had taken a room.

The next morning, Barlow had a pile of flapjacks and hens' eggs for breakfast. The meal was made by the hotel proprietor's wife, and was a far sight better than the poor fare he had consumed the night before. As soon as he finished, he saddled Beelzebub and rode out to Seamus Muldoon's, where a surprised Widow Bridie allowed him to enter. He did, taking off his belt and then heavy coat and hanging them on pegs next to the door.

As soon as he was sitting, a cup of coffee in front of him, he said, "Would you mind sendin' your boy over to fetch your sister-in-law Kathleen?"

The grieving Bridie looked at him in question.

"I need to talk to you and her." He paused. "But I don't want Liam around."

"I understand," Bridie said. She turned. "Tommy, you heard Mr. Barlow. Go and get Aunt Kathleen."

The boy considered protesting, but his mother's stern look and a short *woof* from Buffalo 2 convinced him otherwise. He swiftly put on his coat and cap and hurried off. Because Kathleen lived only a few doors down, the boy and his aunt entered the house minutes later.

Despite the sadness at her brother's death, Kathleen looked genuinely glad to see Barlow. She offered him a small, though warm, smile as she removed her woolen cloak and hung it up.

In moments, the three adults, coffee cups before them, were sitting at the table. "Liam came by to see me at the saloon last night," Barlow said without preamble. "He told me that you two and he had talked after I left here and decided that I should give him the money and that he would handle it for you. That true?"

The two women were shocked. And more than a little irritated. "That skunk," Kathleen snapped. "How dare he."

Bridie said nothing, just stared openmouthed.

"So you two never did make such an arrangement with him, I assume?"

"Of course not," Kathleen said indignantly. "That'd be like having the fox guard the henhouse."

"As I thought," Barlow said. "I may be talkin' out of turn, ladies," he added quietly, "but I think that ol' hoss is a weasel and has only his own interests at heart."

"You're not talking out of turn at all, Mr. Barlow,"

Bridie said quietly. But her voice gave away her sadness and anger. "My brother-in-law is an unbearable scoundrel and if I were a man I'd . . . I'd . . ."

Barlow smiled softly. "I'll have a wee talk with Liam about the discrepancy," he said. "And if he continues being obstinate, I may consider something a bit stronger than a talk to get him to see the error of his ways."

"You should give him a right good thumping," Kathleen said bluntly. "He deserves that and more. Whatever money Seamus left should go to Bridie and the children. Liam has no claim to the estate. At least he shouldn't have. Whatever Seamus did, he did for his family, not our dimwitted brother, that whining degenerate. Nor even me," she added.

Barlow almost chuckled at Kathleen's anger. Well, not at her outrage, but at her expression of it. Her ire at her brother, from everything Barlow had seen, was justified. "I'll use my utmost persuasion to make sure he gets the message that the estate is to go to Bridie here," he said firmly. "And I'll tell you two ladies here and now—if he does try to horn in on the money after I'm gone, don't you hesitate to get word to me in St. Louis. Bellefontaine ain't that far away that I can't make a little paseo up this way to give Liam a fresh lesson in how life works when it comes to family."

"I'll make sure you get word," Kathleen said firmly.

Barlow glanced at her through hooded eyes. He thought he had detected more than a promise of helping her sister-in-law in the statement. He finished his mug of coffee and rose. Stepping toward the door, he tugged on his blanket coat and then strapped his wide leather belt around his waist, taking a moment to adjust the two Colt Walkers in the holsters attached to it.

"I should be back tomorrow, next day at the latest, with the money," Barlow said, facing the women. "Unless we get a storm or somethin'. But I don't expect that." He slapped his hat on. "I wouldn't worry about Liam botherin' you whilst I'm gone. I don't think he'll be comin' round." Then he turned and, with Buffalo 2 at his side, headed out.

The day was frigid, but the sky was a brilliant blue. The sun's reflection off the accumulated snow and patches of ice was painful to the eyes. Barlow pulled himself into the saddle on Beelzebub's back and then headed off down the road south toward St. Louis.

Within twenty minutes, Buffalo 2 warned him that they were being followed. Barlow pulled off the trail a few yards behind some boulders and bare, skeletal trees. He did not have to wait long. As he suspected, Liam Muldoon was the one who was following. The city businessman did not look comfortable on the back of a skittish horse.

Barlow waited until Muldoon was within a few feet of his hiding place before he stepped onto the trail in front of Muldoon.

Muldoon jerked the reins, and the horse reared a little, almost throwing the rider. When the horse's front hooves came back down to earth, Barlow grabbed the reins and calmed the frightened animal. "Get down, hoss," Barlow ordered, glaring up at Muldoon.

A suddenly very nervous Muldoon climbed awkwardly down from the saddle and brushed his coat off as he stood, trying to meet Barlow's glare but not succeeding.

"Makin' a trip to St. Louis, hoss?" Barlow asked sarcastically.

"Yes," Muldoon said, grasping at what seemed to be a reasonable explanation for him being on the road. "Yes, I am."

"Kind of sudden, ain't it, hoss?"

"Well, some business just came up this morning, necessitating this little journey." He tried to chuckle, but it came out more like a gargle.

"Your lies ain't improved any since last night, boy," Barlow said, dropping any pretense at friendliness.

"Whatever do you mean?" Muldoon's nervousness increased considerably.

"I talked with Bridie and Kathleen this mornin', hoss.

They never agreed to let you handle the money from Seamus's estate."

"Perhaps they didn't understand," Muldoon blustered. "You know how women are when it comes to finances and such. Especially when the women are grievin' over the loss of a loved one. You should know they just can't . . ."

"We can stand here all day and argue the fine points of women's abilities, hoss," Barlow snapped. "But I ain't of a mind to. Now I'm gonna warn you just this once—you keep yourself away from the money when I give it to Bridie. It's hers."

"But I'm his brother and as such . . ."

"Close your pie hole, hoss," Barlow growled. "Seamus wanted me to make sure Bridie got it. He told mc so just before dyin'," he lied unabashedly. "He didn't have time to write out his last will, but he made it verbally before he died."

"You're lying," Muldoon seethed. "You . . ."

Barlow slammed a fist into Muldoon's stomach. The man doubled over and fell to the cold, icy ground. His face went through several color changes as he tried to get air into his lungs, and had an incredible amount of trouble doing so. He began to panic, wondering if he would ever be able to draw another breath.

Barlow knelt beside Muldoon. "Relax, hoss, and your breath'll come back soon." He paused, waiting to see if Muldoon followed his instructions. When he did, Barlow added, "As I said, hoss, the money goes to Bridie. If she decides she wants to give you some, that's her doin'. But don't you dare let me hear that you pressured her into doin' so. I do, and you'll pay in ways so horrible you can't even contemplate 'em, hoss. You understand me, boy?"

Muldoon wheezed, but did not say anything.

Angry, Barlow slapped him in the face. "I asked you do you understand what I said, boy?"

Muldoon managed to nod.

As Barlow rose, he grabbed Muldoon's coat and pulled him to his feet. The man stood there, still gasping, but almost able to catch his breath now.

"You go on back to Bellefontaine now, hoss," Barlow ordered, "and tend to your business. And stay away from your sister-in-law." He spun on his heel, gathered up the reins to Beelzebub, mounted the mule, and rode off without looking back. Muldoon's wheezing rang in his ears for some minutes.

5

BRIDIE MULDOON SAT at her table, tears flooding from her red-rimmed blue eyes and streaming down her pale, beautiful face. "I . . . I . . . don't know what to say," she stammered as she ran her hands through the coins overflowing from the open metal box sitting on the table.

"Ain't nothin' to say, ma'am," Barlow said, a little embarrassed. "I just brought you what's yours."

"How . . . how much did you say was here?" Bridie asked, voice awed.

"Five thousand two hundred twenty-seven dollars, ma'am," Barlow repeated.

"Lordy, Lordy," Kathleen Byrne breathed, "you're a rich woman, Bridie." She was genuinely happy for her sister-in-law.

"I'd as soon trade all this money in to have my Seamus back," Bridie said, still trying valiantly but unsuccessfully to stem the flood of tears. "The money doesn't mean much without him."

"I know, Bridie," Kathleen said, scooting her chair closer to her sister-in-law and placing an arm around her shoulders. "But at least Seamus made sure you'd be taken care of." She paused, wondering if she should add the obvious—that if it hadn't been for Barlow's good heart, she would have neither husband nor money. She decided it didn't need saying. "You won't have to worry about keeping a roof over the children's heads."

Bridie nodded, still sobbing, though it was winding down a little, if for no other reason than it couldn't continue forever.

"I'll tell you again, ma'am," Barlow interjected, uncomfortable with all the weeping, "that if Liam pesters you again about the money, you get word to me, and I'll discourage such doin's on his part. I've already had one little chat with the insufferable skunk, and I don't think he'll be so foolish as to come round lookin' for some of that money. 'Specially since he has no idea of how much of it there is. I never told him."

Bridie nodded, finally beginning to have some success against the tears and sobs. "I do thank you for all you've done for me, Mr. Barlow," she said, her voice still quivering with her tender emotions. "There's many a man who would've just taken the money for himself, and I would've never known what happened to Seamus or been able to support my family."

"It were the right thing to do," Barlow said, embarrassed anew at the compliment. "I ain't ever been rich, but I can't see any need to take money from women and children just for my own doin's. Such a thing wouldn't set well with me." He shrugged. "Money ain't that important to this ol' chile. Leastways not important enough to keep it from a family who needs it a heap more than I do."

"What will you do now?" Bridie asked. She ran her fingers through the coins again, assuring herself that they were real.

Barlow shrugged again. "I can find me work for the winter back in St. Louis. There's plenty of jobs to be had. Once spring comes, I'll figure out somethin' else. Most likely head to the mountains again. This city livin' ain't for this chile for very long."

They sat in silence for a few moments, then Bridie started, as if coming out of a trance. She starting counting out some of the gold coins, making a little stack of them. Then she suddenly pushed the neat pile across the table. "Take this as a token of my appreciation, Mr. Barlow," she said quietly. "For all you've done."

"No, ma'am," Barlow responded, wrapping a big hand around the money and starting to push it back.

Bridie's thin, soft hands on his stopped the action. "I insist, Mr. Barlow," the woman said firmly. "It's not much, and I'm not taking anything away from my children. It's just a small amount to thank you for your kindness—and your friendship toward my husband."

Barlow looked into her bright blue eyes, which were dulled now with her grief, and saw that she meant what she said. He nodded. "I'm obliged, ma'am," he said quietly. "And mighty touched by your thoughtfulness."

Bridie managed a wan smile and pulled her hands from his. He scooped up the money and plunked it into his small possible sack, not bothering to count it. As a guess, he figured it was a hundred dollars or thereabouts, a tidy enough sum to get him through the winter without having to work steadily.

Barlow rose. "Well, ma'am, I best be on my way. You have things to do and you don't need this ol' chile sittin' here takin' up your time." He went and got his coat, slipping it on, then hooking his belt around his waist outside the garment.

Bridie and Kathleen rose, too, and waited until he was finished. Then Kathleen said, "Could I impose on you to escort me home, Mr. Barlow?"

Barlow looked at her, trying to stifle his surprise. She had never shown any indication that she was afraid of walking the town's streets, especially since she lived so close to Bridie's home. Then he realized—or perhaps it was hoped—that she had an ulterior motive in the request. He nodded. "It'd be no trouble at all, ma'am," he said, slapping on his hat. He took Kathleen's cloak from the peg on the wall and held it out for her.

She slid into it and then tied a bonnet on her head. She turned back into the room. "You come and get me if you need anything at all, Bridie," she said.

Barlow could see Bridie, but not Kathleen, and he was aware of the startled look that passed across the features of Seamus's widow, and he wondered what Kathleen had mouthed or hinted to spark such a reaction.

Then Kathleen faced him, holding out her arm, bent at the elbow. "Shall we go, Mr. Barlow?" she asked.

"Yes'm." He nodded at Bridie. "It was a real pleasure to have met you, ma'am," he said. "I just wish it could've been under better circumstances."

"That would've been nice," Bridie agreed as tears began to well up in her eyes again.

Barlow and Kathleen left, walking into the face of a biting wind. They were silent as they walked the short distance to Kathleen's house, a neat, trim home very much like Bridie's. At the door, Kathleen looked up at Barlow and asked, "Would you like to come in for a spell, Mr. Barlow?"

"I would," Barlow said evenly. "If you don't think it'll cause people to talk. I'd not want to bring embarrassment on you."

"The only one who'd cause a commotion over it would be my dear brother, and since you've talked to him, I would think he's plannin' to give me—and Bridie—a wide berth for some time to come." Kathleen opened her door and walked in.

Barlow, with Buffalo 2 at his side, followed her. The dog wandered around the front room of the house, sniffing at everything.

Kathleen hung her cloak and bonnet up, then took Barlow's belt and coat and hung those, too. Then she turned and without warning, stepped up, wrapped her arms around Barlow's neck, and kissed him hard on the lips.

Barlow was startled by the suddenness of the warm

attack, but he recovered in a moment and returned the assault with equal fervor.

Kathleen pulled back after some moments, her face flushed. "I hope you don't think I'm too forward, Mr. Barlow," she said, panting a little.

"Just forward enough, ma'am." He smiled brightly.

"Then I think we should make our way to the room in back, Mr. Barlow. Don't you agree?"

"I do. But only if you stop callin' me 'Mr. Barlow.' My name's Will, and considerin' what we're about to do, I expect it'd make a heap more sense to use that, ma'am."

"Well, Will, if you stop calling me 'ma'am,' we have a deal." She smiled invitingly. Then she took his hand and led him toward the bedroom at the rear of the house. Inside it, he stopped and took a moment to take it all in.

The room was neat and trim, reflecting its owner. A large four-poster bed, with a thick, colorful quilt, dominated the room. On either side of the head of the bed was a small table, each with an oil lamp and a tin cup full of matches. Against one wall was a chest of drawers on which rested a comb and brush and two books, as well as a heavy family Bible. A table with two chairs rested in front of a window that looked out the back of the house, offering a bleak view at this time of year. A pitcher and basin sat on another small table next to the bureau. A potbellied stove in one corner radiated a decent amount of warmth.

Barlow turned back to Kathleen, who was busily undoing strings, hooks, and buttons, shedding various items of clothing as she did. It seemed to Barlow that it might take a while, but the woman was making swift progress. With a shrug and a smile, Barlow quickly divested himself of his own garments, feeling a surge of pride at Kathleen's gasp of delight at his swollen manhood. He climbed into the bed, sliding under the quilt, and laced his hands behind his head. He watched as Kathleen hurried to finish undressing.

When she was done, Kathleen stood for a few moments, giving Barlow an eyeful. Then she turned in a circle, twice, very slowly, allowing Barlow to have a good look at her from all angles.

Barlow enjoyed the view considerably. After Dulcy Polzin's skinny body, Kathleen Byrne's lush figure looked heavenly. Her breasts were heavy, round, womanly. Her slight pudginess lent a solidly inviting look to her that Barlow thought would be carried over into touch. A fine, round ass tapered to well-formed legs, and a triangle of soft curly reddish-gold hair barely covered the enchantingly pronounced mound of her womanhood.

Kathleen sashayed toward Barlow, yanked the covers off him, and climbed onto the bed, straddling him on hands and knees. Her long, red-gold hair hung in thick waves, brushing his chest.

Barlow smiled up at her. He reached up and cupped her heavy breasts, which were hanging enticingly within easy reach. He ran his thumbs over the rapidly hardening nipples, feeling them pucker with delight. "Your body plumb shines with this ol' chile," he said, smiling.

Kathleen's womanhood brushed the tip of Barlow's erect lance, sending a shiver through her. "You have a mighty fine body yourself, Will," she said, her voice reflecting her lust.

Releasing one of her breasts, Barlow reached up and grabbed Kathleen by the back of the neck. He gently pulled her head down until her lips were on his. Their tongues danced, explored, tantalized.

Barlow finally allowed her to pull her head back. "Bring your other lips up here where I can kiss them, too," Barlow said hoarsely. "They deserve such a thing, don't you think?"

Kathleen wasn't sure she could speak even if she had wanted to respond verbally. She just pushed up off her hands and began squiggling her midsection upward, caressing his body with her wetness, until her lower lips were positioned over the lower half of Barlow's face.

Barlow grabbed Kathleen's pleasingly fleshy hips and

inched her down until his tongue was able to part the silky hairs over her mound of Venus. He worked his tongue in deeper, until the tip encountered her love bud and flicked it.

"Oh, Lordy," Kathleen gasped. She wriggled her hips, trying to grind her mound against his face. But Barlow's strong hands on her hips would not allow it. He continued to tease her labia and pleasure button, eliciting a growing series of moans from her. Her pleasure intensified steadily until a climax shook her, though she made little sound other than a long sighing gasp.

Not sure she had really reached a first pinnacle, Barlow continued his delicious assault on her privates, lips and tongue working magic that soon had her uttering another drawn-out sigh that Barlow now realized was the vocal sign of her release. Her body shuddered, too, with the pleasure of her climax, and her fingernails dug divots in his shoulders.

Continuing to lap at her womanhood with tongue and lips, Barlow let go of Kathleen's hips and began to gently knead her tits, rolling the thick nipples between each thumb and forefinger. Kathleen almost smothered him as, unfettered, she ground her love mound into his face, wanting as much of his mouth in her inner parts as she could get. She shook as another zenith swept over her, sucking her breath away.

Barlow grabbed her hips again, and lifted her a bit off his face so he could draw in some air. Then he gently pushed her up and over completely off him. She glanced at him, her green eyes glassy with desire. Barlow scooted out and rose to his knees. He shoved her gently so she was on hands and knees again, and then he positioned himself between her legs from behind.

Kathleen glanced over her shoulder at him, pure lust flushing her face. "Yes," she muttered, wriggling her backside at him.

Barlow needed no further encouragement. Taking himself in hand, he introduced the head of his lance to her womanly opening, rubbing it up and down the slot to moisten it.

"Yes," Kathleen whispered again.

Barlow slammed himself to the root into her, giving them both a jolt of pleasure. He stayed there a few moments, savoring the feel of her wet, silken sheath. Then he pulled back almost all the way out and began a smooth, calculated back-and-forth movement, sliding powerfully in and out of her.

Within seconds, Kathleen emitted another of her long sighs and her body spasmed as pleasure roared through her.

Barlow slowed, allowing her climax to run its course, then picked up the tempo again, increasing his speed and force.

Twice more Kathleen reached her almost soundless pinnacle before Barlow began to plow her furrow with an insistent and wild intensity. He finally huffed and puffed as he filled her with his essence, back arched, veins on his neck and forehead bulging with the potency of his own powerful climax.

He finally flopped to the bed beside her, landing on his back, breathing heavily.

Kathleen pulled out his arm nearest her and curled up inside it, her body pressed against his. "That was . . ." she gasped.

"Shinin'. Plumb shinin'," Barlow finished for her.

"That it was," Kathleen agreed wholehcartedly.

They lay there for some time, not really moving except once when Kathleen pulled the quilt up over them against the chill. They were silent, too, not really needing to say anything. Both were content to savor the experience they had just had together.

Then Kathleen pushed the cover away again and reached for Barlow's manhood. She grasped it lightly, smiled up at him, and said, "Time you had some special attention." She squiggled down the bed and took him in her mouth.

• • •

They spent the rest of the day and much of the night in such pursuits, before sleep finally overtook the two exhausted lovers. And in the morning, after a wonderful breakfast and before Barlow took his leave, they replayed some of their love adventures.

6

SPRING SEEMED TO be in no hurry to arrive, but long before it fully bloomed, Barlow could feel hints of it. And it stirred an uneasiness in him, an eagerness to be gone from the cloying closeness of the city. While he liked Dulcy Polzin and enjoyed his time with her, after being cooped up with her all winter, he had a yearning to be away.

To be truthful, there was also the pull of the West, of the mountains. He needed to see the towering purple peaks, to breathe the scents of pine and chokecherry instead of the rank odors that inundated civilization, to drink of the cold, pure water that flowed in rushing streams and not the foul liquid of the States. He needed the freedom the mountains gave his soul, though that yearning was tempered by the loss he would have to face again when he returned there. Anna's spiritual presence—as well as that of his slain wife, Sarah, and son, Will Jr.—would permeate that land, he knew, and would haunt him constantly. Still, he was certain in his heart that being in the mountains and knowing their spirit was with him, would be far better than sitting in this cramped, ramshackle cabin in a busy, overpeopled, stench-ridden, profane city with its vastly ill-humored population. Just the thought of it made his essence shrivel and cry out for relief.

There was also the fact that he had nothing to keep him in this area. His family in St. Charles was as gone to him as Anna was, though their absence from his life meant almost nothing to him. He would miss his mother a little, but his brothers not at all.

On the downside of yearning to return to the mountains was the fact that he knew he would eventually have to return to Fort Vancouver in the Oregon country to tell Anna's grandparents what had happened to the little girl. He did not relish the prospect, but it would have to be done. They deserved to know, and he was not one to shirk unpleasant duties forever.

His main problem was in deciding what to do. With the beaver trade long dead, trapping was out of the question, though he did consider hunting other animals whose fur was still valuable. But such a thing just didn't sit well with him. Besides, even with some of the money Bridie Muldoon had given him remaining, it was nowhere near enough to outfit himself for trapping.

He put off thinking about it as much as possible, but he could not avoid the question forever. And spring was fast approaching, though the temperatures and the occasional snow that still fell made that hard to believe.

A solution came out of the blue one evening as he was sitting in a saloon, sipping a beer and considering whether he should join a card game at a nearby table. A man he knew a little from his mountain days spotted him and wandered over.

"You're Will Barlow, ain't you?" the man asked.

Barlow nodded, trying to come up with the man's name, but was unsuccessful.

"We met some years ago at Rendezvous one time," the man said, holding out his hand. He was a tall fellow, well dressed in a wool suit over a starched white shirt and wool vest. He wore no hat, revealing long light brown hair that was graying and thinning. His face showed some of the ravages of a hard life lived in the wilds, though there was now a softness about it that indicated he no longer had to rely on the wilderness for his livelihood.

Barlow shook his hand and said, "I remember. But," he added, somewhat embarrassed, "your name don't come to mind."

"Hugh Samuels. Mind if I sit?"

"Suit yourself," Barlow responded noncommittally.

Samuels sat and ordered a beer for himself and another for Barlow, as well as a shot of whiskey for each. They jolted down the latter and took a few sips of the former. Then Samuels asked, "You aren't, by happenstance, looking for work, are you Mr. Barlow?"

"Might be," Barlow allowed. "I reckon it depends on what kind of job you're offerin'."

"I've come a long way from the mountain times, Mr. Barlow," Samuels said, somewhat unnecessarily, and with more than a touch of pride. "I'm a successful businessman now. I started supplyin' you boys out there at Rendezvous, and built up from there. Now I own stores here and in Independence, Westport, and St. Joseph. Much of my business is outfittin' wagons headin' for the Oregon country."

Barlow nodded, bored. He was not really all that interested in Samuels's history or success. "What's all this got to do with me, hoss?" he asked. He was certain Samuels wanted him to work in one of his stores, something that he had no intention of doing.

"One of the wagon trains I'm outfittin' has asked me to find 'em a hunter and guide. When I come in here and saw you just now, it occurred to me that I might have my man."

"Why me?" Barlow's tone did not betray the fact that he was suddenly interested.

"You're an old mountaineer, which is good enough for me. But beyond that, if I remember correctly, you had brought some missionaries to the Oregon country. That means you know the route. At least the hardest part of the route—west of Bill Sublette's old post. The one they're callin' Fort Laramie these days. That'd be a big plus for the man hired for such a venture."

Barlow sipped some beer, thinking it over, though he quickly realized there wasn't much to really consider. It was a job he could do well, would give him a certain amount of freedom, and would take him back to the mountains and—eventually—to Oregon, where he would finally talk to Anna's grandparents, relieving himself of the burden he had carried with him for so long.

"The job pays three hundred dollars," Samuels said in encouraging tones.

"Five hundred," Barlow said almost unconsciously. He was ready to take the job, but he could see no reason not to get as much money for it as he could.

"Four hundred," Samuels countered.

"Plus whatever supplies and such I'll need."

"Done," Samuels said without hesitation. "The emigrants decided to leave from St. Joe instead of Westport Landing. You'll leave there in three weeks. You'll meet the emigrants there. The feller they elected their captain is a small but feisty Swede named Mattias Ohlmstead. He seems like a competent man."

Barlow nodded. "Should I stop by your store here or the one out by the jumping-off spot?"

"Might as well do it out there, unless you need some supplies to get you to St. Joseph."

"Probably will need a little. Just a few of the basics for the short jaunt over to St. Joseph. I'll stop by just before headin' out that way and pick up what little I need. About a week and a half. That'll give me just about enough time to get out there, meet this Ohlmstead feller, get what goods and gear I need, and see that everything is all right before we have to leave out."

"I'm obliged,"

Barlow shrugged. Since it would benefit him at least as much as it would Samuels, he saw no need for thanks. He did, however, have one concern that he wanted to address right away, before Samuels left. "When do I get paid?"

"I'll see that you get half when you pick up supplies at my store in St. Joe," Samuels said evenly. He had his mind made up on this, and while he did not want to insult or anger Barlow, he wanted him to know that this was the way it would be. "You'll get the other half when you get to the Willamette Valley."

"That suits," Barlow said. He could see no problem in such an arrangement. He didn't need all the money up front, with Samuels supplying him. And he had no worries about getting the other half in Oregon. He would have no trouble taking it by force if Ohlmstead was foolish enough to be reluctant to give it to him.

Samuels finished his beer, stood, shook hands with Barlow again, and then sauntered out.

Barlow lit his pipe. One problem was solved, but now he faced another—telling Dulcy Polzin that he was leaving so soon. He knew she cared deeply for him; far more than he did for her, though she tried to hide it. But he was not about to stay tied down here, to her, when there was traveling to be done and time to be spent in the mountains.

He finally finished his beer and stood. "C'mon, Buffler," he said, "let's go get it done with."

At home, he ate, perplexed again at Dulcy's lack of improvement in culinary skills over the past few months. After the meal, they tumbled gleefully into bed.

More than an hour later, after they had calmed down and were lying close to each other, Dulcy comfortable in the crook of his arm, Barlow took a deep breath, let it out slowly, and then said bluntly, "I'll be leavin' soon, Dulcy."

She had always known such an announcement would come, though she had hoped it would not. She could not say that she was surprised, but she was disappointed despite herself. "For good?" she asked in a small voice.

"I expect so." He squeezed her a little, hoping to take some of the sting out of his words, but he didn't think it worked. "It ain't likely that I'll be back in these parts."

Dulcy said nothing, but Barlow could tell by the tightness of her body where it rested against his that she was considerably upset.

"Where are you going?" Her voice was caught between anger and hurt.

"I've been hired on to lead a wagon train to the Oregon country," he explained quietly.

"I see." Her voice was now icy. She wondered how he could leave the comforts she offered him for a long, dusty journey across forbidding lands.

"I leave in a week and a half," he added uselessly. He wished he could do or say something to make Dulcy feel better, but he couldn't. The only thing that would work, he knew, was deciding to stay here with her forever, and he would not—could not—do that. He finally fell asleep, but it was rather fitful.

The tension between the two of them over the next couple of days was palpable, and Barlow tended to stay out of the small house as much as possible. Then he came home one afternoon and dropped a piece of paper on the battered table.

"What's this?" Dulcy asked, torn between interest and fear. She picked it up gingerly by one corner.

"Read it."

"I can't read so well," Dulcy admitted, her face reddening in embarrassment.

"Neither can I," Barlow said flatly. "It don't matter none." He paused, then added softly, "That paper is the deed to this place. I had it put in your name."

"You what?" Dulcy was shocked.

"I had the house put in your name, Dulcy. I know this place ain't much, but once I leave, it'll be all yours. You can do with it what you will. Stay here, or sell it, if you're of a mind to, and use the money to move elsewhere."

"I understand what it means," Dulcy said, close to tears. "But . . . why?"

Barlow shrugged, somewhat embarrassed. "It's the least I could do for you, Dulcy," he said honestly. "You've been a kind and warm and pleasin' companion these many months, and it just wouldn't be right for me to go on and leave without makin' some plans for your livin' arrangements." His voice trailed off. What he had said was true, but when he spoke it, it sounded mighty stupid to him.

"And you wonder why I care so much for you, damn you," Dulcy said, crying freely now. She came up and rested her head on his broad chest, locking her arms around his midsection.

Barlow wrapped his arms around her, feeling awkward. "I ain't really all that good a feller, Dulcy," he offered. "I just thought this'd be right. You deserve to have the house after all you've done to make it such a homey place."

"Well, it was a mighty nice thing to do. Nobody's ever done anything like this for me before."

"Weren't nothin'," Barlow insisted. "Just make sure you watch who you let in here once I'm gone. You don't need no more visitors like Claude and them others."

Dulcy trembled at the recollection. "I'll be careful," she vowed.

Though she was still brokenhearted to know that he would be going soon, Dulcy warmed up to Barlow again because she was touched by his gesture. And though she would not admit it, even to herself, she still harbored a slight flicker of hope that he might change his mind after all and stay with her. Or, at the very least, come back here after his trip to Oregon.

The time passed far too quickly for Dulcy, though to Barlow it dragged. He didn't particularly want to be away from Dulcy; he just wanted to be on the trail.

The day before he was to leave finally arrived, however, and Barlow went to Samuels's store, where he got enough supplies to last him on the trip to St. Joseph, which he expected would take about ten days.

After getting back to the house, he and Dulcy made love for a while, and then she went to make supper for them. When she placed plates, coffeepot, and mugs on the table, Barlow smiled at her and set several gold coins on the table next to her dinner plate. It was what he had left of the money Bridie Muldoon had given him.

"That should tide you over for a spell, Dulcy," Barlow said. "It ain't very much, but it's about all I have left."

Dulcy fought back tears—tears of joy at his generosity, tears of sadness that he would be leaving in the morning, so they had only a few more hours together.

That night, as he and Dulcy were sitting at the table finishing up dinner, Buffalo 2 suddenly started growling, eyeing the door warily. A moment later there was a knock.

Picking up one of his Colt Walkers, a surprised Barlow headed to the door and flung it open. His surprise grew when he spotted two of his young nephews, Derek and Clyde.

"Howdy, Uncle Will," Derek said.

7

"WHAT THE HELL'RE you two doin' here?" Barlow asked, still recovering from the start they had given him.

"We come lookin' for you, Uncle Will," Derek said. He was trying to sound confident and adventurous, but the worried look in his eyes betrayed him.

"What'n hell for?"

"We want to go with you."

"Go where?"

"Wherever you're goin'," Derek said matter-of-factly. "We figure you're headin' for the mountains again, and we want to go."

"I can't . . ."

"Invite them in, for heaven's sake, Will," Dulcy said.

"Yes," Barlow said, shaking his head, trying to get over the shock at seeing his two nephews appear out of nowhere and make the pronouncement they had. "C'mon in, boys. You hungry?"

Both youths nodded as they entered the house. They petted Buffalo 2 on their way to the table, then sat. Their faces and hands were dirty, their hair was matted, and their clothes were worn through in spots. Dulcy brought them ham and fried potatoes and coffee. The two dug into the food, not seeming to mind that it wasn't very tasty.

"Will, please introduce our guests," Dulcy suggested.

Barlow realized that the woman had no clue as to the identity of the young men, other than that at least one of them was his nephew. "Dulcy Polzin, these here critters is Derek and Clyde Barlow, my nephews."

Each youth nodded when his name was mentioned.

"Derek's the oldest son of my oldest brother, Finlay. Clyde is Clyde Jr., eldest son of the middle Barlow brother."

"Pleased to meet you," Dulcy said sweetly, though nervously. She was not quite sure how to act around the two boys. After all, she and Barlow were living in sin, and she wouldn't know what to say to them should they ask about her status.

The youths nodded, but said nothing. They were still too interested in their food to worry about the marital status of some woman in their uncle's house.

"Your folks know where you are?" Barlow asked.

Derek shook his head, his mouth too full of food to say anything.

"Tell me again why you're here," Barlow commanded.

"We want you to take us with you," Derek answered after he swallowed.

"Why?" Barlow asked.

"We're tired of the farm, Uncle Will," Derek said seriously, his eyes owlish as he stopped feeding for a moment to stare at Barlow. "We see our mas and pas and the way they're livin', and it just don't seem like the way to live."

"Nothin' wrong in being farmers, boy," Barlow said, hoping it did not sound as false to the two youths as it did to his own ears. "It's honorable and important work. So's raisin' a family."

Derek and Clyde shrugged as one. Barlow was surprised at how much they resembled him more than their own fathers. Though young, they were already beginning to look like him, with his massive torso, stout legs, and bull neck. He could see his brothers in them, too, but he realized that just in the few months since he had seen the boys last, they had changed in body—and, apparently, in spirit—to become more like him. It was a disconcerting thing to see himself reflected so clearly in these two youths. He hadn't expected such a thing until he had children—boys—of his own. Well, he really hadn't thought of it since little Will Jr. had been killed. He had assumed then that his son would have grown up much like him.

"That's hogwash, Uncle Will," Clyde said firmly. He stared almost defiantly at Barlow, before turning to look at Dulcy, his expression pleading for more food, though he did not ask.

The woman smiled and got them more to eat. She was pleased that they seemed to not notice that her cooking was quite poor. Not that Barlow had ever said anything to her about it, but she knew how he felt about her cooking. Their frequent jaunts to one or two local eateries where the fare was fairly decent were a good indication of that.

"That's right," Derek agreed. "We're lookin' for some adventures, like the ones you talked about."

"Besides," Clyde added, "we're gettin' some tired of the beatin's we've been given regular since . . ."

"Beatin's?" Barlow asked, a spark of anger planted inside of him. "What's this about beatin's?"

"Pa and Uncle Clyde have taken to whuppin' us regular," Derek said "Ever since you visited us."

"They're whuppin' you because of tales I told?" Barlow demanded. His anger was rising fast.

"Yep," Derek said with a firm nod that was copied by Clyde.

Barlow was about to fly into a tirade, but he managed to calm himself and sat there thinking for a moment. Finally he said, "That don't make no sense, boys. My broth-

ers ain't the most compassionate folks I ever knew, but I
can't seem them whuppin' your hides just over a few tales
I told you a couple months ago. I think you boys're lyin'
to me. Or at least not tellin' me the whole truth. Now
'fess up, boys. What's brought these beatin's on from
your fathers?"

"You might say, I guess, that me'n Clyde have become
a tad rebellious after you come visitin' us, Uncle Will,"
Derek said sheepishly.

"Rebellious?" Barlow repressed a smile. These boys
were turning out more like him every moment.

"Slackin' off some on our chores and such," Derek
said. He was still somewhat subdued, but he had returned
to eating. "We often went off lookin' for adventures
around the family places." He shrugged. "Not that there
was much of it to find out there in the middle of the
winter."

"They treated me much the same way," Barlow admitted. "Leastways, till I got big enough to keep 'em from
tryin' to whup on me. They always were much more like
my pa than I was. Hardworkin', diligent, mighty self-
righteous in many ways."

"That's the way it is for us," Clyde said with a firm
nod.

"Just what makes you think I'm goin' anywhere?" Barlow countered after a few moments of silence. He glanced
at Dulcy out of the corner of his eye, wondering what
Dulcy would think about his question to the boys. She
didn't seem to be bothered by it, to his relief.

"Pa says you're too footloose to stick round these here
parts," Clyde said with a shrug. "He even said he figured
you was long gone from here already."

Barlow bit back a smile. Despite their lack of contact
over the past decade, his brothers—or at least Clyde—
knew him pretty well. "So, then, where do you boys think
I'm headin'?" Barlow questioned, somewhat bemused.

"Don't matter none," Derek said. He finally pushed his plate away from him, sated. "We just want to go with you. Wherever it is you're plannin' to go."

"That's right, Uncle Will," Clyde added. "We figure there'll be adventures aplenty wherever it is you go."

Barlow fought back a grimace. While he was not ashamed, really, of anything he had ever done, he didn't like having such a reputation with his nephews. Plus there was the fact of their innocence. They had no idea of what they would face if he took them along. He had made the tales he told them sound too interesting, too much like fun. He should have told them the truth—or more of it anyway. Things like how bloody and painful—and potentially deadly—an encounter with hostile Indians could be. Or how the temperatures in the mountains and even on the plains would be so cold as to freeze a man to death in minutes if he wasn't careful. Or how often starving times came upon a man, times when he would eat anything, from handfuls of ants to his own moccasins, just to stay alive. Or the blazing heat in some of the deserts, places where a man could go for days without water, until his tongue swelled up like a bloated, drowned buffalo carcass. Or the pain from a bullet or arrow wound or from being gored by a bull buffalo. Or the loneliness that could come over a man, driving him almost to the brink of madness sometimes. Or the smallness one could feel in the shadow of the towering mountains or the vastness of the plains.

He sighed, realizing they would not have believed any of that anyway. He wouldn't have at their age. They were at an age where they felt invincible, that nothing could hurt them; that there was nothing they could not overcome with youthful exuberance. No, they would have to learn the hardships for themselves.

Besides, and Barlow almost smiled at it, though he managed to contain it, there was a lot of good out there in the wilds. The yearning he had felt for the mountains just a few weeks ago was a real thing, and its causes were something every young man should experience, he thought. There were good friendships to be had. Friendships with men like White Bear, the British sounding Shoshoni, or Sim Rutledge, Charlie Watters, and Caleb Simon, the men who had taken him into the mountains and shown him the ways there. There was fine eating, too—buffalo liver, or heart, or lungs, eaten raw, still warm, torn from fresh-killed cow; or roasted hump meat or fleece, and boudins sizzling just off the fire. And then there were the women, ones like Mountain Calf, the beautiful Nez Percé, and Raven Moon, the delightful Flathead. Yes, he decided, there was much good to be said about the wilderness and its inhabitants and adventures.

Only one thing bothered him about it, though, and he voiced that concern: "You boys're mighty young for such doin's as traipsin' round the mountains lookin' to take part in the kind of excitin' exploits your imaginations've conjured up."

"No, we ain't," Derek protested.

"Hell, boy, you ain't but twelve years old," Barlow countered. "And Clyde there's not even that yet."

"I'll be twelve in a couple weeks," Clyde said fiercely.

"And I already turned thirteen," Derek added just as fervently. "More'n a month ago now. And that's plenty old enough."

Barlow sat there thinking about it for a while. He had been a lot older than they when he had headed west. Of course, he had been getting into all kinds of trouble around St. Charles around the same age as these boys were. And, he well knew, Indian youths were ready for the hunt and the war trail when they reached thirteen. Plus, Derek and Clyde were big for their ages.

Barlow was torn, unsure of what he should do. He could plainly see that the boys were much like him, and would never make good farmers. If he didn't take them, they would end up the way he had been going before he headed west—always in trouble, drinking and fighting. They would either run off on their own, and probably get killed with no one to watch over them and help them learn how to survive in the wilderness. Or they would end up in a local jail, or worse, hanged, for killing someone in a drunken rage or something.

Still, they were kind of young yet, and they were his brothers' sons. While he had no love for his brothers, he debated in his mind whether it would be right to bring Derek and Clyde back to their homes. That would, he knew, be the right thing in his brothers' minds. But if the boys were truthful about their fathers beating them—and he had no reason to doubt them, really—then returning them wouldn't be right.

What finally made up his mind for him, however, was simply time. He had no time to spare. He had to leave tomorrow to get to the jumping-off point on schedule. He could not really afford to take the time to make the ride to St. Charles—with two reluctant youngsters in tow— and then head to St. Joseph. Plus there was the little matter of how annoyed it would make his brothers when they found out that their oldest sons had run off to find adventure with their old reprobate of an uncle. He almost smiled at that.

"All right, boys," he finally said. "You can go with me. But," he added hastily, cutting off their whoops of celebration, "you best listen to what I tell you, or the whuppin's your fathers gave you will seem like lovin' caresses from your mamas once I get through with you."

"Yessir," both youths exclaimed, trying to look serious. But the somberness lasted less than a minute, and they were up doing their version of a war dance around the battered table.

Once they had settled down and sat again, and were sipping coffee, Barlow asked, "How the hell'd you two critters ever find me anyway?"

"We just come down here hopin' to find you," Derek

said. He looked at Dulcy. "May I have some more coffee, ma'am?" he asked politely. When she had poured it for him, Derek said, "We weren't sure you'd be in St. Louis, but it was the best place to start."

"It was the only place to go," Clyde interjected. "We couldn't have made it to Westport or someplace like that."

Derek nodded. "As soon as we got here, we just started askin' around for a big feller with a giant black dog." He grinned. "We just kept askin'. It wasn't too long before we found people who'd met you. They sent us from one place to another. Until finally some feller in a store told us he thought you were livin' here."

Barlow chuckled. He supposed he was easy to find, considering the figure he cut through town and the furry companion who was constantly at his side.

Soon after, Barlow said, "It's robe time for this chile, boys." He was glad Dulcy had made him put the curtain up again to make a bedroom at the back. Despite that, he sat there considering sending the youths out to sleep in the lean-to stable out back.

He glanced at Dulcy, and realized she had the same thought. She would not be put off from making love to him on his last night with her, but she did not relish the thought of doing such an intimate thing with two youngsters sleeping a few feet away, even if there was a curtain to hide their actions. It certainly wouldn't blot out the sounds of their lovemaking.

He nodded and gave her a quick grin. "You boys," he said, "are about to get your first wilderness experience. There's an old lean-to out back where we have Beelzebub, my mule, and some horses stabled. You can spend the night there. I'll come get you in the mornin'. Early."

While he was speaking, Dulcy had gotten some blankets. She handed them to the boys. "You should be plenty warm enough," she said, trying not to look—or sound— embarrassed.

Neither youth seemed put out by the command. They

had slept outside—without blankets—twice on their journey to St. Louis from their homes near St. Charles. They grabbed the blankets, petted Buffalo 2 for a few moments, then headed out the door, chatting excitedly.

8

DEREK AND CLYDE didn't grumble too much when Barlow roused them in the morning. They were used to getting up early on the farm, and while they were tired from their journey and would've liked more sleep, they were excited. This was, after all, the first day of what they expected to be a long series of adventures.

After a breakfast of hens' eggs and more ham, as well as Dulcy's fine coffee, Barlow led Buffalo 2 and the two boys out to the lean-to. He saddled Beelzebub and walked the mule outside. Then he helped the youths saddle the three horses that had belonged to the men who had invaded his home while he had been gone, using the dead men's saddles. They mounted up and rode off, heading toward the center of an awakening St. Louis, Barlow towing the third, riderless horse behind him.

The three pulled up in front of Hugh Samuels's store, tied the animals there, and went inside.

"You on your way out, Will?" Samuels asked as he shook Barlow's hand.

"Soon's I pick up a few more things here," Barlow replied.

"Oh?" Samuels questioned, a little surprised. "I thought

you had everything you need to get you to St. Joe."

"I did," Barlow said with a small grin. "Till these two critters showed up at my door last night. Hugh, meet my nephews, Derek and Clyde Barlow."

The two suddenly shy youths each solemnly shook Samuels's hand, then stepped back a little.

"You takin' 'em with you?" Samuels asked, looking at Barlow in question.

Barlow nodded. "So I need a few things for 'em."

"That ain't part of our deal, Will," Samuels said, suddenly all businesslike.

"I know that, hoss," Barlow said a bit harshly. He hadn't expected Samuels to give him the goods he planned to get for his nephews, but he hadn't expected such a reaction from the store owner either.

Samuels relaxed a little, and some of his usual jovialness returned to his face and manner.

"I got an extra horse outside, with saddle and all," said Barlow. "I expect that'll cover whatever I need."

"Well, let's go take a look," Samuels said, stepping out from behind the counter.

They all went outside, where Barlow pointed out the horse he planned to trade. He had determined before they left which of the three would be best suited for the two boys.

Samuels spent a few minutes looking the animal over, as well as checking out the saddle. It didn't take long, then he stepped back. "I can give you seventy-five dollars for the horse and the tack."

"That suits." Barlow thought he could get more somewhere else, but he had neither the time nor the desire to go around St. Louis dickering over a few dollars. Samuels's offer was fair enough and would cover what he needed to purchase.

Back inside, Barlow ordered a bit more jerky, flour, sugar, and coffee. Then he asked, "What do you have in the way of halfway decent rifles these boys could learn to handle?" Barlow asked. "You know what they'd need to use 'em for, but I figure I can't afford none of Mr. Haw-ken's fine rifles."

"I have an older Dickert and an older Henry. A lot like the one you're still carryin' after all these years."

Barlow grinned a little. "It's a fine gun, and I ain't about to give it up."

"Don't blame you."

"I'll take those rifles and all the accoutrements for 'em."

Samuels turned and took down two rifles from a rack on the wall. He set them on the counter, then added two powder horns, two powder flasks, a pair of bullet molds, a roll of patch material, and a pair of small tool sets. He tossed in a couple of worn buckskin saddle scabbards for the rifles.

"Anything else?" Samuels asked.

"Let me have a couple of them little Colt Paterson re-volvers, too, Hugh."

Samuels nodded and placed the two weapons on the counter. He added the accessories for them, too, including a pair of small, hard leather pouches of paper cartridges. "You need holsters for the pistols?" he asked.

Barlow shook his head. "A couple of decent belts'd do, though," he said after a glance at his nephews. He could see through their open coats that they had rope holding up their pants. He considered getting them new coats, too, since the ones they wore were pretty worn, but he decided against it. The garments would last another couple of weeks, and by then they would be unneeded with summer coming on.

"And might's well see if you got some pants and shirts that'll fit these critters, too," he added.

"Anything else?" Samuels asked after he had laid four pairs of pants, four shirts, and two pairs of working boots on the counter.

"I reckon that should do, hoss," Barlow said.

A few minutes later, the new supplies were wrapped in thick brown paper. Barlow and Samuels dickered over the six more dollars Barlow owed, until Samuels gave in and just called it even. Barlow and the boys went outside and stored their goods in sacks hanging from the boys' saddles. Samuels had wandered outside, and stood there watching. Barlow tied the scabbards to his nephews' saddles and stuffed their rifles—unloaded—into them.

Barlow told the boys to mount up, but before he did so himself, he walked over to where Samuels was standing. "I'd be obliged if you could get word to my brothers about the two boys," he said. "Finlay and Clyde have farms outside St. Charles. Just tell 'em that the boys are safe and with me. No need to tell 'em where we're headed, though I suppose it won't hurt none. Tell 'em the boys wanted some adventure and were dead set against becomin' farmers."

Samuels nodded. "Consider it done. I have a man headin' out that way day after next."

Barlow nodded.

"Fred Turner's my man in St. Joe," Samuels said. "Talk to him when you get there. He'll see that you get everything you need."

"Obliged." Barlow climbed into the saddle on Beelzebub. With a tip of his battered hat at Samuels, Barlow turned his mule and rode off, his nephews close behind, Buffalo 2 trotting nearby.

Barlow pushed the boys some, but not too hard. He had no time to dawdle, but he didn't want his nephews worn out in a couple of days and then be unable to keep up. They made better than thirty miles a day of steady traveling, even though they did stop for an hour or two now and then so Barlow could teach the boys some of the things they would need to know to survive, not the least of which was how to use the single-shot, muzzle-loading, cap-lock rifles and the small five-shot revolvers he had bought for them.

The youths learned everything quickly, soaking up the knowledge, and within a couple of days, their camps were

swiftly made and broken with a minimum of fuss. By the
fourth day, Barlow had Derek and Clyde took turns hunting, usually deer and some antelope—animals big enough
to make a relatively easy target for them, yet not as large
as a buffalo, which were much harder to take down.

Around the fire at night, as they sipped on heavily sug-
ared coffee after a meal of fresh deer meat or something,
Barlow would regale the two youths with tales of his adventures. He realized sometimes that he was probably giving them a false sense of what they faced, but he couldn't
help it. He did include in his stories some of the dangers,
but somehow the excitement and thrills always out-
weighed the poor times. The one thing he avoided, however, was any mention of Sarah, Anna, and Little Will,
because he had absolutely no desire to relive that pain.
Not until he had to.

But that plan died when Clyde asked one night, "Was
you ever married, Uncle Will?"

"Of course he wasn't married," Derek retorted. "He
ain't met no women out there but Injin women, and you
can't marry them. You're such a damn fool, Clyde."

"Am not," Clyde snapped, almost pouting.

"Are, too," Derek teased.

"Enough!" Barlow growled, shocking both boys a little.
He sat there, pain in his heart, wondering what, if anything, he should tell his nephews about his lost family.
He could, he knew, take the easy way out and not say
anything, basically agreeing with Derek's assessment. But
he thought that would be unfair to the youths.

"Somethin' wrong, Uncle Will?" Derek asked, quickly
growing worried.

Barlow appeared not to hear him. "Yes, I was married,
boys," he said, his voice sounding far away. "Sarah was
an Injin. Well, half Injin. Her pa was a trader, her ma a
Chinook. We got married and had us a little place near
the Willamette River in the Oregon country." His voice
trailed off.

"Is that where we're goin'?" Derek asked, suddenly scared.

Barlow nodded, still distracted. "We had us two kids. Two fine children, a gal, Anna, and Little Will."

The two boys sat wide-eyed, interested but worried. They had never seen their uncle in such a state. While they had not been with him for very long, he had never acted this way before, and it was somewhat frightening to them.

Barlow shook his head, trying to clear away the gloom. He wasn't entirely successful, but managed a little. "Anyways, boys, some Injins called Umpquas attacked our cabin whilst I was off huntin'. They kilt Sarah and Little Will."

Derek and Clyde gasped in shock, and they cast troubled glances at each other.

"Those fractious sons of bitches carried my sweet little Anna off."

Clyde seemed close to tears. "Did they kill her, too?" he asked in a quavering voice.

"No, Clyde. No, they didn't," Barlow said quietly, seeming to become himself a bit more. "They took her off to their village. I went after her, but . . . well . . ."

"You never found her, did you?" Derek asked, his voice cracking with horror.

Barlow sucked in a deep breath, and then let it ease out. "No, boys," he lied flatly, "I never did find her." He clamped his mouth shut and fought to control himself. After a minute or two, he said, "Well, boys, it's robe time for this ol' chile."

The two youths had a fitful night's sleep, and when they awoke the next morning, they cast worried, wondering glances at their uncle. Barlow was himself, though, and greeted them as warmly as usual. Derek and Clyde, however, were, despite their young ages, astute enough to know not to broach the subject of Barlow's family around him again, though they did occasionally talk about it between themselves in hushed voices, wondering what their uncle was feeling inside, and how they might react if the same thing ever happened to them.

"Maybe this adventure thing ain't gonna be so much fun," Clyde whispered to Derek one night when they were certain that Barlow was asleep.

"Aw, that ain't ever gonna happen to us, Clyde," Derek said, sounding a lot more certain than he felt. "I ain't plannin' to ever marry some Injin woman anyway."

"Might not have a choice out where we're goin'—if we even ever decide we want to be married. I ain't so sure about gettin' married at all. I can't see no need for it."

"You'll change your tune soon enough," Derek said with a false authority. "Once you learn about women."

"You don't know nothin' about women, you knothead," Clyde insisted.

"You'll see."

They made good time on the trip, slowed only once by a spring snowstorm that suddenly swooped down on them, slowing their travel to a crawl for the best part of a day. And once, a storm that poured sleet and rain down on them made for slow going for an afternoon. But they made up the time on the day after each, pushing hard.

Ten days after leaving St. Louis, they rode into the small but bustling hamlet of St. Joseph, Missouri. Since it was late in the afternoon, Barlow stopped at a hotel and got them a room.

"Best enjoy it, boys," Barlow said as they dropped their gear in the room. "It'll likely be the last time you have a roof—a real roof—over your head for some time to come."

They took the animals to a livery and cared for them, then had a fine supper in the eatery attached to the small, pleasant hotel. They were rather surprised at the quality of the fare, especially Barlow. "I sure wish Dulcy had been able to cook this good," he said, grinning. "I might not've left St. Louis if she had."

After eating, they strolled through the town for a short while, finding Samuels's store, which was closed now, as Barlow had figured it would be, and then headed back to the hotel. Tired, they hit the two beds—Barlow in one, the youths sharing the other—straightaway.

In the morning, they breakfasted at the hotel restaurant, and then headed to Samuels's store. Fred Turner, the head clerk, was busy with other customers, but handed them off to a junior clerk when he learned that Barlow was there. He hurried over and introduced himself.

"Mr. Samuels said I was to make sure you were properly outfitted, Mr. Barlow," he said. "So whatever supplies you need, you just let me know. He also told me to give you this."

Barlow opened the parcel he handed to him. It was half of his pay.

Barlow spent the better part of the morning picking out supplies for himself and his nephews. Turner did not argue, and Barlow was not all that concerned. He figured that if Samuels objected to outfitting Derek and Clyde, there was little he could do about it unless Barlow ever went back to St. Louis. That was unlikely, and even if he did, he would worry about the few dollars at that point.

As part of outfitting himself for the long journey, Turner took Barlow and the youths to the livery, where he picked out almost two dozen mules. Two or three would carry his supplies; the others would be used to tote meat while he was hunting on the trail.

Finally everything was chosen and packed. Barlow, Turner, and the youths saddled up, and Turner led the way out to where the emigrants had gathered with their wagons in anticipation of leaving.

A short, swaggering man with bright blond hair and brighter blue eyes saw them coming, and was waiting for them when they stopped.

The newcomers dismounted, and Turner said, "Mr. Barlow, this is the man elected captain by his fellow emigrants, Mattias Ohlmstead. Mr. Ohlmstead, this is the man Mr. Samuels hired as your guide and hunter, Will Barlow."

The two men shook hands, and when Ohlmstead looked curiously at the two boys, Barlow introduced them. "They'll be comin' along," Barlow said flatly, letting Ohlmstead know that he would brook no argument about it, should the Swede be so inclined.

Ohlmstead simply shrugged and said, "Velcome. Come, ve vill put your mules vit da other animals. Then I vill show you around."

9

THE MEMBERS OF Ohlmstead's wagon train were about what Barlow had expected—a mix of people from various states and other countries looking for a way to get ahead to put behind them whatever failures plagued them, or to chase a dream that had grown since childhood. A few spoke little English, if any at all. All were rather poor, and many—especially the men—had a haunted look in their eyes, as if they thought this was their last chance to make something of themselves. Many of the women looked worried, having followed footloose or dreaming husbands to this point, and while they were ready to continue following them, they were frightened and unsure about what the future would bring.

Barlow was a little surprised to see that they were pretty well outfitted. Each wagon had at least three yoke of oxen, and some had four. Their big Conestogas were, for the most part, in good shape, and looked capable of making the long journey, which was more than Barlow could say about some of the people he spotted.

Mattias Ohlmstead introduced Barlow to only a few of the emigrants. There were too many of them for Barlow to learn their names, and he would have few dealings with most of them anyway. Then the captain and guide sat sipping coffee and puffing pipes, talking in the sparse shade offered by a willow that was just sprouting its new growth. Buffalo 2 sprawled on his side a few feet away, uttering high-pitched sounds now and then as he chased rabbits in his sleep. Derek and Clyde had wandered off, talking to some other youths about their own ages, and Barlow was certain that Derek had his eye on a brown-haired girl of about thirteen who was just blossoming into young womanhood.

"Is everyone ready to leave, Mattias?" Barlow asked.

"Ya," Ohlmstead responded. "Ve have been vaitin' for you to come along so ve could be on da vay." He did not sound accusatory.

Barlow nodded. "Good. We'll leave out come first light, then, if that suits."

"It does." Ohlmstead seemed eager to be on the trail.

"You think these folks're ready for such a trip?" Barlow asked.

Ohlmstead shrugged. "I don't know dese people for too long, but I t'ink most of dem vill do vell."

"It's gonna be mighty arduous, you know, hoss," Barlow commented, emphasizing his words with a few jabs of his pipe stem.

"I have heard dat, ya." Ohlmstead paused. "Vhat vill ve face?" he finally asked. "Ve have seen some books from others who have made dis trip, but, vell, I ain't so sure I belief dem."

"It's a good thing to be skeptical, hoss," Barlow said flatly. "From what I've heard, most of the fellers who wrote them books don't know their ass from a chuck hole." He paused to relight his pipe and finish off his coffee.

When Ohlmstead's wife, Agneta, came over to refill it, the captain spoke to her in their own language. She nodded and hurried off. She returned moments later with a small jug and handed it to her husband.

"A bit of vhiskey vill make dat coffee better, ya?" Ohlmstead said with a grin.

"That idea plumb shines with this chile, hoss," Barlow agreed, holding out his tin mug.

Ohlmstead poured a decent dollop of whiskey into Barlow's mug, then did the same for himself before setting the jug down beside him on the burgeoning grass. *"Till vår framgången,"* Ohlmstead said, holding up his cup to touch Barlow's. "To our success."

"And a safe journey," Barlow added.

They drank a bit. Then Ohlmstead said, "So, Mr. Barlow, tell me vhat ve vill be facing out there."

"Nearabout anything you can think of, hoss. This time of year, we can still get snow or sleet. Maybe some hail. Rain. Later we'll hit desert, where there ain't no water to speak of. Another month or so and the heat'll fry you where you walk. There'll be game aplenty most of the way, but out on the plains, there ain't much in the way of firewood for cookin'. You'll have to rely on booshwa for . . ."

"On vhat?"

"Booshwa," Barlow said with a small chuckle. "Dried buffler shit. It burns fast, but it burns hot and gives fresh meat an almost peppery flavor. There'll likely be sickness along the way. Wild critters can cause a heap of grief, especially snakes. There's some reptiles out there whose bite'll kill you easy, though you'll be in pain for some days before the end comes. There'll be some mighty big rivers to cross, something that don't shine with this chile a-tall. And all that's before we get to the worst of the mountains.

"And we'll have to get to the Oregon country before September," Barlow added. "Or we could see some poor times for certain. Up in the mountains, the snow starts along about September. Now, seein' as you come from a place of cold and heaps of snow, that might not mean much to you, hoss, but believe me, you don't want to be travelin' with wagons through mountain passes in the snow."

Ohlmstead shook his head in amazement, beginning to

wonder if any of them would make the journey alive.

"Then there'll be the trouble amongst your people. Such hardships as they'll see on the trail can bring out the worst in men. Enmities will build and fights'll break out. You'll have to keep a tight rein on some of them folks if they start gettin' fractious."

"I vill do dat, never fear," Ohlmstead said firmly.

Despite Ohlmstead's rather small stature, Barlow believed he would do just what he said, though Barlow was somewhat amused at the sight of Ohlmstead and his wife together. Agneta was a good half foot taller than Mattias. She was also an extremely attractive woman, one who would draw plenty of attention from men who had little or no decency about them. Barlow figured Mattias had been called upon more than once to discourage such unwanted advances, another reason why Barlow thought the Swede would be able to handle himself under the toughest circumstances.

"Speaking of fights," Ohlmstead said, "vhat about Injins? Do ve have to vorry about dem soon? Or later in da trip?"

Barlow laughed a little. "Far's I know, hoss, we ain't got to worry about 'em at all."

"But I t'ought . . ."

"Despite what you might've heard, Mr. Ohlmstead," Barlow said, "Injins ain't madmen. They got too much sense to attack a wagon train with this many people. It's a good way for 'em to get kilt, and whilst they're brave warriors, most of 'em, they don't like gettin' kilt no more'n you or I do, hoss."

"They're not hostile?" Ohlmstead asked, surprised.

"Sure, some of 'em are. Some of 'em can be downright plumb mean critters. But they ain't gonna attack so many travelers. 'Sides, they got no reason to attack a wagon train. Most of the time they attack ain't just to rub out some folks. They usually attack for personal gain—which, to all Injins I know of, means horses. And since you ain't got many of those, they have no reason to attack."

"But everyt'ing on da vagons?"

"Injins got no use for it. What the hell's some damned Arikara warrior gonna do with a spinnin' wheel?" He grinned.

"The oxen?"

"No self-respectin' Injin's gonna eat oxen when there's so many buffler they can block your path for days at a time. Hell, ain't no man, white or red, who makes his life in the wilderness gonna eat ox when buffler's so easy to be had. Ain't no better eatin' for a man than buffler. You'll see, once we get a couple days out from civilization, where the buffler are roamin' all over."

Before Ohlmstead could say anything, Barlow added, "Now, if somebody goes wanderin' off by theyselves or somethin', there might be a chance some roamin' war party'd snatch that person up and run off with 'em, 'specially women or kids—a man they'd as likely kill as not, dependin' on their humor at the time. But they ain't about to attack a whole wagon train."

"I'm beginning to t'ink it's a good t'ing you're our guide and hunter, Mr. Barlow," Ohlmstead said firmly. "Vhile you have mentioned many t'ings dat can go wrong out dere, you have soothed some of my concerns—ones shared by most of the travelers."

"I just hope I can live up to your expectations, hoss," Barlow said modestly. He was proud that Ohlmstead felt that way, but he didn't necessarily want the responsibility of his high expectations.

"Vill ve make any progress—distance—at all tomorrow?" Ohlmstead asked.

"Ain't likely. We'll be plumb lucky if we can get everyone across the Missouri alive—and with all their wagons, animals, and goods intact—by day's end."

"As I t'ought." Ohlmstead paused. "Perhaps ve should have done it a few days ago and vaited for you over dere."

"It don't matter none," Barlow said with a shrug. "It might've saved a day or two, but it's still early for travelin', and it shouldn't make any difference to the journey in the long run."

"Vell," Ohlmstead said, pushing to his feet, "I better go see dat everyvon is ready so ve have no delays tomorrow."

Barlow nodded. "Oh, just one more thing," he called. When Ohlmstead turned back, Barlow asked, "You mind if I hitch my mules to your wagon once we get rollin', hoss? I'll be off huntin' much of the day most times, and I ain't plannin' to haul along my supply-laden mules whilst doin' so."

"Ya, dat vould be all right. Yoost tie 'em to da vagon." He turned and wandered off, his walk cocky.

The camp was bedlam in the morning as people ran around trying to get their wagons lined up, ready to cross the Missouri River. Oxen and mules and horses kicked up choking clouds of dust. Whinnies and brays joined the shouts of the people, creating a cacophony that rolled across the prairie and the river.

Barlow saddled Beelzebub, then he and Buffalo 2 rounded up Derek and Clyde. They saddled their horses, then headed for the ferry. They rode across the river, and then positioned themselves on a rise a little way west of the riverbank. It would provide a good vantage point, Barlow figured, for watching the progress of the wagons as they crossed.

It was not exactly an exciting way to spend the day, and the two boys soon began pushing and shoving each other, then wrestling. Barlow put up with it for a while, then growled, "You boys best go on and see if you can help some of your new friends before you ruffle my feathers and I'm forced to give you a worse whuppin' than your fathers ever gave you."

The youths were all too happy to oblige. They leaped on their horses and galloped off, down the rise.

Barlow shook his head. Then he smiled. Their behavior had annoyed him considerably, but he could remember acting just like they had been doing, and he wished he could go back to those days, at least for a time.

Ohlmstead joined him soon after, and they sat watching the progress for a little while. Then they rode down the rise away from the river and headed west. Less than a mile away, Barlow stopped and nodded. "This'll do, Mattias," he said. "Have your people move to here for the night. It's far enough from the river and looks to have enough new grass for the animals."

Barlow had been a little surprised when Samuels had told him that the wagons would be leaving from St. Joseph instead of Westport Landing, but now he was glad that decision had been made. While crossing the Missouri was hard, the area around it was unused, so there had been grass for the animals while the emigrants waited to jump off. And this way they should beat most of the other wagon trains to the main part of the trail, leaving them in good shape for wood, water, and game for the long journey. Since they would not have to rely on the leavings of other wagon trains, the trek would be much easier.

Ohlmstead nodded and rode back the way he and Barlow had come. Barlow stayed there, waiting for the wagons to arrive. Ohlmstead's was the first. Agneta walked alongside the lumbering vehicle, expertly snapping a whip over the head of the oxen. Her three children, ranging in age from four to eleven, scampered about the wagon. Agneta pulled the wagon to the far side of the glade, next to where Barlow was waiting. Barlow tipped his hat to her, then rode off, back toward the river, passing a steady stream of wagons along the way.

He spent a little more time on the ridge overlooking the river, and was soon joined by Ohlmstead. Not long after, the two went back to the camp. Agneta had unhitched the oxen and set them out to graze. The children had gathered wood, and Agneta had started a fire. A pot dangled from a tripod over the flames.

"You vill eat vit us, Vill?" Ohlmstead asked.

"Reckon I could use a bite," Barlow said with a nod.

They sat on the ground, and Agneta served them up plates of wonderfully aromatic stew and tin mugs of coffee, doing it all with a warm smile.

As Barlow ate, he more than half wished that Agneta and Mattias were not married. He would purely enjoy spending some intimate time with the tall, statuesque woman. He sighed. She was, from all appearances, a warmhearted, loving woman, and she apparently had eyes only for her husband. Barlow respected that. Besides, he had spied several other attractive young women among the emigrants. He wasn't sure if they were unattached, but he would make it a point to find out. So he turned his attention to his food, which tasted as great as it had smelled. He had to smile to himself a little—it tended to make Agneta even more desirable, especially after a few months of eating Dulcy's poor cooking.

"You are velcome to eat vit us for every meal, Mr. Barlow," Agneta said as she poured him more coffee.

Barlow glanced at Ohlmstead, who smiled and nodded. "Ve discussed it before," the Swede said.

Barlow smiled at Agneta. "I'd be honored to take my meals with you, Mrs. Ohlmstead," he said warmly. He meant it, too. "Your cookin' plumb shines, ma'am."

"Tack så mycket," Agneta said. "Thank you very much."

"Your nephews are velcome, too," Ohlmstead added. He grinned. "If dey have not made other arrangements."

Barlow laughed. "They just might have, hoss. Tell you true, Mattias, I might not ever see them boys again till we get to the Oregon country." He paused. "Well, I reckon that ain't such a bad thing, seein' as how they seem to be makin' a mite good lot of friends already."

"Dey are good boys, ya," Ohlmstead said. "I been t'inkin' maybe my Gunnar should spend some time vit your nephews."

"I reckon them two boys of mine'd get along just fine with Gunnar," Barlow said, glancing at Ohlmstead's eleven-year-old son, who was sitting with his back against a wagon wheel.

The two men finished their meal, and then rode off again, back toward the river. At the rise, Barlow stopped, planning to just keep an eye on things, while Ohlmstead kept going, ready to offer his assistance wherever it was needed with the wagons still crossing the river.

Just before dark, the final wagon pulled into the campsite. There had been, much to the relief of Barlow and Ohlmstead, no injuries or losses. The two men wandered through the sprawling camp, making sure everyone was all right, and advising the emigrants that they would be on the trail early in the morning. Before long, the camp was quiet, with all but a few of the later arrivals asleep.

10

BARLOW WAS GLAD he was just the guide and hunter for the wagon train, not the captain of it. He knew he would not have been able to stomach the bickering that started within days of the emigrants leaving the St. Joseph area. Barlow led them north, following the Missouri River for several days, then turned west and a little north, crossing the Big Blue River a few days later, following it in a northerly direction to its West Fork, which they followed for a couple of days. Finally, after a day of traveling away from the river, they reached the wide, shallow Platte River, whose course they followed generally west.

Barlow was up early each morning and, after a fine breakfast cooked up by Agneta Ohlmstead, he would ride out, Buffalo 2 at his side, laying out the course the Conestogas were to follow. He would mark water holes and likely midday stopping points. He would also mark the most reasonable site for the overnight camp, though that was usually late in the day. He would hunt as he traveled after finding a midday stopping point for the wagons, ranging out to the sides of where the wagons would travel, in something of an arc. As he sought game, he also kept his eyes open for an overnight campsite.

Hunting was pretty easy after the first couple of days—when they had put enough distance between them and civilization—and Barlow never failed to bring in several mule loads of buffalo, deer, or antelope meat each day.

He had planned to take his nephews with him on the hunts, but decided they were making new friends and there would be plenty of time later for teaching them. After a couple of days, he almost regretted not taking them, if only to have them do the worst of the butchering. But again, he figured there was more than enough time for them to do their share of such work on the months the journey would take.

Once the game was down, he would take off his shirt, despite the fact that it was still rather chilly most days, then cut the hides off where they were. Right from the start, he decided he would keep the hides. He would tan them himself, at least until he could find or train someone else to do it for him. He was sure he could trade them at Fort Vancouver for some extra cash. After peeling the hide, he would butcher the meat out, usually taking just the best cuts. Then he would move on and hunt some more, until his mules were laden. Often, though, he found a campsite along the way, and would mark it. Then, after he had gotten his take of meat for the day, he would return to the site. If he hadn't found a site by then, he would ride with the laden mules until he did.

There he would finish up the butchering, again stripping off at least his shirt to keep from getting so much blood on it. He divided the meat up into portions that would be doled out to each family based on the number of people in it. When the mood struck him, Barlow would also gather firewood and buffalo chips, if wood was scarce. He would stack it near the meat, so that when people came by for one, they could also get some of the other.

Barlow would clean up as best he could. He was usually close enough to the river to at least half bathe despite the frigid water. Then he would often take a nap, stretching out on the still-sprouting grass, pulling his hat down over his eyes to block out the sun, and dozing off. Even if he didn't have the time for that, however, he especially enjoyed this time. If he couldn't have female companionship—and he was working to change that—he preferred being alone.

But inevitably, the wagons would begin arriving, and with them came the people and all their feuds, arguments, complaints, and problems. During the time the camp was made, the place was a madhouse of activity, noise, and dirt. It was the time he disliked most. Once the camp was made, and the travelers sat down to their suppers and began preparing for bed, things calmed down again, and it wasn't such a bad place to be.

Barlow ate with the Ohlmsteads each night, and afterward, he would often saunter through the camp, Buffalo 2 at his side, meeting people, and introducing himself to potential female companions. Sometimes Ohlmstead accompanied him, and the two would settle disputes, issue warnings where needed, soothe nerves when necessary, and proffer threats, if that seemed to be the right thing to do at the time. Afterward, Barlow and Ohlmstead would discuss the humor of the people in the wagon train in general, and make plans to head off any major trouble either of them might suspect was about to break out.

It was during one of his evening strolls that Barlow met Dora Lee Openshaw. Dora Lee was a widow of only nineteen. Her husband had drowned almost a year before in a river near their Kentucky home. They had been married less than five months. Dora Lee was a short, slender, vivacious woman with chestnut-brown hair, lively gray eyes, and a ready smile. She was traveling with her sister's family, helping her sister watch over her four children, as well as assisting in all the other chores her sister had. She didn't seem to mind, and was always cheerful. That was one of the many things that had attracted Barlow to her in the first place.

Two weeks out from St. Joe, Barlow began spending more time around Charlie Penwell's wagon. And within days of that, Dora Lee began joining Barlow and Buffalo 2 on their daily walks around the evening camp.

"What do y'all do during the days when you're gone, Will?" Dora Lee asked during one of their strolls a few nights later.

Barlow explained it, trying to make it sound more difficult than it really was.

"Take me with you tomorrow," Dora Lee said, her voice sounding a little strained to Barlow.

He glanced at her. "I don't think that's wise, Dora Lee," he said evenly.

"Why not?" she demanded, stopping and grabbing his sleeve, halting him and turning him to face her.

"Such doin's ain't for a woman," Barlow said gruffly. "It's mighty tedious and, once the huntin' is done, godawful bloody."

"I've butchered animals before," Dora Lee said matter-of-factly.

"Nothin' the size of a buffler, though," Barlow countered.

"True," Dora Lee admitted, "but butcherin's butcherin' and blood's blood. 'Sides, I ain't aimin' to do none of the butcherin'."

Well, of course not, he thought. He wondered why he had even mentioned it, since he wouldn't let her do any of the butchering even if she asked to help.

"Well, none of the big butcherin' anyway," Dora Lee added, smiling a little. "There ain't no reason I cain't help y'all divide up the meat for the families like you do."

He grinned, teeth flashing whitely in the darkness. "I usually strip down some for it so's I don't get covered in blood," he teased.

"That's jist common sense," Dora Lee said, surprising him a little.

"It's also dangerous out there, Dora Lee," he noted, his mind still distracted by her presence and request.

"I'll be safe with y'all," she said evenly. She shocked him considerably when she stepped up, threw her arms around his neck, and then kissed him hard, her mouth hotly devouring his.

He wrapped his meaty arms around her, his hands gripping her backside, and pulled her close to him, making sure she could feel his rapidly growing hardness.

The move only served to increase the ardor of her kiss.

Both were panting when they broke apart. "I reckon I can take you with me," Barlow gasped, his voice cracking with lust. He wanted this woman bad, here and now. He fought for control.

"I'll need a horse," she said, her breathing almost back to normal, though her own desire made her eyes sparkle in the moonlight. "And a saddle."

Barlow nodded, then asked, "Where'n hell am I gonna get a sidesaddle?"

"I can ride astride."

Barlow nodded again. Taking her arm in his, he started walking again, eventually heading back to Penwell's wagon, where he left Dora Lee.

Since neither Derek nor Clyde were using their horses much these days—they were too interested in being with new friends, who had to walk alongside the wagons—Barlow just usurped one of the animals and saddled it in the morning.

"What're you doin' that for, Uncle Will?" Clyde asked.

"Takin' somebody with me today," Barlow muttered, embarrassed and not wanting to explain to his nephews—or anyone else.

"Who?" Clyde asked in childlike innocence.

"None of your business, boy," Barlow growled. "Now go on about your business for the day."

He ignored Mattias Ohlmstead, who glanced suspiciously at him as he walked the horse, Beelzebub, and the string of mules away from the Swede's wagon. Since Ohlmstead's Conestoga was the lead one—parked with its fork pointing in the direction they would travel that day—Barlow walked that way. He met Dora Lee almost a quarter of a mile away, out of sight of the camp.

She was sitting in the new grass, and rose when she saw him approach. She smiled, then kissed him when he got to her.

"What'd you tell your sister?" Barlow asked after he had reluctantly pulled his lips from hers.

"Jist told her that I was gonna travel with someone else today," Dora Lee said with a grin. "It ain't none of her beeswax anyway."

"It might not be," Barlow said seriously, "but you could do harm to your reputation."

Dora Lee shrugged. "I'll worry about my reputation. Y'all don't need to."

"You sure you want to do this today?" Barlow asked, needing to make sure. He had become a little concerned about her safety more than her reputation. However, he hadn't seen any Indian sign yet, and was not unduly worried.

Dora Lee grinned widely. "Y'all havin' second thoughts, Mr. Barlow?" she countered in a mock-teasing voice.

"Nope," he responded, grinning back. "Just makin' sure you weren't havin' any."

"I'm quite ready for the day, sir." She paused, brushing his furry cheek with a slim hand. "Now, help me on that horse and let's git movin'."

He did as requested and they rode on, his eyes constantly scanning the ground, the horizon, the land around him; hers never leaving him. As the morning wore on, he relaxed a little, and began pointing out signs to her, where some Indians had passed several days ago, where buffalo had wallowed recently, some speedy antelope off in the distance, naming the hawks and other birds that soared effortlessly overhead.

In late morning, having marked off a place where the wagons could stop for the midday meal, Barlow began looking for game in earnest. It was not long before he spotted several buffalo cows grazing placidly a mile southwest of the Platte. He moved to within seventy-five yards, then stopped. Holding a finger to his lips to keep Dora Lee quiet, he dismounted, aimed his rifle, and fired. He reloaded and fired twice more. Three buffalo went down.

"That's some shootin', sir," Dora Lee praised him,

He grinned, a little embarrassed. "Weren't hard," he said honestly. "Not when I been doin' this for so long."

They stopped near the first cow and Barlow peeled off his shirt. Dora Lee dismounted and sat in the grass nearby. With his big knife in hand, Barlow slit the hide along the legs and the length of the belly. Cutting a couple of holes in the hide, he tied ropes through them, and then used the mules to pull the ropes, tearing the hide smoothly off the carcass.

Then Barlow waded in, knife in hand, and began hacking out cuts of meat. One of the first things he cut out was the liver. He held the dripping thing up and took a bite, grinning at Dora Lee's sudden horror. "Want a taste?" he asked, his bloody grin a frightening thing.

"No, thank you!" Dora Lee exclaimed, looking a little paler than usual.

Barlow took two more bites, then went back to work, occasionally tossing hunks of meat to Buffalo 2, who happily wolfed them down.

Suddenly the dog's head cocked to the side, and he let out a small *wuff*.

Barlow glanced at the dog. He could tell by the animal's stance that the Newfoundland had sensed something out of the ordinary. Barlow jammed the knife into the buffalo carcass and grabbed a piece of old cloth to wipe the blood off his hands. He straightened and looked around. He saw nothing, but that, he knew from long experience, didn't mean nothing was out there. "What is it, boy?" he asked, looking at the dog.

The canine's nose quivered as he sought scents in the steady breeze. Barlow stared in the direction Buffalo 2's nose was pointed. He still saw nothing, but the dog's growing agitation was beginning to concern him. He picked up his rifle and stood tensely.

"What's wrong?" Dora Lee asked, rising and looking around in fear and wonder.

"Ain't sure," Barlow snapped. "Now hush." A few moments later, he muttered, "Oh, shit," as a grizzly rose up on its hind legs, sniffing the air, only twenty yards away, a small dip in the land having hidden it as it had walked on all fours toward Barlow and Dora Lee.

Dora Lee stifled a scream, but not before it alerted the bruin.

The big animal snuffled, trying to find the source of the sound, as well as the source of the blood that had attracted it in the first place. It dropped down on all fours again and began moving forward, unseen until it came up on a small rise.

"Stay there, Dora Lee," Barlow commanded. "C'mon, Buffler." He began trotting toward the bear. Buffalo 2 raced up and paced him. "Go get him, Buffler," Barlow ordered.

The dog bolted forward, and began barking as he neared the bear. The startled grizzly reared up, and Buffalo 2 raced in, nipping at its heels. The bruin dropped down and swiped at the Newfoundland with a massive paw. The canine easily darted out of the way, and rushed in and bit the grizzly just above one rear paw.

The bear roared in pain and swung around, again trying to whack Buffalo 2 with its front claws, but missing. The animal reared up again, and Barlow, now only five yards away, skidded to a stop, threw his rifle up to his shoulder, and fired.

The ball sent up a big puff of dust when it plowed into the grizzly's chest, but it did not stop the massive animal, which only roared in annoyance.

Buffalo 2 darted in again, and bit the bear on the other heel. The bear dropped down onto all fours and swung around, trying to grab the quick, agile dog, with no success. The Newfoundland had the grizzly spinning, trying to get him.

"Back, Buffler," Barlow bellowed as he dropped the old Henry rifle and pulled out one of the heavy Colt Walker revolvers. He thumbed back the hammer as the dog raced away from the bear, which turned to watch the dog, presenting his side to Barlow.

Barlow fired all five shots he kept loaded in the pistol. The heavy, .44-caliber balls punched holes in the grizzly's side, sending forth clouds of flies, puffs of dusts, and howls of rage and pain.

Barlow slid the empty Walker into the holster and drew the other.

But the bear, still growling fiercely, slumped down. It wasn't dead yet, but it was no longer a threat. Barlow put the pistol away and reloaded his rifle. He knelt and aimed carefully, before sending a .50-caliber ball through the grizzly's spine at the neck.

The bear's growls stopped abruptly, and though it quivered a bit, it was dead.

11

"YOU KEEP A watch over that ol' b'ar, Buffler," Barlow said as he reloaded his rife, flicking wary glances at the grizzly. Then he hurried over to where Dora Lee stood, hands pressed to her mouth. "You all right?" he asked, worried.

The woman's face was ashen with fright, but she appeared calm enough. She nodded, then said, "Yeah. I'm fine."

"You certain?"

A little life began to return to her face. "I'm certain." She managed a weak smile. "I cain't say, though, that I've even been in such a situation before."

"I told you it could be dangerous out here, Dora Lee," Barlow noted. "You want I should take you back to the wagons now?"

"Is that bear dead?" she countered.

"Reckon so," Barlow said. "If he ain't, he will be before long. I aim to have that critter's hide."

"Then there's no more danger," Dora Lee said bravely. "I wanted to be out here with y'all today, and I aim to stay now that I'm here." She was recovering quickly.

Barlow nodded. He could insist that he take her back,

but that would take a lot of time, and he had little of that
to spare if he was to fill his quota of meat for the day.
And she seemed to be doing well. Anyone who was not
used to the wilds was bound to be frightened by an encounter with a grizzly. It didn't mean that person was
ready to give up. And Dora Lee Openshaw did not seem
to be a woman who would run very easily. Instead, she
gave the appearance of being one very determined young
lady.

Barlow went back to the buffalo he had been butchering. He took the few minutes first to reload the Colt Walker he had emptied into the bear, then set back to work
on his butchering.

It took several hours, but he eventually finished butchering the three buffalo and the grizzly—he took the hide
off the latter, and even some of the meat, as something
different for himself and the Ohlmsteads. He cleaned himself up as best he could with the old cloth, then mounted
Beelzebub. They rode off, towing the string of meat-laden
mules behind them.

It was another couple of hours before Barlow found a
reasonable camping site for the night. It was close by the
Platte River, with plenty of new grass for the animals.
Blossoming willow trees ran for some distance, with
plenty of deadwood on the ground providing more than
adequate fuel for that night's cooking fires.

Barlow stopped amid some of the trees, which provided
a barely adequate amount of shade. He suggested to Dora
Lee that she rest against the trunk of one tree while he
worked. He unsaddled Beelzebub and Dora Lee's horse,
then unloaded the meat and hides from the extra mules.
Then he pulled off his shirt and drew his knife, ready to
get back to work.

Dora Lee stopped him, though, stepping up behind him
and sliding her hands around his midsection, locking her
fingers over his stomach. She rested her head on his broad
bare back. "I think that can wait awhile, Will," she said
quietly.

He managed to turn around in her embrace, and wrapped his arms around her. "Just what did you have in mind, ma'am?" he asked, his voice low and urgent.

"I think you know that, sir." Dora Lee looked up at him, mouth partly open, waiting.

He obliged, bringing his lips down on hers, his tongue entering her willing mouth, toying, teasing.

"That ol' dog of yours is a pretty good watchdog, ain't he?" Dora Lee breathed into his mouth some minutes later.

"Yep. You saw that."

"Jist makin' sure."

They kissed again, their passion growing. Barlow's big stubby fingers began clumsily working at the buttons at the bodice of Dora Lee's dress, trying to undo them. Dora Lee allowed him to struggle for some minutes, too distracted by her rising heat to want to stop kissing him to help him. But finally she decided that if she didn't help, either he would not accomplish what he was trying to do, or he would end up tearing her dress, which she could not afford to have happen.

She stepped back a bit. "Let me do that," she whispered, her voice having deepened almost to huskiness with desire. She swiftly undid the buttons, and then shoved the worn dress off of one shoulder, then the other, then pushed it down, baring her small, highly pointed breasts, then over her firm hips, and let it drop to the ground.

"Damn, you are a fine sight, woman," Barlow breathed.

Her skin was so pale as to be almost translucent, making her wide areolae and female triangle seem even darker than they really were. A splash of freckles across her upper breasts and her shoulders provided a little more color. Despite their smallish size, her bullet-shaped breasts, capped by tiny buds of nipples, rode proudly above the gentle rise of belly, which swooped down to that thatch of curly hair that hid her female treasure and a pair of perfectly formed legs. Her plain, worn shoes detracted only a little from her sexiness.

"Thank you," Dora Lee said, the demureness of her voice belied by the brazenness of her nudity and stance.

Swallowing hard, Barlow undid his belt and eased it to the ground. Then he slipped off his pants, exposing his hardness to her eyes. He left his moccasins on.

"Oh, my," Dora Lee said with a little gasp when she saw him naked, one hand fanning her face and chest. "You certainly are a manly feller, Mr. Barlow."

He smiled, cocky. "C'mere, woman," he growled softly.

She sashayed the few steps to him, then suddenly leaped up, throwing her legs around his waist and her arms around his neck. She kissed him hotly. When she pulled her head back sometime later, she held on with one hand and reached down with the other. She grasped his hard lance and introduced it to the opening of her silken sheath, then bobbed up and down on him, working her way down the length of his shaft until it was fully buried in her.

She began bounding up and down on his manhood, now slick from her wetness, quickly increasing her tempo and fervor. Barlow had no trouble bearing her slight weight. He just stood there, legs slightly spread, braced, as she bounced on him with increasing abandon.

Suddenly she let loose a yowl that Barlow was certain would be heard by the wagon train, no matter how far back it might be. She almost smothered him as she pulled his head forward and mashed it against her breasts, and she shook like a sapling in a hurricane.

"Enjoy that, did you?" Barlow asked dryly when she had recovered somewhat.

"Lord A'mighty, yes," Dora Lee gasped. "And by the stars, I'm ready for some more." She paused, squinting at him. "That is, if y'all ain't used up yet."

"Does it feel like I'm used up?" he asked with a grin.

Dora Lee tightened her womanhood on him and sighed. "Not nearly," she said gleefully.

"Damn right, woman. I'm just gettin' started."

Dora Lee began rotating on his shaft, alternating it with a forward-and-backward rocking movement. "Can you hold me up awhile longer?" she asked, grinning as she stared into his eyes.

"Quite a while longer, woman."

She did not appear to hear him, however, as she concentrated on the passions that were fast rising anew inside her, soon overwhelming her once more, and she screamed out her joy and release. She slowed only momentarily, though, before she was riding toward the crest of another explosion of bliss.

Breathing heavily, she finally unlocked her ankles from around his waist and let her feet slide to the ground. She clung to him, however, as she stood somewhat shakily. She grinned up at him and kissed him hard again, allowing him to savor her sweet mouth.

Hand in hand, they walked to a nearby tree. Barlow silently directed her to lean forward, bent at the waist, and put her hands against the tree trunk. Stepping behind her, he smiled as she watched him over his shoulder. Then he entered her from behind, her eyes widening with exhilaration.

She watched as he began a slow, steady rhythm, moving in and out of her soft, enchanting love sheath, picking up the pace gradually until he was pounding her with powerful thrusts that soon had both of them breathing hard and climbing toward a burst of ecstasy that rocked them to the core.

Rubber-legged, Barlow finally pulled out of Dora Lee and plopped down on his rump on the grass, then stretched out on his back, sucking in huge gulps of air.

Dora Lee fell next to him, an arm and one leg thrown across him. Her cheek on his shoulder. "Y'all sure know how to make a woman feel like a woman," she panted.

"My pleasure, ma'am," Barlow wheezed, grinning and

giving her a little squeeze. " 'Sides, woman, you make it easy."

Dora Lee smiled warmly in pleasure, though he could not see it. She was thrilled. She pecked his cheek, and then rested her head on him again, content to lie like that for a while.

Eventually, however, her hand strayed to his flaccid manhood, and began teasing it, trying to restore its former glory.

Barlow lay there enjoying the sensation for some moments, then said quietly, "There's a better way to bring that ol' hoss back to life, you know."

"Oh?" Dora Lee pulled her head up to look at his face, her eyes questioning in their innocence and interest.

Barlow outlined her lips with a stubby forefinger. "With this," he said, his voice growing husky.

"I don't know what to . . ."

The thick finger cut off the flow of words. "Use your imagination, Dora Lee," Barlow said, his voice thick. But he managed a small grin. "But not your teeth."

Dora Lee stared at him for a few moments, letting her mind mull over the suggestion, and eventually to begin to grow accustomed to the idea, which became more and more intriguing with each passing second. She smiled in delightful wickedness, then pushed herself up. On her knees, she shuffled downward and then slipped between his legs. She bent and with one hand, gently lifted his soft manhood. She pushed her hair out of her face with her other hand. She studied his shaft for a few seconds, before lowering her head and gently engulfing it with her soft, warm mouth.

"Oh, Lordy," Barlow breathed as pleasure soared from her soft orifice, straight through his lance, and spread through him with the speed and power of a buffalo stampede. He groaned more loudly and with more intensity when Dora Lee's tongue and lips began experimenting, adjusting in reaction to his swiftly expanding length and girth and his fast-increasing moans of pleasure.

Barlow grabbed her by the hair and held her head as he let her control her movements, though he guided her. His ass squirmed in the dirt as enjoyment rocketed through him, and he wondered with some distant part of his mind if he should let her finish him this way, or if he wanted to be inside her womanhood again. He finally decided for the latter. He tugged her hair, pulling her head up.

She glanced at him in alarm. "Did I do somethin' wrong?" she asked, worried.

"Nope," Barlow said with a lusty grin. "I just want to be in you. Climb on atop me, woman," he ordered gruffly.

Grinning hugely, Dora Lee swiftly positioned her womanhood over the top of his lance, then helping herself a little with one hand, eased down on him, sighing as pleasure washed over her. Once she was fully impaled, she rested there, smiling at Barlow. "I think I like this here," she whispered.

"I do believe it plumb shines with this ol' chile, too, woman," Barlow agreed.

With his hands on her hips guiding her, she began rocking back and forth on him, the movement sending sparks of passion skittering through her body, until they lit an all-consuming flame that burned hotly and intently, grew out of control, and was finally muted to embers in the moments after Dora Lee's roaring climax.

Barlow let her create her own tempo and direction as Dora Lee began moving again. His hands gently fondled her breasts, tugging softly at her smallish nipples, rolling them between thumb and forefinger.

Dora Lee quickly began soaring to another peak, which she reached with a yell and grand shudder. She paused atop him, trying to regain some of her equilibrium, but his insistent hardness and wriggling hips would not let her rest for long. She sensed that he wanted her to move differently this time, so she began sliding up and down on his long lance, slick now from her womanly wetness. She could feel him begin to tighten in anticipation, and she bounced faster and faster, with her sudden scream of joy mingling with his hearty howl as they crested the pinnacle together.

"I reckon I best get back to that butcherin', Dora Lee," Barlow said after they had rested for some time.

"I'd rather jist stay like this," she responded, scrunching a little closer into his embrace.

"So would I, woman," he admitted. "But some things got to be done, and that's one of 'em."

Dora Lee sighed in mock annoyance. "Well, if you'd rather mess with some old buffler meat than with me . . ." she said. Then she laughed.

Barlow laughed with her and gave her a little pinch on the behind. "You best behave yourself, girl," he warned with false seriousness. He pulled his arm from around her and pushed himself up. "You can stay right there like that if you're of a mind to," he said with a grin. He rather enjoyed having her naked around him.

She smiled coquettishly. Then she rose, too. "I might's well help you, Will," she said. Before he could object, she added, "I told you before I've done my share of butcherin'. And all the hard butcherin's been done. What's left ain't nothin' more than what I did back in Kentucky. It'll go all the faster with help."

Barlow looked a bit doubtful yet.

Dora Lee grinned impishly. "And don't go worryin' about the blood. I aim to help out dressed jist the way I am."

Barlow decided that her help in such a way would be a wonderful thing. He returned her smile. "Let's get to work, then."

Once they actually got down to the job at hand, they grew serious, and it went quickly. When they were done, they were both pretty bloody. "Looks like time for a washin'," Barlow said.

"I was plannin' it, even if y'all weren't," Dora Lee said, grimacing at herself. She knew she looked a fright.

They walked the short distance to the river, which was a little deeper here than in many parts, but not much. They lay down side by side in the cold water, to get themselves wet, then spent some minutes scrubbing each other clean with the lye soap Barlow had brought with them. They finally went to the sandy, flat bank, where Barlow had earlier spread out a blanket.

He lay on his back, looking up at Dora Lee. She was cold and shivering a little. "I know what'll warm you up, girl," he said with a devilish grin. "C'mon and kneel over me." A moment later, he said, "No, not down there. Up here, by my face."

Without questioning, but with a decided interest, Dora Lee Openshaw did as she was bid, resting on her shins, her womanhood hovering inches from his lips. He grabbed her firm backside in his big hands and pulled her gently down to his waiting mouth.

She almost jumped out of her skin when his tongue first touched her; then she settled down with a sigh. "Oh, my, Will," she breathed, "that's jist divine. It's . . ." Her words were replaced by moans as his tongue burrowed into her most secret cavity and his mouth kissed and sucked at the sensitive button hidden in the folds of her delectable nether lips.

Before long, she was screaming in passion, hands holding his head in a death grip. She shook and squirmed, until it was difficult for Barlow to hold her in place despite his great strength.

As her climax waned, Barlow continued his loving actions, bringing her to peak after peak over the next ten minutes, until she was fairly begging for mercy. He finally relented, and allowed her to slump down, half on him, half on the blanket. It was some time before she could speak, and when she was able, all she could find to say was, "Lordy, Will, that was glorious. Absolutely glorious."

"I'm glad you enjoyed it some," he teased.

"Some," she snapped in mock anger, slapping him gently on his broad, scarred chest.

He kissed her hard, and her hand came over to grasp his new rigidness.

"But what about y'all?" she asked.

"Whatever you want to do is just fine with this ol' chile," he said honestly.

She thought for a moment, then smiled. "I think I got me an idea." She moved down to where she was kneeling between his legs. Her tongue flicked the underside of his hard shaft, eliciting a gasp of pleasure from him. "I reckon I can finish off what I started afore," she said with a wicked grin. Holding her hair back with both hands, she bent her head forward and swallowed as much of his length as she could. She began sliding her mouth up and down on him, bringing her tongue into play, as he had with her. From his sudden powerful grip on her head to the moans that soon were an unending stream from him, she knew she must be doing her job well.

She was rather startled when he grunted softly but insistently, and exploded, but she gamely kept her place and accepted all he had to give her.

She kept up her mouth actions for some time afterward, until he finally said hoarsely, "That's fine, Dora Lee."

She looked up and smiled in pleasure at the sated look in his eyes. "I did all right?" she asked, certain she had, but somehow needing to hear it from him.

"You done more'n all right, Dora Lee," he croaked. "It plumb shined with this chile. Plumb shined."

She smiled and crawled into his embrace, the chill spawned by the cold river and cool day long forgotten.

12

BARLOW AND DORA Lee looked quite prim and proper by the time Mattias Ohlmstead's wagon, which, as always, was in the lead, creaked into the campsite, followed by the others. Ohlmstead looked at the two a little suspiciously, but said nothing, deciding that whatever had gone on—if anything—was none of his business. Barlow had provided plenty of meat, as usual, had marked the trail well, and had chosen a fine spot for the wagons to stop for the night. Thus, Ohlmstead had no reason to complain or to question anything Barlow did.

As soon as Charlie Penwell's wagon entered the campsite, Dora Lee hurried off to help her sister, Laura Lee, and brother-in-law, Charlie, care for the animals, take care of the children, and prepare the evening meal. As she left, she made sure no one was looking and blew Barlow a kiss. He smiled in return.

Barlow stayed busy for a while distributing the meat he had taken that day. Most everyone rejected his offer of the bear meat, though a few venturesome folks raised their eyebrows but took a portion. Ohlmstead looked at him with distrust when he offered some to the wagon captain, then shrugged and accepted. "If anyvon can make dis meat taste good, it's my vife," he pronounced.

Proving the truth of his observation, the stew Agneta Ohlmstead made with the grizzly bear meat was splendid. He wondered how she did it. He considered asking her, but he didn't really need to know. Besides, he could hear her reply without asking: "I yoost take some seasonings and put dem in. Ya, sure." He grinned to himself.

As they ate, Ohlmstead asked innocently, "So, Vill, how vas your day?"

"About the same as always, I reckon," Barlow responded noncommittally.

"How did you come by gettin' dat bear meat? Dat's not so usual, ya?"

"We're eatin' bear meat?" Clyde asked, revulsion suddenly coloring his face.

"Just keep feedin', boy," Barlow snapped. "You thought it was just fine before you knew what it was."

Clyde grimaced, then shrugged and waded back into eating with gusto.

"So?" Ohlmstead pressed on. "How'd you come to get dat bear meat?"

"Some ol' griz come sniffin' round whilst I was butcherin' a buffler. Bears're scavengers when need be, and they'll eat meat if they come across it. I figure he smelled the blood and come round to investigate it." He shrugged. "He came to a bad end once he started nosin' round too close to this ol' chile."

"Didn't you have a guest vit you?" Ohlmstead asked, glancing askance at Barlow.

"I did," Barlow said flatly.

"And dere vas no danger?"

"Not really. Me'n Buffler took care of that ol' griz before it could be any trouble to anyone."

"Are you going out alone tomorrow?" Ohlmstead questioned, trying not to sound too interested.

Barlow shrugged and continued eating. "Depends."

"Maybe you should take von of your nephews vit you. For safety reasons."

"Them boys're busy with their own doin's," Barlow said, beginning to get annoyed. " 'Sides, I don't need no lookin' after. Buffler here's plenty good enough at warnin' me of danger—and helpin' me if times call for such doin's."

"But you vill . . ."

"Enough, Mattias," Barlow said sharply. "What I do out there is my concern, as long as I do what I'm bein' paid to do. You got complaints about that, voice 'em. If not—and you shouldn't since I ain't shirked my duties any—then keep your nose outta my doin's."

"Ya, sure. I do dat," Ohlmstead said, ashamed at having been spoken to in such a way in front of Barlow's nephews as well as his own children. But he had asked for it, he knew, and had no right to complain about it.

Barlow considered apologizing for his harsh words, but then decided there was no reason for it. It *was* his own business, and Ohlmstead had no right to question him about it.

So he continued to take Dora Lee Openshaw with him on his daily rides. He would hunt, they would make love when they found a site for the wagons to stay the night, she would help him divide the meat, they would bathe together in the river, make love again if there was time, and then wait for the wagons to arrive. There were, to Dora Lee's relief, no more encounter with grizzlies or any other large, dangerous critters.

Their only trouble came from within the camp, when Charlie Penwell confronted Barlow and Dora Lee as they wandered about the camp one night about two weeks after Barlow had first started taking her with him.

"I want to know jist what y'all's attentions are toward my sister-in-law," Penwell demanded, planting himself in front of the two. He suddenly glanced worriedly at Buffalo 2, who had stopped, too, and growled, edging up on the man.

"It's all right, Buffler," Barlow said, not taking his eyes off Penwell. "Just where'd you ever get the notion that such a thing was any of your concern, hoss?" Barlow countered.

"She is my wife's sister, and I'm responsible for her. I took on that chore when I allowed her to come along on this journey. She was to help Laura Lee with the young'uns and anything else we saw fit for her to do. It was her payment for us takin' a widow, who's all alone and in need of carin', to the Oregon country."

"Mighty goddamn high price for somethin' she could've done easy without your 'help,' hoss," Barlow said flatly.

"That's for me'n Laura Lee to decide on, y'all," Penwell said with a smirk. "She's as good as bound to us."

"That true, Dora Lee?" Barlow asked, not looking at the woman.

"Only in his mind," she replied. "And maybe in my sister's, too, if he's poisoned her against me."

"You ungrateful bitch," Penwell snapped, raising his hand as if to strike Dora Lee.

Barlow grabbed the man's arm and easily held it. "I wouldn't do that if was I you, hoss," he said harshly.

"Jist who the hell do y'all think you are, boy?" Penwell questioned, trying to jerk his arm free of Barlow's grip. He was unable to do so until Barlow allowed it.

"I'm the chile who's gonna keep you from abusin' this woman and any other you think of lashin' out at, hoss," Barlow said matter-of-factly.

"Y'all're makin' a big mistake here, boy," Penwell hissed.

"Only mistake I might be makin', hoss, is not rubbin' you out here and now." He paused, glaring at Penwell. "From now on, you got no responsibility for this woman. I'll tend to her. Now get your dumb ass back to your wagon before I change my mind about puttin' you under."

After Penwell had taken a few steps, Barlow called out, making the man turn, "By the way, hoss, if you touch Dora Lee's sister, I'll come and pound your ass from one end of this camp to the other. Keep that to mind, boy."

Penwell scowled as he spun on his heel and walked away.

"Did y'all mean what you said?" Dora Lee asked moments later.

"About what?"

"About takin' care of me." She seemed nervous.

"Sure," Barlow said with a shrug. "Leastways till we get to the Oregon country. I can't promise you anything after that. But there's a heap of fellers out there who'll be powerful grateful to have a woman like you."

"You don't want me?" Dora Lee looked crushed.

"Now, I didn't say that, woman," Barlow growled. "Don't you go makin' me out as sayin' things I didn't say. I just said that I couldn't promise nothin' beyond gettin' to the Willamette Valley."

"And you'll watch over me till then at least?" Dora Lee had brightened some.

"That's what I said."

"Where'll I stay on the trip?"

"Well, I usually take my meals with the Ohlmsteads, and sleep near their wagon. They won't be much put out at feedin' you, too, if I ask 'em. They don't like it, we'll eat at our own fire. I ain't so sure about the sleepin' arrangements, but we figure somethin' out for that, too, if the Ohlmsteads make some fuss."

"I don't mind eatin' with them folks, if they'll have us. But our own camp a bit away from 'em might be good thing." She grinned puckishly.

"Might be at that," Barlow agreed. The more he thought about it as they started walking again, the better it seemed. The Ohlmsteads might not make any objections, though he wasn't sure of that, but his nephews might be around too much, and he had no desire to want to try to explain to them what was going on between him and Dora Lee Openshaw.

They strolled to the Ohlmsteads' fire, and sat. Agneta poured them coffee from the ever-present pot. "You mind if Miss Dora Lee here starts takin' her meals here with me, Mattias?" Barlow asked.

"Vell," Ohlmstead said slowly, thinking as he went along, "I t'ink maybe dat's all right. Mama?" he questioned, looking to his wife, who sat across the fire darning a pair of pants belonging to one of the children. "Is dat all right vit you?"

"Ya, sure," she replied, glancing up and smiling.

"Vhere vill you . . . ?" Ohlmstead suddenly looked embarrassed.

Barlow knew what he meant. "We'll make us our own little camp off to ourselves," he said.

"Yoost make sure it's not too close to our wagon, Mr. . . ." Ohlmstead started.

"Papa!" Agneta interjected, stopping him. "You leave dese nice people alone. Dey vill make a camp vhere dey vant, and not too far from us, I'm t'inkin'." She smiled at Barlow and Dora Lee. "And if you two need anyt'ink, you yoost ask."

"Mighty obliged, Mrs. Ohlmstead," Barlow said.

Soon afterward, Barlow and Dora Lee headed off, taking Barlow's sleeping robe, which was plenty big enough for the two of them. Though it was still fairly cool in the nights, they would be warm enough in the robes, and saw no reason for a fire. Buffalo 2 disappeared for a little while to take care of his business, then trotted back. The dog stretched out on his side a few feet from where Barlow and Dora Lee snuggled in the sleeping robes.

"You all right with this arrangement, Dora Lee?" Barlow asked, yawning.

"Yep. Why, y'all have troubles with it?"

"Not me, woman. I'm just wonderin' if this'll cause you some grief with all the other emigrants here."

Dora Lee shrugged, causing an interesting movement of her naked breast against the side of his chest. "I don't know most of them folks. Just Laura Lee and Charlie, really. Might be a few others who know who I am, but what I do ain't none of their concern."

"Just makin' sure, Dora Lee, that's all," Barlow said easily.

"But, Will, y'all best keep an eye on Charlie," Dora Lee warned. "He's a vindictive man and has a mean temper."

"He don't scare me none," Barlow said, dismissing the implied threat.

"I know that, Will. But he ain't fool enough to come against y'all from the front, man-to-man. He'll try'n ambush y'all or somethin'."

"I'll keep an eye out," Barlow promised. "But I ain't concerned. I ain't survived all these years out in the wilds to go under at the hands of some dumb ass like Charlie Penwell. 'Sides, I got Buffler to watch my back for me. You know that."

"I know," Dora Lee said with a sigh that was half resignation, half contentment. "I worry about y'all is all, though, Will."

"Well, quit your frettin', Dora Lee. We'll be just fine."

The usual problems of a wagon train heading west soon began appearing as the emigrants entered the sand hill country. With frightening—and irritating—regularity, wagons began breaking down on a seemingly daily basis and sickness started showing up. Although there had been no deaths yet, that was bound to change, Barlow knew. Bickering among the travelers cropped up with increasing frequency and intensity.

Mattias Ohlmstead handled most of the former problems himself, though he often talked them over with Barlow in the evenings. He dealt with them capably, for the most part, but the real problems created involved the delays that naturally followed such incidents. That, in turn, made Barlow's job more difficult, as he had to be more circumspect in choosing a site for the camps at night— and midday. It meant that the wagons traveled shorter distances each day, so Barlow had to find camps less far-

ther afield than he had been—not that the wagons would
arrive any sooner.

The situation also was one of the causes of the increased altercations. The travelers were growing tired,
sick of being ill. Water, at times, was becoming scarce,
adding to the overall aggravation. As did the delays and
the frustrations of having to spend time repairing each
others' wagons, though most of the emigrants continued
moving on while a few people struggled with repairs.
That, in and of itself, was another source of anger among
the people. Many of the travelers grew enraged as they
watched their fellows passing them by without bothering
to offer assistance.

Barlow was often called upon to try to help quell the
disturbances that regularly flared up at night, especially
after the late wagons straggled into the camp. Ohlmstead
frequently asked Barlow, with Buffalo 2, to accompany
him to mediate a dispute over some real—or, more likely
than not, imagined—grievance one family had against another. More than once, Barlow had to give someone a
good thumping to get his point across, though he tried to
keep that to a minimum. He got no enjoyment out of it,
and resorted to violence simply when no other recourse
seemed available. Or when one of the emigrants was foolish enough to attack him for appearing to take the other
party's side in whatever dispute was at the forefront at
the time.

It all annoyed Barlow more and more. His irritation
grew with each passing day. There were many times when
he wished he had not taken on the job, or thought about
just leaving the emigrants to their own devices, riding off
one day for his daily hunt and guiding duties and just
keeping going, without waiting at a campsite. He could
take Dora Lee with him and be happy. He could easily
make it to Fort Laramie, or even farther, on his own.

But he knew he could not—would not—do that. First
off, he had hired on to see these people to the Oregon
country, and he was not the type of man to renege on a

promise, which is what he considered his hiring. When he had taken Hugh Samuels's money, he had, according to his lights, made a promise to fulfill a contract. He would not go back on that.

There was also the matter of his nephews. While the two youths spent most of their time with new friends their own age, they were, when it came down to it, his responsibility. And, though he had made no promises about that, taking care of them was an implied vow.

So he kept his temper as best he could, spending his days making love to Dora Lee when the work was done, and trying to keep the wagons moving as quickly and smoothly as possibly.

13

WITH EACH PASSING day, troubles mounted, not the least of which was the steadily increasing temperatures. Combined with the more frequent lack of water, it served to raise already volatile tempers. On his nightly meanders through the camp, Barlow began to hear more and more grumbling from the travelers. Finally he had had enough, and on a Sunday, a day on which they generally still traveled over the protestations of the more pious among them, Barlow had Ohlmstead call a halt for the day. After allowing the emigrants to hold services, Ohlmstead gathered the men around for a meeting.

The men sat out on the prairie, softly cursing the heat, the travel, the insects, the dust, and anything else that crossed their minds. They puffed on pipes or hand-rolled cigarettes while sipping at mugs of coffee or cups of water; a few even surreptitiously nipped from flasks of whiskey.

Finally Barlow stood. "I understand some of you boys ain't real happy with the travelin' these days," he said flatly. Over rumbles of assents, he snapped, "Well, boys, all I can say is too goddamn bad. You best get used to it, 'cause it's only gonna get worse."

"To hell with you, Barlow," one man snarled. He at least had the nerve to stand up to verbally confront Barlow. "If you knew what you was doin', this journey wouldn't be near so bad."

More undertones of agreement.

"That a fact?" Barlow asked, his sarcasm lost on the gathered group. "And just what brings you that notion?"

"It just stands to reason," the man said, gaining confidence. "Our night campsites was jist fine till lately. It's only since you took up with that goddamn trollop you been haulin' out there every day that our night spots've gotten so poor." He looked smug.

Ohlmstead leaped up, easily seeing what the man was too stupid to notice—the rage that had suddenly sprang into Barlow's eyes. "Now, vait a minute dere, Phil," Ohlmstead said in a voice he hoped was soothing, "dat's not a very nice t'ing to say. You don't know dis voman. She's a fine voman, she is. Ya. And you shouldn't say such t'ings about her. You shouldn't say such t'ings about nobody else neidder. Especially if you don't know dem."

"Oh, sit down and shut the hell up, Ohlmstead," Phil Crunkleton snarled. "You're supposed to be the captain of this outfit, but you ain't done a goddamn thing to help out."

If Barlow wasn't still so enraged, he might've laughed at Crunkleton's stupidity. The man simply could not see that he was treading on mighty thin ice here, insulting both the wagon train's captain and guide.

Ohlmstead was speechless with anger, prompting the increasingly foolish Crunkleton to say unctuously, "What's a matter, Ohlmstead? Cat got your tongue?"

Though Crunkleton was a tall, rangy fellow, he did not have a chance under the sudden assault Mattias Ohlmstead launched at him. The little Swede smashed Crunkleton to the ground with two quick punches to the face, and then began stomping on the man's body wherever he could reach.

Barlow, almost grinning at the justice of it, let it go on

for a minute or so, then marched over, grabbed Ohlmstead around the torso, and lifted him up. He carried the frantically kicking, swinging, swearing Swede off a few feet and set him down, but did not release him.

"You best calm down, Mattias," Barlow said sternly. "Knockin' that ol' hoss's dick in the dirt ain't gonna do us no good."

"Ya, sure, easy for you to say, you big oaf," Ohlmstead snapped. "You yoost let me . . ."

"Relax, hoss," Barlow said more sternly.

Suddenly realizing that dealing with Barlow was a far different case than dealing with Phil Crunkleton, Ohlmstead quit resisting. He was still furious, but he knew that continuing to fly off at the handle the way he had been would solve nothing. He nodded. "I'm all right, Vill."

"You certain, hoss?" Barlow asked dubiously.

"Ya, sure."

Barlow released him and stepped back a bit, but kept a wary eye on him.

Ohlmstead composed himself and faced the group of men again. Crunkleton had been helped to his feet, and looked blackly at the Swede and Barlow. His face was already beginning to color with bruises. "Do any of you others feel da vay Phil does?" Ohlmstead demanded, eyes angrily scanning the crowd.

Mumbled agreement floated from many of the men on the breeze.

"Den you should elect a new captain here and now," Ohlmstead said flatly. "Any of you who t'inks he can do a better job dan me is velcome to da post."

"We don't want a new leader, Mattias," someone called out. "We just want our guide to find us better places to spend the night. Like we used to have."

Ohlmstead listened to the chorus of agreement until it had died down. Then he said, "Maybe Mr. Barlow vill vant to talk to you about vhy dese places haven't been so good lately." He glanced at Barlow, who nodded.

"Have any of you goddamn fools taken a good look

around lately?" Barlow asked, glaring at his audience. "This whole country is poor. Grass is sparse enough, but with at least one emigrant train havin' been this way before us this year, it's even worse. Water's scarce. Hell, even the Platte's way down, which ain't unusual this time of year."

"But . . ." the same man started.

"What's your name, hoss?" Barlow asked, cutting him off.

"Marty Stavely," the man said, torn between defiance and fear of this broad, dangerous-looking hulk.

"I'll tell you what, Mr. Stavely," Barlow said evenly, his rage at Crunkleton having ebbed considerably after the beating Ohlmstead had administered to the offensive man. "How's about I take you with me the next day or two. We'll look for noonin' spots and night camps together. You can see what the lay of the land is and see if you can find us some better places. What d'you say, hoss?"

"Well, I don't know," Stavely stuttered, suddenly unsure of himself, and silently cursing himself for having spoken up.

"Well, now, hoss," Barlow said curtly, "have you changed your mind about the job I'm doin'?" He glowered at the man, his anger beginning to rise again.

"Well, I wouldn't say that exactly," Stavely stammered. "It's jist that I, well . . ."

"Go with him, Marty," someone yelled, a call that was soon echoed by a number of men in the crowd.

"I got my family to think of," Stavely said more firmly. "I cain't go traipsin' about out there in the wilds doin' this here feller's job for him. It ain't right."

"We'll care for your family," someone insisted. That, too, brought a chorus of agreement.

Stavely looked around the crowd, appearing for all the world to be a treed raccoon. Finally his shoulders slumped. "All right," he muttered. "I'll go along for a day or two." His head rose. "But no more'n that," he insisted.

"And goddammit," Crunkleton said, shaking off the

men who were helping him stand, "I'm goin' with you both."

Barlow shrugged. "You'll have to supply your own horse and such." He did not like the idea of Crunkleton being along, but he decided that he would not be unwilling to finish the beating Ohlmstead had begun giving the hotheaded emigrant. He looked at Stavely. "I'll let you use one of my horses, hoss," he added.

"I ain't got no horse," Crunkleton snapped.

Barlow shrugged again. "That's your lookout, hoss. You know when I leave out each mornin'. You want to come along, you'll be there on a horse. I ain't aimin' to wait around for you."

"What about your other horse?" Crunkleton demanded.

"What about it?" Barlow countered.

"Why cain't I use it?"

"'Cause I don't want you to," Barlow said simply, bluntly.

"So your whore can use it?" Crunkleton asked with a smirk, which quickly froze on his face.

Barlow was livid, and it took all the strength he had in his formidable mind, spirit, and body to keep from hammering the man into a bloody pulp.

Ohlmstead, who saw Crunkleton's death in Barlow's speckled brown eyes, quickly stepped in front of the big man, gulping in concern as he did. "Don't do it, Vill," he said urgently. "He is not vort it." He knew he was spouting nonsense, but he had to try to keep Barlow from killing Crunkleton.

"You're an odious little shit, hoss," Barlow said tightly to Crunkleton. "And I won't inflict you on some poor animal that ain't done no one any harm." He paused. "And heed my words, you sorry piece of shit. If you ever speak ill of Miz Openshaw again, or if you ever cross me again, I will tear your goddamn heart out with my bare hands and feed it to Buffler."

He turned and walked away, and even the obtuse Crunkleton had enough sense not to say anything further.

• • •

To Barlow's surprise—and great disgust—Crunkleton was waiting out on the prairie when Barlow was ready to set out in the morning. With Buffalo 2 trotting around them, Barlow, Crunkleton, and Stavely rode out, towing a long string of pack mules behind, moving fairly swiftly to put some distance between them and the first wagons. Barlow was surly, not only at having the loathsome Crunkleton along, but also because he was accompanied by Stavely, and thus had decided to leave Dora Lee behind for the day. It was going to be a long, lonely—and intensely annoying—day for him, he was certain.

They rode in a small arc, from the Platte River on the north, bowing out to the west, and several miles to the south. The scenery was, by and large, pretty bleak: The sandy soil did not allow a lush growth of grass, and what was there was pretty well cropped down by the previous wagon train. The Platte, never very deep at the best of times, was, in many places, a broad muddy puddle. Trees were virtually nonexistent, even along the river. The passage of the previous wagon train was well marked by dead oxen and mules, discarded belongings, and occasional graves. Game was scarce, and the sun was an unrelenting ball of heat that seared the earth and everyone on it.

Barlow finally found a spot where there was some water that was relatively clean, and marked it for a nooning site. Though it was still only mid-morning, the heat was intense, and the men and animals took a short break. Barlow loosened his saddle and made his two companions do the same, allowing Beelzebub and the two horses to breathe. Then the men sat, gnawing on some jerky and sipping judiciously at the muddy river water. Buffalo 2 lay on his side near Barlow, tongue lolling, breathing heavily to try to cool himself.

"We been pretty lucky so far, boys," Barlow said flatly. "If you've been observant at all, you've seen what the earlier emigrant train's been through. We ain't lost but two or three animals so far, and nobody's had to toss out any belongin's, but that's comin'. And the only one who's gone under has been ol' Mr. Sedgewick when he got run over by his wagon last week. We ain't even had much sickness, but I expect that ain't gonna last neither."

Crunkleton looked rankled by the information, and the dawning knowledge that Barlow was not shirking in his duty.

Stavely, however, was thoughtful, thinking back on the morning's travel so far, and what he had seen. It did not look good to him, and that was beginning to worry him.

"Maybe I was some hasty in thinkin' you wasn't payin' full attention to your duty, Mr. Barlow," Stavely said seriously. "Unless you been leadin' us on a strange course to confuse us—and I ain't sayin' you done so 'cause I don't think that's the facts—what you said about it bein' difficult to find decent sites for our night camps must be true."

"Oh, quit your mewlin', boy," Crunkleton snapped. He might've seen the same things Stavely had, and come to the same conclusions, but he was not about to seek forgiveness, especially in the whining way he thought Stavely was doing.

"Is there no end to your ignorance, hoss?" Barlow asked. He was still furious at Crunkleton, yet managed to be amazed at the man's intemperate remarks.

"Go to hell, Barlow," Crunkleton snapped. He was irritable from the heat, and from the knowledge that he had been wrong.

"You can't be too fond of livin', boy, with remarks like that one," Barlow growled. He pushed himself up and added, "Time to be our way, boys." He jerked the saddle cinch so hard that Beelzebub shied away. Taking a deep breath to calm himself some, Barlow tightened the cinch properly, then mounted the mule and rode out, neither knowing nor caring if the two men were following him.

Barlow waited until fairly late in the afternoon before actively looking to make meat. He had not wanted to butcher the animals in the worst heat of the day, nor did he want to carry the meat with him for too long, lest it go bad before he could even distribute it. But eventually he had to hunt where he could. He managed to bring down a pair of buffalo. Because there were only the two, he decided he would take as much meat off each carcass as he could, rather than just the better cuts, as he often did.

After using the mules to pull the hides off, Barlow said, "Come on and help out here, boys."

Stavely dismounted and headed toward Barlow.

But Crunkleton remained on his horse. "Piss on you, Barlow," he said with a sneer. "I ain't been hired for doin' such work. That's what you're bein' paid for, boy."

Barlow jabbed his knife into the carcass of the buffalo and wiped the sweat off his forehead with a sleeve. He headed toward Crunkleton, speaking as he walked. "I've about had more'n my fill of your troublesome ways, you sack of shit. Now get your dumb ass down here and help." He stopped beside Crunkleton's horse.

"Or what?" Crunkleton's smirk spread.

"Or this . . ." Barlow reached up, grabbed Crunkleton's shirt, and jerked him down from the horse, which sidled nervously off.

Crunkleton hit the dry ground with a thud, sending up a cloud of dust. Barlow immediately pressed a moccasin against the man's throat. "What's it gonna be, hoss?" he asked, his voice mean.

"I'll help," Crunkleton managed to croak.

Barlow nodded once, curtly, and moved his foot. He spun and went back to work. A moment later, an angry Crunkleton joined Stavely in hacking meat off the other buffalo carcass.

Soon after, Barlow, still busy butchering, had worked his way around to the other side of the buffalo, leaving his back toward his two companions. Crunkleton, seeing an opportunity, suddenly charged at Barlow, his knife raised.

Barlow spun when Buffalo 2 began frantically barking, bringing an arm up instinctively as he did. The arm partially blocked Crunkleton's knife thrust, though the blade sank into Barlow's shoulder just below the collarbone on the right side. His own knife went flying off into the dirt somewhere.

As Crunkleton tried to jerk the knife free to stab him again, Barlow kneed him in the stomach, the power of it doubling Crunkleton over and lifting him a foot off the ground. Barlow locked his fingers together and brought both hands down as one on the back of Crunkleton's neck. At the same time, he jerked his knee up, and it smashed into Crunkleton's chin.

Crunkleton groaned and fell, but Barlow was too enraged now to let him lie there. "You dumb piece of shit," he muttered as he grabbed Crunkleton by the hair and hauled him up. With his left hand, he smashed the man's face three times.

Stavely ran over, yelling, "Stop, Barlow! You're gonna kill him." He was too afraid to physically try to stop Barlow, however.

Barlow ignored him. He pulled the knife out of his shoulder and suddenly slid it across Crunkleton's throat, then shoved the rapidly dying man away from him. He tossed his attacker's bloody knife away, seeming to throw off much of his anger with it. He looked down with contempt on the body, then checked out his shoulder. With a very nervous Stavely's help, he managed to bandage the wound. Then the two men finished butchering the buffalo.

As they prepared to ride off, Stavely hesitantly asked, "Ain't we gonna bury Crunkleton?"

"You're welcome to stay here and do so if you're of a mind to," Barlow said flatly. "But I ain't wastin' my time. That critter ain't worth my sweat, hoss."

"But animals and such . . ." Stavely looked rather queasy.

Barlow shrugged. "That damn-fool critter is gettin' his just deserts, hoss." He rode on.

Stavely hung back a few moments, then shrugged nervously and quickly caught up to Barlow.

14

MARTY STAVELY MADE sure that everyone soon knew of Phil Crunkleton's demise—and the reason for it. He also made sure the travelers were well aware of Barlow's truthfulness as to the barrenness of the area through which they were traveling.

That did not stop the grumbling, though the complaints were no longer directed at Barlow, or even Mattias Ohlmstead; it was more of a general griping over the difficulties of the journey; the increasing number of deaths of animals as well as people; the heat; the lack of water overall, and the frequent scarcity of potable water; the rising cases of illnesses; the infrequent though powerful storms that sometimes swept down over them; the occasional paucity of game.

It still made people irritable, and arguments often were the order of the day—or, rather, night—though fights happened less often. The verbal jousting was something the captain and guide could deal with. And Barlow was more than capable of handling the fisticuffs that broke out, even with the minor wound inflicted by Crunkleton. It became real trouble only when one of the combatants pulled out a gun or maybe a knife. None of the emigrants was really skilled in the use of either, at least as an offensive weapon, and it was too easy for some innocent to get killed by mistake.

While Barlow had no fear of anyone, he had enough sense to be mighty wary when around one of these gun-toting travelers. He could as easily get killed by a man unskilled in guns as anyone else. And more than once he had to make a daring move to wrest a gun away from some angry emigrant before someone did get killed. Then, he would usually cuff the miscreant around for a while to teach him a lesson, taking out some of his own anger on the one who had caused it.

The day after Stavely and Crunkleton had accompanied Barlow, he began taking Dora Lee Openshaw with him again, much to her relief, and his own pleasure, at least for a while. Things were not really as great as they had been, though, considering the lack of water.

"Y'all're gittin' a mite rank, Will," Dora Lee said one afternoon as they lay in the grass. Both were sweaty and considerably bloody from the day's butchering, and with the Platte being little more than a mud puddle for a long stretch, they had had no real opportunity to clean up.

Barlow was a little hurt—and annoyed—by the remark. "You ain't so sweet-smellin' yourself, woman," he groused.

She tensed in anger and hurt.

"Well, Dora Lee," Barlow said contritely, "it ain't really our fault, what with no water and all."

"I know," Dora Lee groused, almost whining. "But I don't have to like it none."

"I don't much care for it neither, girl." He considered just going and using what water there was to clean up, but that would leave little, if any, for the wagon train, and making sure the animals had water was a lot more important than him and Dora Lee sprucing up. "But ain't a damn thing can be done about it."

Dora Lee nodded, knowing it was the truth, but not liking it one little bit. However, she chose to stay with the wagons each day for the next couple of weeks, which created a strain between them, a strain that was alleviated only after two days of drenching rain brought back the river and filled the streams. Once again they could wade armpit-deep in the blood of buffalo or deer, but then bathe before enjoying each other's intimacies. One afternoon of fornicating with Dora Lee Openshaw eased Barlow's irritability considerably, to the relief of practically all the travelers.

During the two weeks that Dora Lee did not go out with Barlow during the days, he took one or both of his nephews with him. He figured it was time to start teaching them more about surviving in the wilderness and helping them improve their hunting and butchering. It also gave Barlow a chance to relax a little, as he let the two youths handle the majority of the work.

"Why ain't you helpin', Uncle Will?" Derek asked, his voice full of complaint.

"You boys're doin' just dandy," Barlow announced. "It's good for your souls."

"Wouldn't it be good for your soul, too?" Clyde questioned, stopping and staring at Barlow.

"Reckon it could be, hoss," Barlow admitted. "But I've done more'n my fair share of such chores over the years, and I ain't so sure my soul could use any more goodness. Now quit your bellyachin' and get back to work, boy. You keep stoppin' to flap your gums at me every two minutes, you ain't ever gonna finish, and them pilgrims'll be mighty put out when they got no meat for their supper."

Barlow almost grinned when he heard Derek mutter to his cousin, "Maybe we made us a mistake comin' along on the journey."

Clyde glanced over his shoulder at Barlow, who pretended to be paying no attention. "It sure ain't the way I expected it to be, Derek," Clyde whispered. "But there's nothin' we can do now."

" 'Cept maybe make ourselves scarce in the mornin's when Uncle Will sets out."

Clyde brightened a bit at that. "Just might work," he mused in a low voice.

But having overheard them, Barlow was on to their little scheme, and even before they could disappear in the morning, he was rousing them from their beds.

Dismayed, the youths rose and grumbled through their hasty breakfasts before Barlow had them saddling their horses and pulling out, towing the long strong of pack mules.

The next two nights, Derek and Clyde bedded down with one family, but after everyone was asleep, skipped off to sleep elsewhere, figuring to throw Barlow off, since he knew where they had been at bedtime.

But Barlow was having none of it, and always managed to track them down and wake them before it was fully light. They finally gave up trying to fool Barlow, and grudgingly accepted their fate as drones for their taskmaster of an uncle.

They were relieved when Barlow told them one night that they would be on their own again for at least a few days—Barlow didn't know how long Dora Lee would want to be out there with him every day again. The boys didn't care why, just so they were free for a while.

But Dora Lee's return to going with Barlow did not last long, what with the weather heating—and drying—up again. So soon she was staying back with the wagons, and a reluctant Derek and Clyde were heading out each morning with their uncle. Besides the weather, however, Barlow had begun seeing fairly heavy sign of Indians, and while he did not really want to put his nephews at risk, he was even more reluctant to put Dora Lee in danger. The boys could help if things got touchy. Whether they would be able to or not was something he did not want to contemplate too deeply, though if they wanted to have adventures in the West, they would have to encounter such a thing sooner or later.

With the youths becoming more proficient at both hunting and butchering, Barlow was free to be more wary when the three of them were out ahead of the wagons.

Another storm swept down on them, ripping across the prairie, with heavy, pounding rain, prodigious bolts of lightning, and resounding claps of thunder. The wind pushed the driving rain almost sideways at times. Barlow, never a fan of rain at the best of times, complained heartily that night at their camp. It was not the best camp, though it could have been worse, really. The people had gotten into the habit of picking up extra booshwa whenever possible and carrying it in buckets under their wagons, where it would stay dry and usable. So there were fires this night, though they were mighty poor, seeing as how there was no dry ground on which to build them. But what Barlow was complaining about was the fact of the storm itself.

"Vhy are you so upset vit dis?" Mattias Ohlmstead asked.

"Tomorrow, next day, maybe, we got to cross the river where the Platte divides into north and south branches. With all this rain, that crossin's gonna be tough doin's."

"De Platte ain't been so bad-looking so far," Ohlmstead reasoned. "Neidder vide nor deep. Vhy should it be so troublesome?"

"It's muddy enough at the best of times. Right after a storm, 'specially one's bad as this, the mud'll be axle-deep, like as not. Plus there's liable to be places where there's quicksand. Not deep, but it can really make it hellacious on the animals tryin' to pull the wagons through it."

"Ya, dat makes sense," Ohlmstead acknowledged. "But ve can't change it, can ve? Vait a day or two maybe?"

Barlow considered that for some seconds, then nodded. "Mayhap that might work. If this damn rain stops soon and we get a couple good dry days, we should be able to stop for a day, not much more than that, though. We cain't afford to lose more time."

"Ya, I understand. Ve'll see vhat happens. It's in da hands of da Lord, I guess,"

"Reckon so," Barlow said, unconvinced.

The rain did stop, and the sun came out with a fierce-
ness that was almost malicious. Things dried out rather
quickly, much to Barlow's relief. He called a halt for the
afternoon much earlier than usual, because they had
reached the bank of the river where they would have to
cross. It would be, he told Ohlmstead, who passed around
the word to the travelers, foolish to try to start crossing
that afternoon. He also decided that they should stay there
the whole of the next day, giving the land more time to
dry out before making the crossing.

Barlow was glad he had the travelers wait. The crossing
went off as flawlessly as could be expected. Only one ox
team got bogged down and had to be hauled out. Only
one wagon broke an axle—and that was early on, and
was repaired by the time the last wagons had crossed.
Since the Platte River here was far less wide and deep
than the Missouri had been, the crossing did not take all
day, so they also managed to make almost four miles beyond by the time they halted for the night. Trying to make
up a little time they had lost in waiting the day, Barlow
and Ohlmstead pushed them that night, and got them
moving somewhat earlier in the morning.

Barlow marked a trail a little south of where the previous wagon train had gone, and found much better grass.
Game was more plentiful, too, and he and his nephews
took down four fat, meaty cows that afternoon. As the
boys butchered the beasts, Barlow sat on Beelzebub
nearby, with Buffalo 2 beside them, watching. He spotted
the three riders coming from the northeast before the
Newfoundland got a scent of them and growled,

"I see 'em," Barlow acknowledged. He kept an eye on
the tiny dots as they grew larger. Finally he called to the
youths, "You boys wipe yourselves off and stand ready."

His nephews looked at him in surprise, which quickly
changed to alarm when they saw the set look on Barlow's
face. "What's goin' on, Uncle Will?" Derek asked.

"Visitors comin'," Barlow growled, not taking his eyes off the approaching warriors.

"Visitors?" Clyde mused aloud as he and his cousin looked at each other in wonder.

Then Derek's eyed widened in recognition and some fear. "Injins?" he asked, his voice frightened.

"Yep," Barlow answered perfunctorily. "Now do what I say, boys. And be quick about it."

"What are they?" Derek asked as he and Clyde cleaned themselves off on scraps of cloth.

"Ain't sure yet," Barlow said. "Round here, likely Sioux."

"They dangerous Injins?" Clyde asked.

"Don't know if they're dangerous," Barlow responded. "They are some fierce warriors when they want to be."

"What do we do?" Derek asked as they tossed aside the now-bloody cloths.

"Keep your rifles nearby, but make sure them pistols of yours're ready, and just wait," Barlow ordered. "Don't you do nothin' less'n I tell you to."

The two youths nodded and swallowed hard. They glanced at each other, worried and growing more so with every passing second.

As the three Indians drew close, Barlow said, "They're Sioux, all right."

The warriors stopped within fifteen feet of Barlow, who still sat on the mule. His nephews were on one side, Buffalo 2 on the other. He made the sign for welcome.

One of the warriors returned it. He was in his early twenties, and like his two companions, naked save for breechcloth and moccasins. Each had a bow and quiver of arrows slung across his back, and all were unpainted.

"They're a huntin' party," Barlow said to his nephews without looking at them. He did not take his eyes off the Indians.

"That's good, ain't it?" Derek asked nervously.

"Better than if they was out for hair." With signs, he asked the warriors, "Has your hunting been good?"

The one shrugged.

"What's your name?" Barlow asked in signs.

"Calling Wolf," the man answered in kind.

"You're welcome to some of our meat," Barlow said, still using signs. He waved at the small mound of buffalo meat the youths had already butchered. "Take a little," he suggested. "Just the best. The tongue and the livers."

The warriors talked among themselves for a minute or two; then Calling Wolf looked back at Barlow and nodded. "We will take some," he said in signs. "It is good that you have allowed this."

"I want my Sioux brothers to be happy," Barlow said both in signs and in quiet English, so his nephews could understand. He managed to keep the sarcasm out of his sign language, but not his voice.

"We will take it all," Calling Wolf continued in signs. "And your mules to carry it."

"Like hell you will," Barlow muttered. But with his hands he simply said, "No. Only some. And no mules."

Calling Wolf's eyes narrowed dangerously. "We'll take it all," he signed, hands snapping furiously.

"You try that, and you'll be killed," Barlow said, still with his hands. His look was stern, and his hand movements showed that he meant what he had said.

As the warriors talked among themselves again, Barlow said, "Put your hands on your revolvers but leave 'em in your belts, boys."

Though they tried to pretend they had not seen it, the warriors, Barlow knew, were aware of Derek and Clyde holding the grips of their Colts, ready to draw them. Calling Wolf looked angrily at Barlow, but signed that the arrangement was satisfactory.

Barlow nodded, then jerked his chin, indicating that the Indians should go pick out some meat.

As they did, Barlow said to his nephews, "You boys stand your ground. Let them Injins take what meat they want, but don't let 'em move you out of the way. And don't move on your own. Just stay right where you're at."

Scared spitless, Derek and Clyde tried to wear determined faces as they stood like statues. The three Indians moved toward the pile of meat, bumping shoulders with the youths, who did not move. When one warrior narrowed his eyes at Clyde and looked as if he were about to hit the white youth, Buffalo 2 growled and edged forward. The Sioux changed his mind. Then the three of them took an armload of meat each, mounted their ponies, and trotted off,

Barlow breathed a sign of relief.

Still pale with fright, Derek asked in a shaky voice, "Will they be back?"

"Ain't likely, boy. Most warriors're pretty courageous, but they ain't fools. Them three know that if they try somethin' against us, at least one of 'em, and likely all of 'em're gonna get put under. They might be angry, but they ain't foolish enough to come back and try to take us on."

Barlow surveyed one nephew, then the other. Then he grinned. "Now, get back to work," he said.

15

TWO DAYS LATER they arrived at Fort Laramie. Because the previous wagon train had been there just days before, Barlow suggested to Ohlmstead that they camp a mile or so away in a decent spot he had found. "There's sufficient grass," he told Ohlmstead. "Plus the water's not been fouled by them others who passed through here. And there's plenty of wood for a change."

"Are you planning to stay here awhile?" Ohlmstead asked.

"Couple of days, maybe. Three at most. It's usual for wagons to spend a bit of time here. Repair wagons, maybe trade for some supplies, let the animals—and the people—rest a bit. Maybe even trade in some worn animals for fresh ones. The worst of the trip is ahead of us, and we'll want everyone to be ready for it."

"Da vorst?" Ohlmstead asked skeptically.

"Yep," Barlow responded. "Won't be long before we hit the mountains. It's a week, maybe, till South Pass, the easiest way 'cross the Divide, but then things'll start gettin' a heap more troublesome. Wait'll you see them mountains, boys," Barlow continued, glancing from Ohlmstead to Derek, then Clyde. "They're some awesome, I'm tellin' you, boys. Tall as the sky, all jagged-lookin'. Snow most of the year on some of the peaks, and you can get a snowstorm even in June at times. Some places we'll have to go are so high that you can't hardly draw in a breath. And cold, too, even in summers, at least at night."

"Maybe you yoost better keep most of dat to yourself, Vill," Ohlmstead suggested. "Da emigrants hear some of vhat they'll be facing, and dey might vant to change their minds."

"They do change their minds, they'll be in a pisspot of trouble, hoss," Barlow growled. "Ain't nobody from Fort Laramie gonna take 'em back east, and the folks at the fort ain't gonna let 'em stay here indefinitely. They'll have to go on with the rest of us, or make their way back to the States on their own."

"That shouldn't be so hard, should it, Uncle Will?" Derek asked. "We ain't had that much trouble on the way out here."

"That's mostly true," Barlow agreed. "But they started out with fresh teams, had plenty of supplies and a heap of other folks along with 'em to help out was they to get into some kind of trouble. Plus while Injins ain't likely to attack a wagon train full of pilgrims, they might not be so reluctant to raise hair on one or two wagons on their own. 'Specially wagons that'll be headin' back east. Them Injins'll have the notion—and they'd be right—that those travelers are faint of heart and won't put up much of a fight was they to be attacked."

"Den maybe ve should tell dem," Ohlmstead said. "So dey know yoost vhat dey are getting into. And vhat dey vill face if dey turn back."

Barlow shrugged. "Tell 'em whatever you want, hoss. That's your doin's as cap'n, not mine. I figure they'll have some inklin' of what they're facin', and if they don't now, they will pretty soon. Tell 'em too much now, and you'll maybe scare off the whole lot of 'em." He grinned. "Then you'd be a cap'n without a wagon train."

"Dat vouldn't be very good," Ohlmstead mused. He

grinned, too. "It might even make me look bad."

"Probably would."

Soon after, Ohlmstead and Barlow strolled through the spread-out camp, talking with the pilgrims, telling them all of the plan to stay a couple of days, suggesting that they make sure they fed themselves and their animals well, and suggesting they get to the fort as soon as possible to buy or trade for what supplies and fresh animals they needed—and could be gotten there.

"There's no tellin'," Barlow said to each, "if there ain't another group of pilgrims followin' right behind us. We need every advantage, and takin' too long to get some supplies that might be needed could mean the fort runs out—or sells everything to the folks who arrive with the next wagon train."

Most of the people, Barlow was pleased to see, took his advice, and headed to the fort the next morning to buy whatever they needed and could afford. And over the next couple of days, he was also pleased to note that the people were carefully tending to their animals, allowing them to graze on the lush grass. Barlow and his nephews rode out each morning with the pack mules, and returned in the afternoon with plenty of meat to parcel out to the emigrants, and everyone ate well, and took plenty of rest.

Fortified and with spirits refreshed, the emigrants pulled out two days later, their wagons creaking loudly as they rolled across the grassland. The prairie rose steadily, though imperceptibly to the travelers, heading toward the dim smudge of the mountains they could faintly see at times on the far horizon.

Barlow had decided that it would be safer for Dora Lee to leave her behind with the wagons for a while. Though the chances of an Indian confrontation were slimmer now than before because of the proximity of the fort, there was the possibility that some warriors might strike at a lone man and woman out away from the wagons. The Indians would know that the wagons were freshly supplied from the fort, and might think a pilgrim or two far ahead of the wagons was a tempting target. So he took Derek and Clyde with him.

The two youths were not as averse to going these days as they had been. They had come to enjoy the hunting, though not the hard, dirty, rank work of butchering. And while the brief encounter with the three Sioux warriors had not really amounted to very much, it had imparted at least the smallest aura of adventure—the first such episode in their so-far-tedious journey—and whetted their appetites for even greater adventures. They could boast now that they had faced warriors out on the wide prairie. Sure, they knew it was really a non-confrontation, but the girls traveling with their parents were easily impressed when the two youths embellished the run-in considerably.

It was Clyde who saw the small band of Indians a couple of days later. Or so he thought. Barlow had spotted the warriors some time before, but had not said anything, waiting to see how long it would take his nephews to become aware of the newcomers.

The time gap was considerable, at least to Barlow, and he was only a little satisfied when Clyde pulled his horse to a stop and pointed. "Look," he said, his breath catching in his throat.

"They Injins?" Derek asked, trying to sound braver than he felt when he, too, stopped and saw what his cousin was pointing at.

"Yep," Barlow agreed.

"More Sioux?" Clyde asked. While his uncle might have warned them that the Sioux could be fierce, Clyde had seen no indication of it in their last little meeting with the warriors.

"Mayhap," Barlow responded. "But more likely Snakes, at least since they're comin' from the south and west. Was they comin' from the north, I might think they was Crows." Seeing them, and figuring there was a good chance they were Shoshonis, Barlow could not help but wonder how White Bear was doing. He wished that his old friend were there with him. While having his nephews along was all right, he would have much preferred White Bear's company on this long, wearisome trek. He shook off the sudden gloom. White Bear was back with his people and probably enjoying his life there.

"Snakes?" Derek questioned with a grin. "Crows? Pretty funny names for Injins."

Barlow smiled softly. "Reckon those names do sound queersome. Snakes're really called Shoshonis. They got the name Snakes from the old mountain boys because the sign for them is like a snake." He moved his hand up and down in front of him in a wavy line. "The Crows call themselves Absaroka—the Bird People."

"They mean?" Clyde asked.

Barlow shook his head in amusement. "You boys're sure concerned with the meanness of Injins," he noted. "Both of them peoples're friendly to whites, for the most part. I ain't ever heard of a Shoshoni attackin' a white man. Crows're usually friendly, but it ain't above them to raise hair on a man out by himself, or even a small group of fellers. Say, a man and two boys." He fought back a grin at the shock on his nephews' faces.

Then Derek snorted in derision. "He's just joshin' us, Clyde," he said dismissively.

"Not entirely, hoss," Barlow said, growing serious. "The Crows'll attack small groups of white men if they think they have the advantage over 'em. Damn Crows're about the best horse thieves this chile's ever seen. But they can be fearsome when it comes to war. And ain't no man—red or white—can ride like them boys. Them Injins ride like they was born on the back of a pony."

The youths looked suitably impressed.

"Let's mosey on, boys," Barlow said, urging Beelzebub forward. He kept an eye on the approaching Indians, who were still some ways off, noting their appearance and disappearance as they rode up and down the dips and rises of the undulating land.

Finally he stopped again. He checked his rifle, which lay across the saddle in front of him, and his pistols after suggesting that his nephews do the same. Then they waited.

"Damn," he muttered when he caught sight of the Indians again.

"What's the matter, Uncle Will?" Derek asked, suddenly becoming frightened.

"Them boys're painted for war," Barlow said curtly. "You boys stand fast. Like as not, if they attack, they'll charge at us like madmen just to test our mettle, but they won't do us no harm, 'cept maybe to count coup on us first. You just . . ."

"Count what?"

"Coup," Barlow snapped. "French word. Means they'll hit you with a bow or coup stick or even a hand. Shows how brave they are 'cause they have to get close enough to touch you. Now shut up and pay attention to what I say."

Buffalo 2 was growling, but at the same time, he was looking perplexed. Barlow watched the dog for a few moments, wondering. He glanced up again and got a good look at the approaching warriors. Recognition dawned, and his broad face split into a wide grin. It quickly faded, however, when he spotted White Bear's grim features.

The Shoshoni and his three companions stopped within feet of Barlow and his nephews.

"How's doin's?" Barlow asked tentatively.

"Bloody goddamn poor," White Bear answered flatly.

Barlow nodded. "I figured as much when I saw your face. What's happened?"

"Two women and a child were taken from the bloomin' village," White Bear said harshly, his voice touched with anger. "We're out here to get them back."

Barlow nodded. It was only right that they would do so. "Know who took 'em?" he questioned.

"Bloody goddamn Crows."

"You know this Injin?" Derek asked, looking from White Bear to his uncle in surprise.

"What the hell do you think, boy?" Barlow snapped.

"Mayhap I was just passin' the time of day with some Injin just come wanderin' along?" He looked at White Bear. "How long ago was they took?"

"Two days. Got on their bloody trail as soon as we could." His voice was full of bitterness. "These're the only bloody chaps who'd venture to come along with me."

"How many of 'em did this?" Barlow asked.

"Just three. Bloody bastards stole several of my horses, too." He sounded more angry at that, almost, than at the fact that three people had been kidnapped.

"Who was took?"

"My sister, my wife's sister, and her child."

Barlow nodded, then sat there thinking awhile. Finally he said, "You boys look mighty spent. Looks like you could fill your meatbags some, too. Why'n't you stop here with us for the night."

"What're you three doin' out here anyway?" White Bear asked.

"I'm guidin' a wagon train to the Oregon country. And huntin' for the pilgrims. These're my nephews, Derek and Clyde. They help me out from time to time with the huntin' and butcherin'."

"You want me to stay the night with a bloody wagon train of bloomin' pilgrims?" White Bear asked, not quite incredulous, but getting fairly close to it.

Barlow nodded. "We'll see that you get some supplies and such to maybe make your search easier," he said. "It'll give you and your boys here a chance to rest a bit without havin' to worry about bein' put upon."

White Bear barked a nasty laugh. "You expect us to feel safe surrounded by a bloody wagon train full of pilgrims?" he asked sarcastically.

"Would I make the invite if I didn't think it was true, hoss?" Barlow responded tartly.

"Suppose not," White Bear said with a sigh. "Sorry, old chap. I am bloody well angry—at the Crows, and with my own bloody people, who don't have the courage to come with me to find the lost ones."

"I understand, hoss." He paused. "Look, we need to make meat. Maybe your boys there can throw in with us in doin' so; then we'll find a site for the night's camp and wait for the wagons. We'll talk tonight."

White Bear nodded. "We saw some bloody fat cows back there about half a mile," he said, jerking his chin in the direction from which he and his companions had come.

Barlow nodded. As they all moved off, Barlow asked, "Who's your amigos?"

"The young one is Little Leaf," White Bear pointed. "The one with the red-speckled paint is Eight Smokes, and the other is named Tall Bull."

Barlow nodded, and they rode in silence. Half an hour later, they spotted the small, scattered group of buffalo. White Bear brightened a bit. "Those bloody nephews of yours ever run buffalo?" he asked.

Barlow shook his head, a slow grin starting.

"Then it's bloody well time they did so, ain't it?"

"Reckon you're right, hoss," Barlow agreed.

"What the hell're you talkin' about, Uncle Will?" Derek asked, confused.

"You'll see, hoss," Barlow said, excitement starting to build in him just a bit. "You boys wanted adventure, well, you're about to get some, and shinin' doin's it is, too."

"What do we do?" Clyde asked, the excitement also beginning to infect him.

"Just follow us and do what I do, boy." He looked at White Bear. "You ready, hoss?" he asked.

"Bloody right I am."

16

THE SEVEN MOVED forward, spreading out a little as they did. Little Leaf, Tall Bull, and Eight Smokes talked among themselves in their own language, pointing to various buffalo. Derek and Clyde's eyes wandered from Shoshonis to buffalo to each other to their uncle, as they wondered about what was going to happen in the next few moments. Though he was as excited as the humans, Buffalo 2 knew enough to be quiet, though he did bounce energetically around.

Barlow moved over and forced Beelzebub between his nephews' horses. "See that buffler cow yonder, Derek?" he said, pointing. When the youth nodded, Barlow said, "That 'un's yours. And, Clyde, you take that 'un there," he added, pointing again.

"Easy as pie, Uncle Will," Clyde said. "I can hit that thing from here easy."

"You ain't gonna hit it from here, hoss," Barlow said with a grin. "You're gonna ride your horse right up alongside that buffler and put him under that way."

Clyde looked at Barlow in alarm. "You're joshin', ain't you, Uncle Will?" he asked, eyes wide.

Barlow shook his head.

"But that's mad," Derek interjected, as confused and as worried as his cousin.

"Hell, hoss," Barlow said brightly, "them Shoshonis're gonna do it with just bows and arrows."

Derek's renewed protest was cut off by a sharp yell from Little Leaf, who suddenly kicked his pony into a run. The Shoshoni raced toward the buffalo, which looked up in bewilderment, then began to run, shuffling slowly but rapidly gaining speed. White Bear, Eight Smokes, and Tall Bull were right behind the young warrior, and moments later, Barlow was following the Shoshonis, leaving the long string of pack mules behind.

Derek and Clyde looked at each other, eyes wide with fear. Then Clyde—sometimes the bolder of the two despite his being a little younger—shrugged and slapped the reins on his horse's rump. He howled a challenge, copying Little Leaf, and was off and running.

Not wanting to be outdone by his younger cousin, Derek swiftly joined the chase, pointing his horse toward the buffalo Barlow had picked out for him moments earlier.

Within minutes, the two youths were sitting on their horses twenty yards apart looking at each other in amazement. They were breathing heavily, and their horses were blowing hard after the chase, but each had brought down his quarry. Barlow and the Shoshonis were spread out over some distance, but it looked to the two boys as if everyone had been successful. Glancing into the distance, and seeing that everyone else was beginning to work, Derek and Clyde dismounted and began the long, hard, hot, bloody task of butchering the carcasses.

Two hours later, the meat had been butchered and was loaded on the mules. They all rode off, sweating and tired but pleased with the afternoon's success. Even White Bear had not fallen back into his anger. Barlow stopped them after another hour's ride. Though there would still be plenty of daylight left when the emigrants reached there, Barlow had decided that he needed to talk with White Bear and that this was where the emigrants would spend the night. It would cost them a little time, but Barlow did not care about that right now. He had been thinking about White Bear's quest all during the ride, and was formulating a plan. So he stopped them, and they began unloading the meat, cutting it into portions, unsaddling and tending the horses, finding firewood and more.

The site was along the Platte, on the south bank. The water—and there was a decent amount of it, for a change—had not been fouled here by the earlier wagon train. There was plenty of wood, and sufficient grass for the animals.

"These bloody emigrants're lucky to have you guidin' 'em, old chap," White Bear said to Barlow as they worked.

Barlow shrugged, but he was pleased at the words.

When they were finished with their chores, Barlow looked at White Bear and half smiled. "You best clean that paint off your face, hoss," he said, "lest you frighten those poor pilgrims half to death when they get here." He paused. " 'Sides, with all your sweatin' and the blood and all, that paint ain't fit for no proper warrior."

White Bear started to get angry again, but then calmed down when he realized that Barlow was right. "Suppose so," he said. He almost managed to grin. "Of course, old chap, you're pretty well a bloomin' mess yourself."

"Reckon I am at that."

They headed toward the water, stripped off their clothes, and flopped into the shallow water. Buffalo 2 bounded in after them. Little Leaf, Tall Bull, and Eight Smokes followed them moments later. It was rather easy for them to join in, seeing as how they were wearing only breechcloths and moccasins.

Derek and Clyde stood there watching for a moment, too shy to join in.

"C'mon, you faint-hearted little bastards," Barlow bellowed.

The two youths looked at each other, uncertain. It

didn't seem right to them somehow, though they couldn't really determine why.

"Best get on in here and get yourselves cleaned up, boy," Barlow warned, "or we'll come on out there and help you, which ain't somethin' you'll take enjoyment from."

Derek and Clyde glanced at each other again, then shrugged. They tossed off their pants—having taken off their shirts while they worked—and quickly ran into the shallow water and plopped into it, facedown, hiding their privates while trying to seem as if they were not doing so on purpose.

They all soon cleaned themselves up and then sat out in the sun for a bit to dry off. They redressed, then started two fires—one for the Ohlmsteads' wagon, the other a little ways off that the Shoshonis would use for themselves. They sat at the Shoshonis' fire, which was shielded from what would be the emigrant camp by a thick curtain of willows and cottonwoods. They roasted a little meat, and made some coffee from the Indians' small supply.

As they ate the half-raw meat, and drank the hot, black coffee, Barlow asked, "Why'd you head for me and the boys, White Bear, 'stead of ridin' on around? You should've been able to tell early on we weren't Crows."

"We had bloody well planned to avoid you. Little Leaf had seen a bloomin' wagon train early on. He came back and reported it, and we headed east to get around it."

"That was an earlier one;" Barlow said.

White Bear shrugged. "Then Little Leaf—who was still scoutin' for us—spotted you. We were going to avoid you bloody bastards, too, but then he said he saw a bloody giant dog roaming around. So we came to take a look."

Barlow nodded. They sat in silence for a bit, as Barlow took in the Shoshonis who accompanied his friend. Little Leaf was young—less than a year older than Derek, he estimated—thin, with a hawklike face. Despite his young age, he must be well thought of, Barlow figured, considering that he had been doing the scouting for the small

war party. Such an important task was not given out
lightly. Intelligent, curious eyes looked out over a beaked
nose and thin lips.

Tall Bull was appropriately named—a tall, powerful-
looking man in his mid-twenties with a fleshy nose and
matching lips. A thick scar cut across the nose, as if someone had tried to lop it off. His skin was very dark, and
his wide chest also was marred by scars. He gave off
every appearance of being a tough, seasoned warrior, and
one who would shy away from nothing. His hard face and
the battle scars probably would serve to give enemies
pause before taking him on, Barlow thought.

Eight Smokes was an unhandsome man with deep-set
eyes and a face heavily pocked by a bout with some childhood disease. He was heavy, with a thick, protruding belly
and fleshy limbs. Despite his unprepossessing appearance,
he gave off an aura of toughness and fearlessness. Barlow
would wager that Eight Smokes was a good man to have
at one's side in a battle. Like his three companions, Eight
Smokes wore his hair long and loose, hanging down to
frame his face. All carried an unstrung bow in a rawhide
case attached to a rawhide quiver full of arrows. Each also
carried a knife and an iron-headed tomahawk. White Bear
also wore the two single-shot muzzle-loading pistols he
had had with him in the Mexican lands.

Barlow grinned inwardly as he saw Derek and Clyde
edge closer to Little Leaf and ask him if he spoke English.
He did, and the three youths were soon talking animatedly
about the day's buffalo hunt.

"You have any trouble gettin' back to your village after
leavin' the Mexican lands, White Bear?" Barlow asked.

The Shoshoni shook his head. "It was a bloody boring
trip, to be frank, old chap. How about your journey back
to the States?"

"Weren't quite the same as yours, hoss," Barlow said
flatly. "Turns out most of them fellers hired on by the
trader had bad hearts. They kilt the owner—a feller named
Seamus Muldoon—and two others and made off with all

the specie and goods. I was out huntin', and chased after them critters when I found Muldoon and the other two. Took out a couple of 'em, but they creased my brainpan with a rifle ball and left me to go under."

"Seems bloody obvious you didn't go under out there," White Bear noted dryly.

"Damn, hoss, you ain't lost a bit of your sagaciousness," Barlow responded in kind. "Actually, the goddamn Comanches found me and hauled me back to their village. They was fixin' to raise my hair, but Buffler—who I thought was gone under from a rifle ball—showed up and helped me make an escape from them critters."

"I presume you chased after the bloody bastards who left you out there."

"I did," Barlow answered flatly. "And them boys all paid for their misdeeds, too."

"As they bloody well should have."

Barlow noticed that the three youths had moved on from the topic of the buffalo hunt to the possibility of battles. Or perhaps it was the possibility of living with a woman. He couldn't be quite sure, as animated and relatively quiet as the conversation was.

"You said your wife's sister was one of the women who was took from your village," Barlow said to White Bear. "Did you take another wife when you got back? Or did you just go back to . . . what was her name? The woman you were with when we first met up." He felt foolish for not being able to remember the woman's name.

"Singing Bird." White Bear paused. "Yes, we're together again. She had thought me lost, so she took another husband. But he died in a fight with the Blackfeet more than a year ago. So now she's my wife again."

Barlow nodded. "You happy with her?" It was, he realized, a stupid question, but it was too late to take it back now.

"Happy enough," White Bear said with a shrug. He lightened up a little. "Singin' Bird's a bloody good woman."

"Glad to hear it, hoss. You just treat her right."

White Bear shrugged. He was in no mood to discuss his love life with Barlow, or anyone else. Another time, he would not care, but now was not the time and this was not the place.

There was silence for a while, before White Bear decided he should try to break out of his sourness a bit. "You sure these bloody pilgrims aren't gonna mind me and my mates bein' here?"

Barlow's shoulders rose and fell. "Don't matter none whether they mind or not, hoss," he said evenly. "You're here at my invite, and that's all there is to it. 'Sides, ain't none of them pilgrims gonna make trouble over it. Ain't a one of 'em's got the courage—or the wherewithal—to try anything."

White Bear almost grinned. "It's good to see you haven't changed much over the past few bloody months, old chap," he said.

Barlow smiled. He stretched out, his head on his saddle, pulled his floppy old hat down over his eyes, and fell asleep.

The creaking of the wagons roused Barlow from his nap. He rose, shoving his hat back into its proper place on his head. Then he rubbed his big hands over his broad face, trying to brush away the tiredness that lingered.

"They'll be here any time now," Barlow said to White Bear, who was still sitting. "I'll head on over there by the other fire and wait for the captain of the train—a feller named Mattias Ohlmstead. You and your boys best stay here out of the way till I let Ohlmstead and at least some of the others know you're here."

White Bear nodded and spoke to his companions, who were sitting or lying nearby, in their own language.

"Let's go, boys," Barlow said to his nephews. "Time to go wait for the wagons. C'mon, Buffler."

They all walked over to where they had built the Ohlmsteads' fire, and where they had placed the couple of tons of meat they had brought in earlier. With half an ear toward the increasing creaking headed toward them, Barlow, Derek, and Clyde checked over the pack mules. They had not been looked at in some time, and Barlow figured it was a good time to check the animals' hooves, shoes, and skin for any signs of overuse or pending problems. They found none, which did not surprise Barlow, as he generally tried to treat all his animals with care whenever possible.

Just as they were finishing, Ohlmstead's wagon squealed into view, and Barlow directed it to the spot near the fire.

"Vhat is dis?" Ohlmstead asked, walking over to stop in front of Barlow. "Ve're stopping here? So soon? Dere is plenty of sunlight left in da day."

"I know, but . . ."

"Is dere trouble?" He suddenly looked worried. "Ve are in danger perhaps?"

"No, we ain't in danger, Mattias," Barlow snapped. "Now hush up and let me tell you."

"Vell?" Ohlmstead said, standing there with his hands on his hips, glaring at Barlow. When he got no immediate response, he repeated, "Vell?" A movement in the trees caught his attention, and he looked that way. He blanched. "Are dere Injins in dem trees?" he asked, his voice cracking.

"Yep," Barlow said in what he hoped was a reassuring tone. "They're . . ."

"But I t'ought you said dat . . ."

"Hush, Mattias," Barlow snapped. "They're friends, and they've come on some poor doin's. I want to talk with 'em and see if there's any way I can help 'em a little."

"But you said ve couldn't afford to lose more time. Ve vill lose several hours of traveling time if ve stop now."

"We'll make up the time," Barlow promised. "Look, this is a prime spot for spendin' the night. Plenty of good wood, plenty of water, and good grass for the animals. And we've made a heap of meat."

Ohlmstead still looked skeptical.

Barlow was already tired of the debate. "Look, hoss," he said tightly, "I aim to stay here the night with my friends. If that don't suit you and the others, you can push on. All you got to do is follow the river. You'll be fine. I'll meet up with you on the trail tomorrow."

Agneta Ohlmstead walked up and placed a hand on her husband's shoulders. "It vill be all right, Papa," she said softly. "Ve vill make up da time, like Mr. Barlow says."

"Are you sure, Mama?" Ohlmstead asked, looking at his wife.

"Ya."

Ohlmstead nodded at Barlow. "All right, Vill. But I better varn de others."

"That suits."

As Ohlmstead went to talk to each family as the wagons arrived, Barlow and his nephews began unhitching the oxen, while Agneta Ohlmstead and her children started setting up their camp and preparing supper.

17

IT WAS OBVIOUS from the sidelong glances shot at Barlow and at the Shoshonis, and the angry, frightened murmurs that spread like a prairie fire throughout the camp, that the travelers were not happy with the presence of the Indians in their camp.

After doling out the meat for the day, Barlow went to the Shoshonis' fire, making sure he took some meat for them, too. He left a worried Dora Lee Openshaw at the Ohlmsteads' fire. Derek and Clyde decided to go with Barlow. They were nervous, but had come to like Little Leaf already, and hoped to talk to him some more.

While the small group was feeding on more buffalo meat and coffee—now augmented by the sugar Barlow had retrieved from his personal supplies—Ohlmstead tentatively approached.

"Vill?" he called hesitantly. "Mr. Barlow?"

"C'mon over, hoss," Barlow said. "There's no need for you to be concerned."

Ohlmstead moved closer. "I'd like to talk vith you, Vill," he said, his voice a bit stronger, but still touched by worry.

"Set, hoss," Barlow commanded in friendly tones.

"Whatever you got to say can be said in front of these boys."

Ohlmstead nodded and nervously sat on his shins near Barlow. He was too frightened to look at anyone.

"Mattias," Barlow said with a sigh, "I told you before, these boys're friends of mine. Well, White Bear there is a friend. I just met the others today, but if they're with White Bear, then I figured they're friends, too. There's no need for you to fear these men."

Ohlmstead glanced from one dark face to the other, still not sure of what to think about it all.

"You're welcome to meat and coffee, old chap," White Bear said.

For a moment, Ohlmstead looked like he was going to faint when he heard the British English coming from the mouth of the grim-faced Shoshoni. But he quickly recovered at least to some extent. "Thank you, Mr. . . . um, did Vill say your name vas Vhite Bear?"

The Shoshoni nodded.

"Thank you, Vhite Bear," Ohlmstead went on, gaining a little confidence, "But I'll eat vit my family soon." He looked at Barlow. "The people are vorried about having dese Injins here, Vill." He glanced sidelong at the Shoshonis, wondering how they would take such a statement. To his relief, and a bit of confusion, they seemed quite stoic.

"Why?" Barlow asked. "They ain't causin' no trouble. Nor are they plannin' to."

Ohlmstead shrugged. "You know dese people by now, Vill," he said. "Dey are frightened of everyt'ing dey don't know. Despite vhat you say, dey still vorry dat dey vill be attacked vhile dey sleep, their vives molested, their children taken away. Dey . . ."

He stopped, shocked, as a suddenly angry White Bear abruptly pushed himself up and stalked off deeper into the trees. Ohlmstead looked at Barlow in puzzlement. "Vhat is wrong vit . . . ?"

"He's a mite sensitive right now to talk about people bein' taken away," Barlow said flatly.

"I didn't mean . . ."

"I know, hoss," Barlow said more softly, relenting a little. He sighed. "You go on around and tell all them damn pilgrims they have nothin' to fear from these Shoshonis. They ain't gonna be attacked, their wives won't be ravished, and their young'uns sure as hell ain't gonna be taken away from 'em." He paused to stem the slow rise of anger. "And tell 'em to use their goddamn heads a bit, for chrissakes. Even if the Shoshonis was plannin' some deviltry, they'd be a mite outnumbered, don't you think?"

Ohlmstead nodded. "Ya, sure. I tell dem all dat, but dey don't vant to listen. And dey say dat maybe dese Injins here have friends out dere somevhere vaitin' for darkness."

"Then they're even more goddamn loco than I figured," Barlow said hotly.

"Ya, sure. You're right, I'm t'inkin'. But dere is more."

"And what's that?" Barlow asked, still fighting his anger.

"All da people, they suspect dat something here isn't right. Something about da Injins. Not, maybe, dat da Injins vill attack dem, but that there is something wrong. So dey are afraid of vhat it might mean for dem."

"Well, hoss," Barlow said, regaining control of himself, "it so happens that there is somethin' wrong. But it ain't gonna affect the pilgrims none."

"Vhat is wrong?" Ohlmstead asked, almost instinctively.

"Some Crows raided White Bear's village and made off with a couple of women and a child," Barlow responded in even tones. "White Bear and his companions're are on the trail of the Crows."

"A child vas stolen?" Ohlmstead said with a gulp.

"Yep."

Ohlmstead shook his head, wondering at how anyone

could do such a thing as steal a child away from its mother and family and people. "Dat is yoost evil," he said.

"Damned devilish," Barlow agreed. "And like I said, it ain't gonna affect the pilgrims, or their travel. Go and tell 'em that. And that the Shoshonis'll be gone in the mornin'."

"Ya, I vill tell dem." Ohlmstead stood. "I don't know if dey vill listen, t'ough, but I vill tell dem." He turned and started walking away, then spun back. "I hope your friends find the vuns who done dis evil t'ing and return vit their people to their homes."

Barlow nodded. "Thanks, Mattias," he said.

When Ohlmstead had left, White Bear returned to the fire. He plopped down, cross-legged, and reached for some meat.

"Mattias didn't mean no harm, White Bear," Barlow said soothingly. "And he didn't know about your situation before I just told him."

"I expected as much, old chap," White Bear said, gloom weighing heavily on him. For the first time, he had some real inkling of how Barlow had felt during all those years the two of them had spent searching across the West for Barlow's daughter, Anna. He had sympathized then, but now he felt a surge of empathy. It was not a comfortable feeling. "I don't hold it against him. I just couldn't sit here and bloody well listen to him, though."

Barlow nodded. He lit his pipe and leaned back against a log, puffing quietly. "There anything I can do to help you, White Bear?" he finally asked.

The Shoshoni shrugged. "Not bloody much, I suppose, old chap," he said. "Maybe give us some bloomin' jerky or pemmican, if you have any, so we don't have to waste time making meat."

"Reckon I can do that," Barlow said reflectively. He fell silent again, drawing smoke from his pipe. Unformed thoughts roiled around in his head, and he grew annoyed when they would not coalesce. Finally, however, they slowly started to come together. And that, in some ways, increased his irritation because he quickly realized he should have come to these conclusions right off, instead of having to work his way through a fog of thought.

It was still several hours before dark would arrive when Barlow leaned forward and, using the tip of his pipe for emphasis, said, "I'm goin' with you, hoss."

White Bear's eyes widened. He supposed he should not be surprised by anything Barlow said or did, but he could not help it. The man was sometimes incredibly unpredictable. "That's mad, old chap," the Shoshoni said as he carefully set down his mostly empty coffee cup.

"Like hell it is," Barlow snapped. "I reckon I owe it to you, White Bear."

"You don't owe me a bloody thing, old chap," White Bear said almost vehemently.

"Buffler shit, hoss," Barlow snapped. "There weren't no reason for you to help me look for Anna. Not at first, and sure as hell not after a couple of years of fruitless lookin'. Most other folks would've just headed on home after a spell, even if they'd helped out in the first place. But you, you damn fool, stuck it out with me right till the very end."

White Bear shrugged. "It was nothing, old chap," he mumbled.

"Maybe to you, hoss," Barlow said more quietly. "But it meant a heap to me. Now it's my turn to help you."

"You can't do anything we bloody well can't do ourselves, old chap," White Bear said. "Tall Bull, Eight Smokes, and Little Leaf are quite bloomin' capable of trackin' down and handlin' a few damned Crows."

"Never said they weren't capable, hoss," Barlow responded in reasonable tones. "But you might need some help when you catch them Crows. Hell, we're close to their land now, so it ain't unthinkable that they'll have joined up with some others. If that's true, you might have to face off against a heap more'n three of 'em. And," he added grimly, "lest you forgot, I can more'n hold my own in a fight, whether it's against white men, Mexicans, or goddamn redskins."

White Bear almost managed a smile. "I suppose you're bloody well right about that, you pale-faced devil."

"Then shut your flappin' hole about the whole thing, hoss. I'm comin' with you."

Derek and Clyde, who had ended their conversation with Little Leaf to listen to what Barlow and White Bear were discussing, looked at each other, then back to Barlow. "We want to go along, too, Uncle Will," Derek said firmly.

"I don't reckon that'd be wise, boys," Barlow said. "You ain't used to the kind of doin's we'll be facin' out there. You ain't used to the hard ridin' wc'll have to do. And you ain't ever been in a battle where some fellers're tryin' to raise your hair."

"We can keep up, Uncle Will," Clyde insisted.

"Yeah, and do whatever needs doin'," Derek added.

"What do you think, White Bear?" Barlow asked, looking at his friend.

"Leave me out of this bloody decision, old chap," White Bear said with the barest hint of a smile. "I don't know these chaps, and I have no idea what they can do. You want them along, I won't bloomin' object. You want them to stay behind, it'll probably raise my opinion of your intelligence."

"You're a big goddamn help," Barlow mumbled. He looked at the youths. "I'll think on it." At the sudden brightening of their faces, he added with a growl, "Now don't you boys go gettin' all excited and such. Even if I do agree to let you tag along, this ain't gonna be no church social. When we catch them Crows," he added, utterly confident that he, White Bear, and the others would find their quarry, "we're like as not gonna have to go agin 'em, and those critters can fight."

"We understand," the two youths chorused.

Barlow shook his head in annoyance. His nephews did not seem to be taking the whole matter very seriously. He sighed, deciding that he probably would have been the same way had he been in their position at their ages. There was just something inside all young men that made them think they could undertake anything and come out of it unscathed, no matter how dangerous or tough it was.

"You think these bloody pilgrims are going to let you just wander off with us, old chap?" White Bear asked.

Barlow shrugged, unconcerned. "There ain't a damn thing they can do about it, hoss," he commented.

"You don't have to do this," White Bear noted. "Me and the others were well on our way after those bloody bastards before we come across you. We won't be put out, old chap, if you decide to stay with the bloomin' wagons."

"You got somethin' against me goin' with you, hoss?" Barlow asked. He was suspicious, and a little hurt. He had thought that White Bear would be happy to have him along after all that they had shared. Not that the Shoshoni would prefer Barlow to his tribesmen, but he appeared to not even want Barlow around.

"No, old chap," White Bear said, feeling bad. He could see the hurt in Barlow's eyes, and did not like being the cause of it. "I just want to make sure you know what you're getting yourself into, and what you might have to deal with here before we leave out."

"I know damn well what I'm facin', hoss—both here and out there," Barlow growled.

White Bear let it drop. It was not really his concern. He knew Barlow well enough by now to know that if Barlow made up his mind to do this, no one would be able to stop him from doing it. Not even an entire wagon train of angry pilgrims. And he truly did want his old friend along with him. They had shared a plentiful myriad of adventures and had come through them all mostly unscathed—or at least alive. And, when it came down to it, they *had* found Barlow's daughter. Even if they had had to leave her with a Mexican family in San Diego, way out in California. He and Barlow rode well together and fought well together. A man couldn't ask for a better companion than Will Barlow, White Bear thought. Having him along on this quest would go a long way toward seeing it succeed. Of that, White Bear was absolutely certain.

Barlow was relieved when White Bear quit arguing over it. He realized that the Shoshoni was just trying to do what was best—making sure Barlow was thinking clearly in his decision to join the hunt for the captives and their takers.

He made an effort to shake off the gloomy thoughts. The matter of him going was settled. What wasn't settled was whether he should allow his nephews to go along. He was, after all, responsible for them, and did not want to see them come to any harm. On the other hand, they were young and eager for adventure. And sooner or later, they were, if they stayed in the West, going to face hostile people, whether red or white. It might as well be now, when the chances of them running into a major force of Crows was relatively slim.

Besides, he reasoned, Little Leaf was not much older than Derek, and had been on the war trail for at least a year, and probably the hunt for two or three. However, while Little Leaf would have been raised in the harshness of this life out here, and reared with the expectation that battle was inevitable for men, his nephews had not been brought up under the same conditions, and their outlook on what life might hold for them was vastly different.

Barlow finally decided that he would sleep on the matter, and make his decision just before he and the Shoshonis pulled out to take up the quest again. He hoped that a good night's rest would make the decision a little easier to come by.

"Boys," he finally said, "go'n fetch Mr. Ohlmstead and bring him here. Don't let on what me and White Bear've been talkin' about. Just tell him I need to talk with him at his earliest convenience."

The two nodded, rose, and headed off through the trees toward the emigrants' camp.

18

"I VILL NOT allow it, Vill," an almost apoplectic Mattias Ohlmstead snapped. He rose, seething, pulled himself to his full height, all five feet four inches of it, and paced around the fire the Shoshonis were using. Barlow and the Indians remained seated. "I can't allow it. You should know dat, Vill." He turned an angry glare on Barlow.

The big man's shoulders rose and fell once as he stared benignly back at the irate wagon train captain. "It ain't a question of what you can or can't allow, hoss," he said evenly. "Like I told you, I'm goin' with White Bear and his men to hunt down the Crows and take back the women and child them fractious critters took. You really got no say in the matter, Mattias, that's all there is to it."

Ohlmstead stomped around some more, trying hard to get himself under control. He knew he had to speak calmly and rationally if he was to make his point, and he could not do that when he was as furious as he was. It took some time, but he managed to get a grip on his anger and push it down some.

"You have a contract vit us, Vill," Ohlmstead finally said in mostly reasonable tones. "You are being paid good money to guide dis vagon train and to hunt for us."

"I know that, Mattias," Barlow acknowledged.

"Ya, sure, you know dat. But you von't pay no heed to it. You are being paid a good sum of money to do dese t'ings for us, and you should fulfill your obligations."

"I plan to, hoss," Barlow started.

But Ohlmstead cut him off. "I vould not have t'ought of you as a man who vould go back on his vord, vonce given. I am disappointed in you, Vill," he said, the outrage beginning to rise in him again. "And it makes me angry. Ya. Very angry."

"But I . . ."

"I have put my trust in you all dese veeks—months— since ve left Missouri. And now you vould just abandon us out here, leaving us to find our own vay across de vilderness. Ve don't know our vay out here, and ve have no von who can hunt for us. Not de vay you can."

"Goddammit, hoss, would you close that flappin' goddamn hole of yours for a minute," Barlow snapped, his own choler beginning to surface. He was not used to being talked to in such a way, and did not take kindly to it. When an irate Ohlmstead slapped his mouth closed and glowered, Barlow continued, hoping he was speaking in measured tones. "I ain't abandonin' you and the wagons, hoss. And I aim to fulfill my contract with you and Mr. Samuels."

"Ya, sure you vill," Ohlmstead spat in rage. "And how vill you do dis if you are traipsin' off vit dese Injins here looking for villains." He turned a slightly softer eye on White Bear. "I am sorry about your losses, Vhite Bear," he said. "But dis is about vhat Vill has promised to do for us, and I plan to hold him to his vord."

"As you bloody well should," White Bear said, throwing an ingratiating grin toward his friend. "You can't always trust the white-eyed devils, you know, old chap."

Ohlmstead's eyes bugged out for a minute before he realized that White Bear was needling him. He couldn't decide if that rankled him even more; then he forcibly put it aside. It didn't really matter at the moment whether he was annoyed at it or not. There were far more important matters to be dealt with.

"Look, Mattias," Barlow said soothingly, trying to placate the wagon train captain. "Soon's we find those critters, and get them women and that chile back, I'll scurry on back here quick as I can, and be guidin' the wagons and huntin' for you and the rest of the pilgrims just like I have been from the start."

"No," Ohlmstead snapped. "You vill stay vit us now and do vhat you promised to do. Your Injin friends here vill have to take care of dis business on their own." He glanced at White Bear again, not sure he wanted to talk to the Shoshoni again after having been teased, but wanting him to understand his position on the matter. "I am sorry, Vhite Bear," he said apologetically, "but I must insist dat Vill stay vit the vagons and continue his duties to us."

"I understand," White Bear said, biting back the retort that bubbled close to the surface, fighting for release. "But I better warn you, old chap, that if you force that bloody bastard to stay here when he has his mind set on coming with me and my mates, he's going to be one bloody infuriated fellow, and will be the devil to live with."

"Ya, sure, I expect dat, knowing him," Ohlmstead said with a shrug. "But I am villing to deal vith dat. Da safety of dis vagon train and da people vit it are far more important dan Mr. Barlow's vexation and vounded pride."

White Bear looked at Barlow and said seriously, "He's got a bloody good point there, old chap."

"Buffler shit," Barlow growled, not willing to admit the truth of Ohlmstead's statement. "He just wants to put me on the spot."

"Like hell, old chap," White Bear countered. "Without you—or someone like you—these pilgrims're going to be lost, wandering around the wilderness. Before you know it, they'll be far off the trail to Oregon, and if you don't get back soon enough, they'll likely get stuck up in the mountains when the snow sets in." The Shoshoni was now having serious doubts about Barlow accompanying him and his companions. As much as he would've liked his friend's help, he was not comfortable with the thought of an entire wagon train being lost, its people possibly dying, just to have a reliable old friend with him on the trail of the Crows.

Barlow was having similar thoughts, but he was a mule-headed man, and once having made up his mind, was extremely reluctant to change it, especially if that meant admitting he might be wrong.

"You told me at times," Ohlmstead said in calmer tones, breaking the sudden silence that had grown, "dat many Injins arc smart. Your friend White Bear has just proven dat to be true. Ya, sure. I t'ink you should listen to him dis time."

"We ain't gonna be gone but a couple days at most," Barlow insisted, still loath to give up his plan. "You can't get lost in that little bit of time." He refused to look at White Bear. He knew what the Shoshoni was thinking— that the search for Anna had taken five or six years, and that this quest could be equally as long, though it was highly unlikely. Still, there was a very good chance that the hunt for the Crows would take longer than just a couple of days. Otherwise, White Bear and his men would have run down the Crows already.

"How do you know dat?" Ohlmstead questioned harshly. He was no fool, and knew that out here in this vast expanse of plains and mountains, a search for a small band of Crows could take a long time, especially if, as Barlow and the Shoshonis had indicated, the miscreants were heading into their own territory.

Barlow shrugged, growing more irritated at the increasingly apparent fact that he was incorrect about all this. "I don't, hoss," he grumbled. "I just feel it in my bones."

"Ya, sure, but dat von't bring in meat for da travelers, Vill," Ohlmstead went on, relentless. "And it von't show us da right path. Or find us good water and vood and grass for de animals and . . ."

"I know, goddammit," Barlow snapped. "I know all that," he added, calming himself. "But . . ." He paused, the pain at his daughter's loss rising up in him like lava in a volcano, threatening to overwhelm him. "But White Bear helped me in the search for my daughter, hoss," he finally managed. "I owe it to him for all his help—and his friendship." He looked defiantly at Ohlmstead. "And there ain't a goddamn thing you can say to me to make me change my mind about that, hoss," he added harshly, with finality.

Ohlmstead was a little taken aback by the vehemence of Barlow's determination. And by the rightness of it. Which put the Swede in a quandary. His thoughts had to be of the emigrants and doing whatever was necessary to get them to their destination as safely and as quickly as possible. On the other hand, friendship, especially of the kind that seemed to bind Barlow and White Bear, was almost a sacred thing, and was not to be discounted. However, he had to come up with a decision, and it was certain to mean that one of these two things was going to have to take precedence over the other.

Ohlmstead paced some more, thumbs stuck in his belt, head bowed in thought, as he pondered the situation. Finally he made up his mind. There could be only one choice—the travelers and their concerns had to come first.

"I'm sorry, Vill," he said, stopping a few feet in front of where Barlow sat and squatting to look the guide in the face. "Ya, very sorry, but I must t'ink of da people who have put their trust in me. I must insist dat you fulfill your contract vit us and continue your duties." He craned his neck looking over his shoulder. "I am sorry, Vhite Bear, but it must be dis vay. I hope you vill understand."

White Bear nodded. He was saddened a little. Since he had first seen Barlow earlier in the day, he had harbored the hope that his friend would be able to join his quest, even though he had argued against it some. But he could see Ohlmstead's reasoning, and he even agreed with it, though that didn't mean he had to like it any.

"I'm sorry, too, hoss," Barlow said to Ohlmstead, bringing the Swede's attention back to him. "But I'm goin' with White Bear, and that's all there is to it. I'll be back as quick as I can and take up my duties again then. I owe White Bear too much to let him and his boys ride off without me for such doin's."

Before Ohimstead could object, Barlow held up his hand, stemming the protests. "Look, you can find your way for a spell without me, hoss," he said in even tones. "Foller the Platte for another couple of days. Then just look for the tracks of that wagon train that's been just ahead of us since the beginnin'. You know enough to move off the trail a bit to find grass for the animals. You can see where the water's been fouled by them others before you."

Ohlmstead shook his head, caught between anger, sympathy, and worry. He was losing his argument, that was obvious, and he didn't like that, though the implications for the wagon train were what really bothered him the most. "But vhat about meat?" he suddenly asked. "Vit'out fresh meat, ve vill be suffering soon. And dere is no von vit the vagons who can hunt the vay you can."

"Sure there is," Barlow said with sudden realization. The thought helped lighten his mood—while he was adamant about going with White Bear, he did not feel particularly good about leaving the emigrants in the lurch, which is how he saw it to some extent.

"Ya? And who vould dat be?" Ohlmstead demanded.

Barlow jerked his head at his nephews. "Derek and Clyde," he said. "They've come a long way since we left the States. They plumb shine now as hunters, and they know how to butcher mighty damn well, too. They'll be able to keep you in meat for the short time till I get back."

"But we want to go with you, Uncle Will," Derek said, his face registering his shock. While he was pleased with the compliments, he had no real confidence in his ability to actually provide enough meat for the entire wagon train on a daily basis. It was too much to ask of him. Besides, he wanted the adventure of being out chasing after hostile Indians, not wandering out on the wide prairie shooting down buffalo who were too dumb to get out of their own way. And then having to spend hours up to his elbows in blood and gore while butchering the beasts.

"You'll do what you're told, boy," Barlow growled. Having come up with a solution, he was not about to listen to his nephew sass him.

"But . . ."

"Enough, boy," Barlow snapped.

"Now vait a minute, Vill," Ohlmstead interjected. "I'm not so sure dat dese boys can do vhat you say. Dey're still boys, and all da hunting dey have done has been vit you showing dem da vay—and directing dem in vhat to do. Maybe dey von't be able to find buffalo like you can. Or maybe dey're not as good hunters as you t'ink." He did not like talking about the youths this way right in front of them, but he had no choice. The safety and health of the travelers were far more important than the burgeoning pride of the two young hunters.

"They'll do just fine," Barlow insisted. "Don't you fret about them. I taught 'em well."

"I know dat, Vill, but . . ."

"Hold on, old chaps," White Bear interrupted. "I may have a way out of this whole bloody problem." When they turned to him, he added, "Just sit and shut up a for a time while I talk over the whole bloomin' situation with my friends." Ignoring the other whites, he turned to his Sho-shoni companions and began speaking to them in their own language.

Barlow shrugged and grabbed another piece of meat. He was not really hungry, but it would keep him occupied for a few minutes while he watched the Shoshonis. He could understand a little of what was being said, and got the gist of White Bear's plan. It made sense to him, if he understood it correctly.

It was obvious, however, that neither Eight Smokes nor Tall Bull looked upon the idea favorably. Eight Smokes in particular argued vehemently, with increasing rage. But White Bear finally managed to calm him down considerably after several minutes of soothing words.

Finally White Bear turned to face the whites again. "This'll be pretty bloody unusual," he said evenly, "but maybe this'll be acceptable to you, Mr. Ohlmstead." He paused. "Will will come with me and Little Leaf. Eight Smokes and Tall Bull will stay with you. They'll take on Will's duties of guiding and hunting for you chaps."

Ohlmstead stared at him in disbelief for several long seconds. Then he said in a hesitant voice, "You are yoost joshing me, ya?"

"No, old chap, I'm not."

"Da travelers vill never accept somet'ing like dat," Ohlmstead said, still not certain that White Bear wasn't being facetious.

White Bear shrugged. "You'll have to bloody well convince them, then, won't you, old chap," he said flatly. "You've been around Will long enough to know that once he's made up his mind about somethin', not much is going to change it. And I do believe the bloke plans to join this quest. If he just goes, you'll be left with no one except perhaps the two boys there to guide you and hunt for you. This way, you'll have two chaps who know the trail—at least for some miles—and are top hunters."

Ohlmstead shook his head, hating to be in this position. He knew he was boxed in. It was obvious that Barlow was going to go with the Shoshonis, and that there was nothing he could do to stop him. The emigrants might be a lot more pleased to have to rely on the two white youths, simply because they would not trust the Indians. But Ohlmstead was accountable to the emigrants and for the wagon train, and having two inexperienced men—no, boys yet, really—in such responsible positions as guides and hunters probably would be folly.

Making it all worse was that the Swede was going to

have to sell the idea to the emigrants, which would be some task. Then he sighed inwardly. If the people objected to the plan too much, they might very well relieve him of his duties as captain and select someone else. Or, he could very well just step down voluntarily and let someone else worry about it. Then the onus would be off him. Which, once he thought about it, might not be such a bad thing after all.

"All right," he finally said. He looked at Barlow. "But both your nephews stay vit us, too."

Barlow considered that, then shook his head. "I reckon Derek'll go with me," he announced.

"But what about me?" Clyde said angrily, almost in tears with rage.

"You'll stay here, boy," Barlow said gruffly. He eased his tone then. "Mr. Ohlmstead is gonna need your help, boy. He's gonna have his hands full with tryin' to get the pilgrims to accept a couple of Shoshonis guidin' and huntin' for 'em. It'll make Mattias's job easier to have someone he can rely on to help him out."

"I want to go," Clyde pouted.

"Don't matter what you want, hoss," Barlow said harshly. "What's done is done, and there ain't no use in you mewlin' about it."

19

AS BARLOW WAS saddling Beelzebub in the morning's darkness before dawn, he glanced over at White Bear, who was saddling his pony. "Are Tall Bull and Eight Smokes gonna be all right with these doin's?" Barlow asked.

White Bear did not look up, just nodded.

"You certain, hoss? Eight Smokes especially looked put out by the notion of helpin' out a heap of pilgrims."

"Your nephew Clyde didn't seem much taken with the thought of being left behind either, old chap."

"Ah, hell, White Bear, you know better'n to compare the two. Clyde ain't but a boy. Eight Smokes's a full-grown warrior, and a mean-lookin' cuss, too. He don't look like the type to take such a thing lightly."

"He'll be fine, old chap."

"You don't think he'll cause a ruckus or somethin' soon's we're out of sight?"

White Bear looked over his pony's back at his friend and shook his head. "I bloody well doubt it. He's not that foolish. He'll do what he's supposed to."

"You sure, hoss? Far's I've ever seen among your people—hell, all the Injins I've ever met—even the chiefs can't tell any of their people what to do."

"But the leader of a war band has pretty much bloody absolute power," White Bear countered. "And I'm the leader of this bloomin' war party." White Bear glanced around, making sure no one unwanted would hear what he had to say next. "I did tell him and Tall Bull, though, that if the bloody emigrants start a jolly—a fracas—with them, that they're to take off and either follow us or head back to the bloomin' village. After telling Clyde and Ohlmstead that they're goin'."

Barlow nodded. "Wise thing, hoss. Ain't no reason your amigos should take any guff from the likes of these pilgrims. Not when they're doin' these folks a favor."

"My thinkin', too, old chap."

Finished preparing the mule, Barlow headed to Ohlmstead's wagon, where he packed some of his dwindling stash of supplies—some coffee, sugar, and jerky mostly—into a buckskin sack that he went and hung from the saddle horn.

Dora Lee Openshaw came up as he was doing so. She smiled somewhat shyly up at him, remembering last night. After the discussion and the decision, he had gone to Dora Lee and had made love to her with more passion and power than he had in days. She'd responded with equal fervor, pleased at it. Then she had gotten angry when she learned of Barlow's plan.

"And what about me?" she had demanded.

"What about you, woman?" he'd responded, surprised. "Ain't much changed. You'll travel with the Ohlmsteads, just like you been doin'. They ain't gonna mind. And I ain't figurin' to be gone more'n a few days at most."

She was not satisfied with that, but she knew that arguing would not improve matters. It was better just to accept his decision, since she was not willing to leave him, and to hope that he was back soon. Actually, she had no real choice—she could not go back to traveling with Laura Lee and Charlie Penwell. She just had to trust in Barlow.

Now she approached him, wanting him to know that she was not really angry with him, but simply would miss him. She kissed him warmly on the lips.

He broke it off quickly, and grinned at her. "Much as I'd like to have you again, Dora Lee," he said, "there really ain't the time for it."

"You're no fun," Dora Lee said with a pout that quickly melted into a giggle.

"Not at times like this, I ain't," Barlow said somberly. "The doin's me'n White Bear face are some serious, girl."

"You'll be back, though?" Dora Lee asked, suddenly growing worried again.

"Just as soon as I can, Dora Lee," Barlow promised. "I got to help White Bear. That's important to me. But I got duties here, and I don't take those lightly neither. Plus," he added with a gentle smile, "I got this fine gal waitin' for me." He pulled her close and ran a thick hand over the back of her mane of soft hair as she rested her cheek against his broad chest.

"You best be careful, Will Barlow," Dora Lee muttered into his cloth shirt. Then she leaned her head back to look up at him. "You understand me?"

"Yes'm." He gave her another hug, then said, "You best get back and help Agneta with the mornin' meal."

"You're leavin' soon?"

Barlow nodded. "Soon's we can. We want to be on the trail before the people really learn what's happenin'."

He and Ohlmstead had decided last night that Ohlmstead would tell the emigrants of the plan as the wagons were pulling out this morning. It would eliminate a lot of arguing, since they would be on the move at that point and could ill afford to stop, nor would they want the hassle of halting just as they were starting. The captain and guide were hoping that by the time the wagons pulled into camp that night, the people would be too tired and would have seen that the two Shoshonis who had taken over

Barlow's duties were capable—and harmless to them. And Barlow and Ohlmstead figured that with a decent site for the night's camp, some fresh water, and the prospect of full bellies—the two expected the Shoshonis to bring in meat as plentifully and as easily as Barlow did—they might not be so prone to argue.

"Maybe they'll be too bloomin' frightened of us bloody savages to make much of a fuss, old chaps," White Bear had said the night before, eliciting a belly laugh from Barlow and a nervous chuckle from Ohlmstead.

Derek and Clyde moseyed up as Dora Lee headed back to the wagon. Derek walked through the gathering light with a cavalier stride; Clyde's face was glum. Derek held the reins to his saddled horse.

"You got powder and ball, boy?" Barlow asked Derek. The youth nodded.

"Caps and such?"

"Yep, Uncle Will." He seemed a bit put upon that his uncle would have to ask such questions.

Despite the still-dim light, Barlow saw the look and said flatly, "Don't you get cocky with me, boy. You got no reason for such an air just because me'n White Bear're lettin' you come along with us." He might have thought it somewhat entertaining had the mission on which they were about to embark not been so serious—and potentially dangerous. He could've laughed at Derek's attitude in some other situation, but he wanted his nephew to know right from the start how somber this venture was.

"And you, boy," Barlow said, turning his attention to Clyde, "don't be so damn gloomy. Mattias'll be lookin' to you to stand between the Shoshonis and the pilgrims. And maybe you'll be called on to show Mattias's son, Gunnar—or others—some of what I've taught you about huntin' and guidin' and such, particularly if the emigrants act like the damn fools they are sometimes and drive off the Shoshonis."

Clyde shrugged. All those things might be necessary, but to his mind, they sure were not very exciting. Like his cousin, he wanted action and adventure—tracking down miscreant Indians and battling them as he helped rescue captives they had taken. Such things were the reason he had wanted to come out here in the first place. Not hunting and butchering buffalo for a bunch of cowardly, constantly bickering, ungrateful emigrants. That was almost as bad as farming, he thought.

Barlow threw a huge arm around Clyde's shoulders and walked the youth a little way from the others. "I know you're disappointed, boy," he said gently. "But there'll be plenty of times for you to have adventures. Derek's a bit older'n you, and some bigger, and that might be important in the doin's we have to undertake."

"I know, Uncle Will," Clyde grumbled.

"I'll tell you somethin' else, too, boy," Barlow commented. "Your stayin' here will be a big help to the emigrants, boy."

"You don't have to say such things to try'n make me feel better, Uncle Will," Clyde said morosely.

"I ain't just tryin' to make you feel better, boy. These folks round here ain't gonna like the Shoshonis guidin' 'em and all, and you stayin' behind'll make 'em feel some better, I expect. Sort of soothe their feelin's a heap. 'Sides, hoss, it'll be sort of a guarantee that I'll return. They're gonna know I ain't gonna leave you here and never come back." Barlow stopped and grinned down at his nephew. "You know, boy, I seen both your and your cousin castin' eyes at that there little VanBuskirk gal. What's her name?"

"Charity," Clyde said, brightening fractionally.

"Well, hoss, with Derek off with me and White Bear, he can't be rivalin' you for Miz Charity's attentions now, can he?"

Clyde managed a smile of a sort. "Reckon not," he grudgingly admitted. "Reckon not." His mood eased as he considered the possibilities. He liked the twelve-year-old Charity, and while he knew they were too young for real courting, he wanted to spend some time with the chestnut-haired girl. But he had always seemed to get pushed aside by his bigger, older cousin. Now that wouldn't happen. By the time Derek returned—and it never entered his mind that his cousin would not return; it was simply not something one even thought about when going on an adventure—Charity would likely have forgotten all about his wayfaring cousin Derek.

With a lighter air, Clyde turned and wished Derek well, then scooted off in search of Charity VanBuskirk.

Barlow shook his head. Twelve-year-old boys sure could be foolish critters, he thought. In his recollection, he had been much the same when he had been that age. He smiled into the gray dawn. He was certain that full-grown men were mighty foolish at times, too, especially when it came to women.

"You about ready, old chap?" White Bear asked, walking up beside him.

Barlow nodded. "Reckon so. Can't see no reason to delay. I just want to stop by and bid farewell to Mattias."

"Just be bloody quick about it," White Bear said more curtly than he had planned to. He wanted to be on the trail as quickly as possible now that day was really breaking. Still, he didn't need to snap at his friend, who knew full well the need to get moving now that they had made up their mind as to what they were going to do.

Barlow glanced at White Bear in mild shock, but said nothing. He knew what was going through the Shoshoni's mind. He had frequently felt much the same under the similar circumstances in his search for Anna. He hurried to the Ohlmsteads' wagon, where he greeted Agneta politely, then took Ohlmstead aside.

"We're headin' out, hoss," he said. "I don't know Eight Smokes and Tall Bull, of course, but if White Bear puts his faith in 'em, you can, too. Listen to them about stoppin' sites and whatnot, just like you would to me. Have Clyde help you in whatever you need. And if the pilgrims can't bear to have the Shoshonis around and send 'em packin', rely on Clyde for your huntin'. You can trust him, and you can send Gunnar out there with him to learn huntin' and butcherin'."

Ohlmstead nodded. "I hope dat von't be necessary," he said earnestly. "Most of da travelers're really good folk, Vill. I t'ink you know dat." He paused, and almost managed a smile. "Oh, I know dere are some who're cranky or like to complain, and even a few who take pleasure in causin' trouble, but most're good people who yoost vant to get to the Oregon country. Dey may not like vhat is going on right now vit you and the Shoshonis, but dey vill accept it if it vill help dem get to their destination."

"I hope you're right. If not, tell 'em all to go to the devil and let someone else be in charge. They'll soon learn keepin' a handle on a wagon train like this one ain't such easy doin's."

"Ya, I figure dat already," Ohlmstead said firmly. He drew himself up and held out his hand. As they shook, he said, "*Jag hoppas att du lyckas!* Good luck! I hope you succeed!"

"Thank you, Mattias."

Five minutes later, Barlow, Derek, and the four Shoshonis rode out of the still-awakening wagon camp, Tall Bull and Eight Smokes towing the long string of pack mules. Barlow had, through White Bear, briefed them on how to mark the trail for the wagons, what to look for in a nooning spot, and a rough distance for finding a site for the night camp. Dawn had still not fully broken, and the emigrants had not really seen them leave.

Half a mile west of the camp, the group divided. Tall Bull and Eight Smokes continued mostly west, though beginning to angle a little way southwest, taking the pack mules with them. Barlow, White Bear, Little Leaf, and Derek, with Buffalo 2 trotting alongside Barlow's mule, Beelzebub, splashed across the wide, shallow Platte River and headed northwest. The two adults were silent as they traveled, thinking about the task they faced—and remembering a similar one that had lasted far longer than either of them had expected. But the two youths chatted rather amiably, using English for the most part, though Little Leaf soon began teaching Derek some Shoshoni.

After an hour or so of steady riding, they stopped. White Bear dismounted and searched the ground carefully, eyes examining everything. He spotted some familiar signs and called to his friend. Barlow climbed down off the mule and knelt next to the Shoshoni, who pointed to the signs so that Barlow would be able to recognize them as easily as White Bear could.

They remounted and rode on again, unconsciously pressing a little harder as they kept their eyes on the tracks the Crows had left a few days before. They also paid attention to the rising bank of clouds that had formed to the west and were approaching them, pushed ahead by a strong breeze. Neither wanted the rain, which would wipe out much—if not all—of the Crow sign, but both knew it was coming. The best they could hope for would be to get as far as possible after their quarry before the storm arrived. And hope that it passed quickly.

The rain, when it did come, hit hard and fast. It was a drenching downpour that pounded at them, as if trying to drive them into the ground. The wind, unfettered by tree or bush, whistled across the rolling prairie, buffeting them with powerful gusts. The wind and the rain—combined with the mud the latter quickly produced—made traveling not just miserable, but an ordeal. Still, there was no place to stop in safety, no site that would offer any protection from the raging elements.

Soon lightning began shooting down from the sky in jagged, brilliant bursts, lending an eerie atmosphere to the landscape. Heavy rolls of thunder boomed and cracked, adding to the wretchedness of the day's travel.

The two men and two youths pulled their blankets or coats around them as the temperature sank, and hunched their necks to keep the rain from slithering down their backs. And they rode on stoically, irritated at the vehemence of the storm, but fully aware that they could do nothing at all about it.

They finally gave up on traveling and called a halt. They had still found no shelter, but continuing to ride into the teeth of the storm was doing them no good whatsoever, and was likely to hurt the animals. They stopped, unsaddled their mounts, and sat, eating a miserable meal of jerky.

20

"IS THIS DAMN rain ever gonna quit?" Derek grumbled. When no one paid him any heed, he repeated it, much more loudly, to make sure the others could hear him over the driving rain, rampaging wind, and booming of thunder.

Barlow, White Bear, and Little Leaf swiveled their heads toward the youth and simply glared at him. None of them could see that an answer to such a foolish question was necessary.

They had spent a miserable night out in the open, not sleeping much with the pouring rain and the noise, hunkered down in their heavy coats or blankets, not talking. Despite the thick wool of their garments, water still managed to slip down the backs of their necks, and they ended up sitting in puddles as often or not, since they could not squat or stand forever. The temperature inched steadily down, adding to their general misery.

Dawn, such as it was, finally arrived, announced only by a faint graying of the darkness.

"Well, old chap," White Bear said, pushing himself up and pulling his blanket a little tighter around him, "sitting

around here in this bloody storm isn't doing any good."
He began saddling his pony.

Barlow got up, too, and silently cursing the foul
weather, slapped the saddle blanket on Beelzebub, then
the saddle on top of it. The two youths, Little Leaf and
Derek, did the same.

Soon they were riding out, splashing across the prairie,
horse and mule hooves often slipping on the mud under
the blanket of water that coated most of the plains. Thick
rivulets cascaded down each rise, often pooling at the bottom. Where there were no pools, the grass was flattened
down and slick.

After several hours of riding—broken by an occasional
spell of a few minutes when the rain seemed to lighten
up, thus breeding a brief, though always forlorn, sense of
hope—Derek made his plaintive query. And was ignored
by his fellow riders.

The trail they had been following was gone long since,
and White Bear, who was nominally leading the small
group of travelers, went by instinct. He hoped that the
Crows were also being hampered by the storm and that
when it finally stopped—as it most certainly would, he
kept assuring himself—he would be able to pick up the
sign of his quarry again quickly.

By early afternoon there were occasional breaks in
the downpour, though it never really did stop raining—
the thunderous roar of the downpour simply eased up for
a short spell now and then. Still, it was encouraging. An
hour or so later, they spotted some trees, and soon after,
had entered a thick copse than ran for some yards alongside a fast-running, now rather swollen river.

"How's about we stop here?" Derek questioned. Since
his snub this morning, he had ridden in silence, half sul-
len, half frightened that he had turned everyone against
him for all time. But he needed a rest, and hoped that
voicing his desire would not be considered too harshly by
his heartier companions.

Barlow pulled to a stop and looked at the trees and the

cover they would provide. "The boy makes sense, White Bear," he said. "We need rest—and more importantly, some decent food—and the animals could use a break."

White Bear, who had traveled on a few yards, stopped and looked back at him, ready to argue. Then he realized that doing so would only prove him to be foolish. Barlow was right, and they would gain nothing, really, by continuing to push on under these conditions. It was not as if they had any chance of catching the Crows with another hour or two of hard riding. He nodded. Then he rode up alongside Little Leaf and spoke to him in their own language.

Little Leaf nodded, and rode off.

"Where's he goin', Uncle Will?" Derek asked.

"Make meat, I reckon," Barlow responded. "With any luck, we'll have fresh meat." He turned Beelzebub's head and moved into the cover of the cottonwoods and willows. Plenty of rain still dripped through the thick leaves and heavy branches, but it was damn near dry as far as they were concerned after having spent the previous night out in the open in the midst of the storm.

"You go fetch us some good firewood and such, boy," Barlow said to Derek as they dismounted. "Then get us a fire goin', pronto."

"Pronto?"

"Fast. Now go on and do it, boy," Barlow growled, his temper not far below the surface because of his annoyance at the storm. "I'll see to your horse for now."

By the time he and White Bear had unsaddled the mule and two horses and tended them, Derek had a fire started under the widespread branches of a cottonwood, near to the trunk, where it would offer the most protection from the weather, and a pot of coffee on to boil.

Minutes later, Little Leaf rode in, a bloody deer carcass draped over his pony behind him. He and White Bear swiftly and expertly began butchering the meat out, while Barlow tended to the young Shoshoni's pony.

Before long, chunks and strips of meat were hanging

over the fire, sizzling, sending out enticing aromas as fat dripped into the flames, sending up little sparkles of embers and sound.

Hungry, they all dug in long before the meat had more than gotten seared a bit on the edges. They didn't care. It was warm and full of life-giving richness. But once the first pangs of hunger were laid to rest, they sat back and waited until the meat got a little more done—or at least until it was fairly hot all the way through—and they ate more slowly. They held off as long as they could on pouring themselves coffee, wanting it as hot and thick and potent as they could get it.

Finally, however, they were pretty well sated, and they leaned back, glad to be out of the rain, for the most part, their bellies full, sipping of cups of hot black coffee. Barlow and the two Indians pulled out pipes, filled them and lit them.

"You got an extra pipe, Uncle Will?" Derek asked hopefully.

"Over in my pack there, boy," Barlow said. With the propensity of these small clay pipes to breaking, he always had a couple of extra ones with him.

The youth rummaged around in Barlow's possible sack for a minute, found a pipe, then came back to the fire. He sat and held out his hand, waiting.

"Damn, boy, you want me to light it and smoke it for you, too?" Barlow grumbled good-naturedly as he handed over his twist of tobacco.

"I reckon I can handle those things my own self," Derek said with a grin. He tore off a bit of tobacco, and handed the twist back to Barlow. Then he stuffed the crunchy black leaves into the pipe bowl, lit them with a burning twig from the fire, and sat back, sucking in smoke happily.

The men were quiet then, puffing pipes and sipping coffee. Under the protection of the leafy canopy, the rain seemed far away, with even the sound masked somewhat by the rush of the river so close by. The cracking of thunder frequently, though ever so briefly, overrode even the noise of the water. And the still-frequent lightning lent an eerie cast to the landscape.

Buffalo 2 lay close to Barlow, his back against the outside of his master's thigh. The dog was nervous with all the noise and the lightning, and was comforted by Barlow's occasional petting.

"How far ahead you think them Crows are, White Bear?" Derek asked, not happy with all the silence—or, rather, the lack of talking.

"I have no bloody idea, mate," the Shoshoni said in tones far more surly than he had wanted to use. Yet they were an accurate reflection of his annoyance and exasperation.

"They're probably as caught up in this storm as we are, boy," Barlow interjected into the uneasy silence that had been born the moment White Bear had finished his short comment. "But with White Bear on their trail, it really don't matter how far ahead they are. Soon's the rain stops and the land starts dryin' out again, he'll pick up their trail in no time and we'll catch up to 'em soon after."

"But what if . . ." Derek started. He stopped, however, at the piercing glare Barlow shot at him. He stuck his pipe between his teeth and clamped down hard on it, angry and upset. It bothered him to be treated like a child, and he wasn't about to admit, even to himself, that that was what he was. At least out here. Besides, all he had done was to ask a question. Or try to. Since he was traveling with them—was one of them, and could be expected to fight alongside them when the Crows were found—he at least expected to receive an answer.

Barlow suspected what his nephew was feeling, but he knew the youth had to work through the new emotions rampaging through him on his own. He did not think he could explain to Derek—or that the youth would understand anyway—what it was like to have friends or loved ones in the hands of enemies, and what every delay in following them meant to you. He could not explain the anger that coursed through your veins at such times, or the incredible frustration you felt when you had to sit someplace while the captors of your people either got farther away or were given an opportunity to cover their tracks, or both, and you couldn't do anything about it. No, the boy was too young and inexperienced to understand such things.

Barlow plucked another piece of meat off a small stick braced over the fire and popped it in his mouth, savoring it. It wasn't buffalo meat, but deer meat was fine by him. And this was particularly succulent, considering he hadn't eaten a real meal since breaking his fast with the Ohlmsteads two mornings ago. This meat was hot and filling, and that was important now.

A few minutes later, however, he stretched, yawned, and rose. "It's robe time for this ol' chile," he announced, heading to get his sleeping robe. He spread it out away from the fire, under the thick branches of a tree, tugged off his gun belt and set it inside the robe, then slid in and sighed. He was asleep in seconds.

Derek wondered how his uncle could fall asleep so easily despite the rain still coming down, the sizzling bolts of lightning, the pealing thunder, the rush of the river. As he prepared his own bedroll and got into it, he realized that White Bear and Little Leaf had done the same. He had never really noticed that before. He lay there for a long time, still simmering in anger at his treatment by White Bear and the others, before he, too, was asleep.

The three others were awake and feeding on deer meat and coffee when he opened his eyes in the morning. He got up, trying to rub the remnants of sleep off his face. He crawled out of his bedroll and shivered in the cold. He realized with a sinking feeling that it was still raining, and the day was uniformly gray and dismal. He took a seat by the fire, grabbed his tin mug, and eagerly reached for the coffeepot.

"You thinkin' of movin' out today, hoss?" Barlow asked around bites of meat.

"Bloody right I am," White Bear grunted. "Are you thinking otherwise, old chap?"

"Not so much thinkin' different, hoss, as wonderin' what good it'll do to ride on through this damn storm."

"Just making up time, old chap," White Bear countered. "We might not know where the bloody Crows are, but we can get closer to their country."

Barlow shrugged. "I think we'd be wastin' our time, hoss," he said. "Even if we ain't in their country right now, we're close enough that they'll know it pretty well."

"And what's that supposed to bloody mean, old chap?" White Bear asked with a bite to his voice.

"It means, hoss," Barlow replied with a sigh of exasperation, "that they'll know where the best places are for lyin' low till the storm passes. They'll be well rested and dry and once the weather clears, they can move fast for home. We'll just be out there wonderin' around, wearin' our animals down, gettin' drenched for no damn good reason."

White Bear waited some moments before responding, as if considering what he would say. When he spoke, his tone again was sharp. "Did I ask you to bloody sit and wait for good weather when we were lookin' for Anna, old chap? Or did I ride through bloomin' snowstorms and rainstorms and hailstorms and every other kind of bloody mean weather whenever you wanted to be on the trail?"

Barlow was taken aback by his friend's vehemence. That swiftly gave way to anger combined with hurt. What White Bear had said was true to a large extent, but Barlow was appalled at having it thrown in his face like that, especially in front of others. He was also bothered because White Bear had always been the one with sense—the one to keep him from doing something foolish like charging off in some direction looking for Anna even if there was no real reason to do so.

He fought back the rising anger, then said as calmly as he could manage, "There's one big difference, hoss."

"And what's that, old chap?" White Bear asked tightly.

"Anna was my daughter. My own flesh and blood. And her ma and brother was kilt when she was taken."

"What bloody difference does that make?"

"Weren't nobody kilt in your village when your people was took," Barlow said flatly. "And it weren't really none of your kin. Not really. Not like Anna was—is."

The two glared at each other, their friendship wilting under the heat of their sudden anger and the flicker of hatred that had grown. The tension rose as the silence spread.

Finally, Little Leaf said in English, speaking slowly, unsure of his words and wanting everyone to understand, "I'm ready to go whenever you are, White Bear. But maybe this time you should listen to your friend." He emphasized the last word.

Barlow and White Bear turned to look at the young warrior. Little Leaf refused to be intimidated or to worry that he was overstepping his bounds with his elders. "You told me many times of the experiences you had with this white man," he continued, his voice even, his tone neutral. "You should not let your friendship die over something like an argument over whether to sit out a storm for another day."

White Bear continued to glower at the young warrior for some moments, before turning his gaze back to Barlow. He didn't smile, but his face softened fractionally. "Don't you bloody well hate it when bloomin' little bastards are right, old chap?" he finally said.

21

LITTLE LEAF WENT out hunting again early in the afternoon, taking Derek's horse with him as a pack animal. He returned after little more than an hour with the horse packed high with buffalo meat, a fair portion of which went on the fire almost as fast as it was taken down from the horse.

"It appears you done right well, Little Leaf," Barlow said as he sliced off a hunk of seared-on-the-outside, raw-on-the-inside meat with his knife and then popped it into his mouth. "It's fine fat cow you brung us here, hoss."

The Shoshoni youth nodded stoically, but he could not hide the pleasure in his eyes at the compliment.

"Lo, the bloody great hunter," White Bear said with a heavy measure of sarcasm.

The words instantly wiped the joy from Little Leaf's eyes, leaving him looking slightly wounded.

Barlow considered reprimanding his friend for the harsh words to the young warrior, but decided against it. He could understand White Bear's attitude, and the underlying annoyance and frustration that bred it. Plus Little Leaf would have to learn that life sometimes hit on a man pretty hard, and one had to learn to bear up under it. Being on the receiving end of an insulting comment, even one from a trusted mentor, was not the end of the world. Little Leaf would get over it, and in doing so, probably would become a better and stronger man.

So, instead of saying anything, he just winked at Little Leaf, much to the young man's surprise, and gave him a small grin. He sliced off another piece of meat and chewed slowly. After a pipe, he pulled his hat down over his eyes, leaned back against his saddle, and fell asleep.

The rain began to taper off in the afternoon, and White Bear's moroseness lifted a little, knowing that soon he would be on the trail again.

The men whiled away the afternoon hours in various tasks—Barlow and Derek casting rifle and pistol balls from lead to replenish the ones they had used in the two months on the trail with the wagon train; Little Leaf working on a few arrows he had started a week before leaving his village; and White Bear aimlessly, endlessly sharpening his knife and tomahawk.

The four ate buffalo meat, some of which was constantly sizzling over the fire, and drank the potent black coffee whenever they had a mind to. They cast frequent glances at the sky through the leaves overhead, and began to see occasional patches of blue amid the still-thick black and gray clouds.

By dawn, the rain had stopped, and the sky was a light gray edging toward blue. With little fuss and no real talking, the four—and the big dog—ate. Then the men silently saddled their animals and quickly rode out. White Bear once again led them northwest, toward the yet-far-off Bighorn Mountains, the heart of Crow country. The Crows who had raided the Shoshoni village would head there, and White Bear thought that within a couple of days—if they had no more rain—he would be able to find sign of the band of men he and his friends were chasing.

White Bear soon began riding out ahead of the others, eyes scouring the ground ahead, looking for any clue that the Crows he sought had passed this way. But it was hopeless, at least for now. With all the rain they had had, the enemy warriors could have been by here an hour ago and no sign would be left.

So it was an even surlier White Bear who called a halt for the night in the late afternoon. The day had turned hot, which was the only real bright spot, as it would help the ground to dry out quickly. But even that bit of good fortune could not ease White Bear's anger and frustration.

Figuring it was time that Derek was given some responsibility—and the opportunity to prove something of what he was made of—Barlow had pulled him aside early in the afternoon. "Go out an make some meat, boy," he ordered.

"Do what?" Derek asked, confused.

"Make meat, boy. It's what I've been callin' huntin' and such since we been out here. You know that."

"I know what you mean," the youth said a bit huffily. "I just . . ." He paused. "I just didn't think you'd trust me to do it is all," he finally finished.

"You wanted adventure, boy," Barlow said gruffly. "Here's a start to it, maybe. Now go on and do what I say." As Derek began to trot away, Barlow called him back. "You remember what I taught you about finding animal sign?"

Derek nodded.

"And findin' your way around out here in these empty places?" Barlow demanded.

Once more Derek nodded.

"Then go on, boy. And don't you come back with empty hands neither."

Wide-eyed in wonder and worry, Derek turned his horse's head and trotted off, hoping he was up to the task that had been set before him. It had always been easy under Barlow's watchful eyes, but now that he was going to be by himself, he was no longer sure that finding game, shooting an animal, and butchering it was going to be easy. Plus he would have to do it with the possibility that some hostile Crows might be roaming through the area. Adventure was one thing; fighting off a few Crows all by himself was an entirely different matter.

The youth was pretty proud of himself, therefore, when he caught up with the others after having slain a buffalo and butchering out forty pounds of the best cuts of meat. And he had done so quickly and efficiently—and most importantly, with no trouble from hostile Indians or fierce animals.

His joy soured when Barlow looked at him and said evenly, "Took you long enough, boy."

"But I . . ."

"No need to lie and make up pitiful excuses, boy. It's mighty apparent you took your own sweet time," Barlow said, successfully hiding a grin.

The youth suddenly turned glum, earning a sympathetic look—quickly hidden—from Little Leaf.

"He's just teasing you, you bloody damn fool," White Bear snapped, the needling increasing his already considerable irritation.

Derek, slightly shocked, glanced at Barlow, who put on an air of innocence, refusing to look at his nephew.

Little Leaf rode up alongside Derek and playfully jabbed him in the side, grinning widely. The white youth returned it, suddenly feeling considerably better. As he rode along, he began to realize that his uncle's bantering was designed to let him know that in some small way that he was becoming accepted; that he was a part of this little group of manhunters. Not fully accepted, he knew, though somewhat. That was enough for now, however. And Derek was determined to show his uncle and the Shoshonis, when the time came, that he was worthy of their complete acceptance. With head high, and proud heart, he trotted on, chatting at times with Little Leaf, at other times just thinking of what things would be like when they caught up with the Crows. Such thoughts were exciting, but a bit scary, too, though he could not really believe that Barlow,

White Bear, and Little Leaf would have any trouble defeating any group of Crows.

With the storm having passed and the cloud cover gone, the temperature rose fast and significantly. The heat beating on the substantial amount of water that remained on the ground created a miasma of steam that made traveling an increasingly uncomfortable activity. The men sweated heavily under the unrelenting sun amid the humidity.

It did nothing to lessen their annoyance in general, and indeed, in some ways increased it. By the time White Bear called a halt for the night, they were all in a pique, White Bear most of all. He took care of his pony after barking out orders for Little Leaf to gather wood and start a fire. Then he plopped down at the fire and sat, stone-faced and surly, waiting for the meat and coffee to be done.

Barlow kept a wary eye on his friend as he ate. The Shoshoni was silent, though that was not unusual under the circumstances; even the young men were talking little. Barlow was exasperated, too, though not, of course, as much as his friend. He could well understand White Bear's aggravation; he had felt it many times himself in his quest for Anna. The fruitless searching frayed a man's nerves, ate at him, until he began to wonder if he would ever succeed. He would begin to question himself, and question whether he was really up to the task. He would worry that he was going to fail his loved ones—and himself.

Because he understood it all so well, he could not—would not—say anything to his friend. Besides, berating him for such natural feelings under the circumstances would do no good anyway, and was as likely to increase the vexation White Bear was feeling as anything else. So Barlow kept his silence, stewing in his own exasperation and worry.

It went on like that for a couple of more days, the men all growing more irascible. It was only with a great force of will on everyone's part that they kept from any number of physical altercations. Hardly a word was exchanged by any of them, other than orders that Barlow or White Bear occasionally gave to the youths. Even the youths had almost stopped chatting entirely. Not that they were cantankerous; it was more that they were almost afraid to speak in front of their elders, lest they be reproached by them.

Then, in the middle of the afternoon two days later, White Bear stopped and dismounted. He spent ten minutes scrutinizing the ground, then remounted his pony.

"Well?" Barlow questioned, letting some of his vexation leak out in the single word.

"A lot of bloody Crow sign, old chap," White Bear growled. "It's all over the bloomin' place."

"I can see that my own self, hoss," Barlow answered in kind. "Is there any sign of the bastards we're after?"

"No, there's no bloody sign of the goddamn bloody bastard Crows we're after," White Bear said, his anger and frustration boiling over into his voice.

Barlow ignored the harsh tone. "We're makin' progress, hoss," he said evenly. "Now that the ground's dried up enough to start really readin' sign again—and the fact that we're startin' to see Crow sign all over creation—means it won't be long before we come on the track of the ones we want, hoss."

"You're awful bloody cheerful under the circumstances, old chap," White Bear responded, his voice no less blunt than it had been.

Barlow shrugged. "You know damn well it's only a matter of time now, hoss. A couple of them ponies have such distinctive markin's that pickin' up their sign won't be hard."

"That's bloody barmy, old chap, and you bloomin' well know it," the Shoshoni said, his voice dripping with exasperation.

With an effort, Barlow bit back the several retorts that bubbled up inside him. Instead, he said lamely, managing to keep his voice even, "Just push on, hoss."

Behind them, Derek looked over at Little Leaf and

whispered, "I hope we find them Crows soon. We don't, they're likely to bust and go agin each other like a couple of wild dogs."

Little Leaf nodded in agreement. He was worried, too, but had so far been successful in hiding it. But he knew things could not go on the way they were for much longer before there was an explosion between the old friends, and that could be disastrous. He knew White Bear well, and while he had met Barlow only a short few days ago, he had heard enough about him to feel he knew him, too. And the two were hard as well as hardheaded. If they went at each other, it would not be a pleasant sight.

The tension between Barlow and White Bear rose through the rest of the afternoon, and was almost palpable by the time they made camp that night.

Little Leaf had gotten something of a reprieve earlier when White Bear ordered him to go find meat for the night. But he was wary when he returned, not sure how things would be between the two older men. And he and Derek tiptoed around the camp that night, not wanting to risk treading on the frayed nerves of their elders. Even Buffalo 2 remained rather shy, sticking close to his master, but keeping a watchful eye on him all the same.

Things were no better in the morning. Breakfast was quickly eaten and the small group soon on the trail. A surly White Bear rode a little in front of the others, his head bent as his eyes scanned the ground, looking for sign of his quarry.

Barlow had to forcefully make him stop about midday. "The animals need rest and water," Barlow said sharply.

White Bear was going to argue, then realized Barlow was right, even though he did not like to admit it.

After letting the ponies and Beelzebub breathe for a while, and drink from the remnants of a stream, the men remounted and rode on, White Bear once again taking the lead some yards ahead of the others.

But White Bear found no sign of the men he was hunting, and he finally, grudgingly, called a halt for the night.

The Shoshoni seemed to Barlow to be more despondent than angry or frustrated as he sat by the fire. He ate with a desultory attitude, seeming not to care about the food—or anything else.

"You ain't aimin' to give up, are you, hoss?" Barlow asked quietly though pointedly.

White Bear raised his head, turning sad eyes on his friend. "Not yet, old chap," he said wearily.

Barlow nodded. "Glad to hear it, hoss," he commented. Then he lightened his tone a little. "We'll find them critters, White Bear," he said. "Don't you fear."

White Bear shrugged and went back to his melancholy feeding.

The Shoshoni still seemed despondent in the morning. But he took the lead again, and seemed to be every bit as observant to possible sign as he always had been.

Barlow was relieved to see it, but he continued to closely watch the Shoshoni for any indication that he might be losing his attentiveness. That wore thin after a few hours, though, and Barlow almost began to doze in the saddle. He jerked awake at a shout from White Bear. "You find somethin', hoss?" he asked, his tiredness evaporating. He hurried toward where the Shoshoni had just jumped off his pony and knelt.

22

"IT'S THEM ALL right, hoss," Barlow acknowledged as he squatted next to White Bear. "Damn if it ain't."

"I know, old chap. I bloody well know." For the first time in days, White Bear sounded almost excited. He rose. "Let's go, old chap. They're only half a day ahead of us. We might be able to bloody well catch them before nightfall."

As Barlow climbed up into the saddle on Beelzebub, he decided not to tell White Bear he was being overly optimistic in his assessment as to how long it would take to find the Crows. He did not want to destroy White Bear's newfound elation. Besides, there was always the possibility that the Shoshoni was right; now that the Crows were in their homeland again, they might very well be traveling slowly, or would stop early for the night or something.

As they traveled on, pushing harder now, Barlow could feel his own excitement starting to increase. He looked forward to finding the Crows, to rescuing the women and child, and then getting back to the wagon train. He wanted this to end; memories of the long, often-fruitless search for Anna were still fresh in his mind. He did not want this to drag on indefinitely.

Derek and Little Leaf picked up on their elders' renewed enthusiasm, and while they tried not to show it too much, began gabbing a little with each other again. Even Buffalo 2 perked up as the big Newfoundland sensed the change in attitude.

The excitement continued throughout the day, and even when they stopped for the night. White Bear ate more heartily than he had the past couple of nights. He still didn't have much to say, but eagerness burned in his eyes for everyone to see.

Barlow, anticipating White Bear's eagerness to be on the move, was up before dawn the next morning and had meat roasting and coffee heating. As soon as White Bear began to stir, Barlow roused the two youths. The three of them got the mule, horse, and two ponies saddled and ready, though White Bear was awake and moving before they finished. They all hurried through their meal, wanting to get on the trail as quickly as possible. After eating, it took only minutes to douse the fire, pack up their few cups and coffeepot, and mount their animals.

An eager Buffalo 2 headed out ahead of the men, though White Bear quickly caught up to him. The man watched the land while the dog sniffed his way along, seeming to know now who was being hunted.

Riding Beelzebub, Barlow stayed back a little ways from his friend and dog, watching them with a bemused smile on his face. A certainty caught spark inside him and began to grow steadily that today would be the day they found their quarry. He glanced over at the two youths, wondering how well they would do in battle. He was pretty sure Little Leaf would be fine, but he did not know about his nephew. Derek had never been in anything even remotely like a battle with hostile Indians—men who were well hardened to war. He hoped that Derek would be all right.

Derek didn't seem at all concerned. He and Little Leaf

talked as they rode, their bodies indicating expectation and eagerness. With the sense of invincibility that seemed inherent in all males their age, they could not conceive that they would be harmed.

They were in the foothills at the far southern end of the Bighorn Mountains now, and the land was generally slanted upward, though not so steeply as to make the traveling difficult, for the most part. It flattened out with some frequency, and in some places, the land even dipped a little.

With White Bear's head tilted to constantly watch the ground, Barlow kept his eyes focused on the horizon, swiveling his head slowly to take it all in, except in the direction from which they had just come. Late in the morning, he stopped, and stood in his stirrups. He leaned a little forward and squinted, staring across the open landscape. Then he nodded once, satisfied that he had seen something.

Plopping his backside back into the saddle, he slapped the mule on the rump and trotted up to White Bear and stopped him. "Over yonder," he said, pointing to the north, when the Shoshoni looked at him with a question in his eyes. "There's smoke, hoss."

White Bear shaded his eyes with a hand and stared hard in the direction Barlow had pointed. "Small bloody fire producing it, old chap," he said after a few moments.

"Campfire, or maybe cook fire," Barlow announced.

They paid no heed to the two youths, who had ridden up and stopped. Derek and Little Leaf sat on their horses and looked into the distance, trying to spot the smoke their elders were talking about.

"I think you're right, old chap." White Bear paused, fighting to control the burst of excitement that surged through him. "It's likely them, don't you think?"

"Likely is," Barlow agreed. "The sign we're followin' is headin' right that way."

"Then let's bloody go, old chap," White Bear said, eagerness shining in his dark eyes.

"Don't go rushin' off now, hoss," Barlow warned. "We don't know how far off they are, how many of them there are, and what kind of defensive position they might have."

"Going bloody yellow on me, old friend?" White Bear asked, not entirely in jest.

"C'mon, hoss," Barlow said derisively. "That's such a damn-fool statement it don't even merit a response."

"Then why're you bloody well hesitating to go on over there and rub out those bloomin' Crows?" White Bear demanded.

"Now, I never said no such thing, and you damn well know it, hoss," Barlow retorted. "All I'm sayin' is that it'd be a damn fool thing to just go chargin' on over there not knowin' anything about those critters or how they're fortified. We just need to take it slow, scout out their camp, and then do what we have to do." He paused. "Hell, we ain't even sure it's the critters we want."

"That doesn't matter," White Bear said sourly. "They're Crows, and that's all I need to know."

"I don't mind killin' Crows no more'n you do, hoss," Barlow said, growing a little heated. "But if they ain't the ones we want, and one of 'em escapes and spreads the alarm, we're gonna be ass-deep in angry warriors. They'd either put us all under or send us skedaddlin' back to where we come from, and we'd never find them kinfolk of yours."

White Bear shrugged, unwilling to acknowledge the sense of Barlow's statement.

"Look, hoss," Barlow said, calming a little, "I ain't rode all this way just to have my hair raised by them goddamn Crows. Now, I'll fight the entire Crow nation if'n that's what it takes to get your people back. But I'll be damned if I'm gonna lose my hair for no goddamn good reason."

"You know, old chap," White Bear said in resignation, "you're a great bloody goddamn annoyance when you make sense." He paused and sighed. "All right, mate, we'll do it your way. But," he added, looking pointedly at Barlow, "I sure as bloody hell hope it's the ones I want."

"So do I, hoss," Barlow agreed. "So do I." He could understand White Bear's desire to have this quest over, and to rescue his fellow Shoshonis. Once the captives were ensconced in a Crow village somewhere, they would be so much harder to find—and to save. And chasing after them was becoming mighty wearying on them all.

Barlow climbed down off Beelzebub. "Let's give the animals a bit of a rest before we press on," he said, not really waiting to see if White Bear agreed or not. He loosened the saddle a little, letting Beelzebub breathe.

The others followed suit.

Barlow knelt and called Buffalo 2 over to him. When the dog came and sat in front of him, Barlow petted the big dog's head. The Newfoundland's tail whisked briskly back and forth, sending up some dust and pieces of grass.

"We're gettin' close, Buffler," Barlow said quietly. "We're gonna need your help to find them critters we're lookin' for. So you be a good boy and keep our nose in the wind for us. Understand?"

The dog's tail wagged a bit faster, and his tongue lolled. He didn't appear to understand at all, but Barlow was not worried. Buffalo 2 had never failed him in any quest or in any order he was given.

Barlow rose and stood, looking around. He stared for a while, making sure the smoke was still there. Five minutes later, he and the others climbed back into their saddles after tightening them.

They rode toward the smoke, which seemed to be at least a couple of miles off. Despite their eagerness, they traveled slowly. Without having to follow the sign, they could all keep their eyes on the land around them rather than the ground right in front of them. No one said anything, but it was understood that they had better be on the lookout for any Crows who might be coming their way.

The heat bore down on them as they rode, but they paid it—and the resultant sweat—little mind. They were too near the end of their quest, or so they hoped, to worry about such minor inconveniences as blistering temperatures and perspiration.

Time seemed to drag as they rode slowly along, spreading out a little to try to keep to a minimum any dust they might kick up. Barlow was glad the land was still thick with short, green grass. It, too, helped keep them from stirring up any dust, which might give them away.

It seemed to take forever, but finally they seemed to be making real progress toward the smoke, which they eventually saw rising in two thin spirals. When that became apparent, Barlow trotted over to White Bear. "Looks like two fires, hoss," he said.

White Bear grunted acknowledgment.

"Means there's more of 'em than there were when they raided your village," Barlow added. "If it's them."

White Bear glanced sharply at his friend. He had been so focused on getting to the enemy—and what he would do to them when he arrived—that he had thought of little else.

"No reason why three warriors so near to home would make two fires," Barlow reasoned.

White Bear pondered that for some seconds, then nodded. "Noted, old chap," he said flatly. It was good to be forewarned, though he would not be deterred in doing what he had to do.

Early in the afternoon, they could clearly see the streams of smoke, and knew they were getting close. They stopped on the southeast side of a rise and dismounted.

"Derek, you and Little Leaf stay here with the animals," Barlow ordered. "Me'n White Bear're gonna take us a look-see from up on the ridge there." He pointed, though it was unnecessary. "Keep your eyes open, boys. There's liable to be Crows all over the place here."

"What'll we do if we see some, Uncle Will?" Derek asked. He looked rather pale.

"Little Leaf will know what to do, old chap," White

Bear said. "You just bloody listen to him and you'll be all right."

"Yessir," Derck said with a gulp.

"You stay here with the boys, Buffler," Barlow ordered. Then he and White Bear turned and headed up the hill, which they soon found to be far stonier than it had looked at first. Still, plenty of grass covered it, and the rocks were little problem until the two men had neared the top and dropped to hands and knees and scrabbled to the crest.

At the top, they slithered on their bellies to where the ridge began to head down again. Barlow set his hat aside, and then he and White Bear crept the last few feet to where they could look down on whatever kind of Crow camp was there.

They scanned the small encampment, trying to spot the captives, to make sure they had the right group of Crows, for there were a number of Crow warriors there.

It was more than a minute before White Bear pointed. "There," he said. "The one with her hair loose is my sister, Yellow Deer. The other's my wife's sister, Lost Bird."

"I don't see the chile," Barlow noted.

"Me either," White Bear grunted.

"Girl or a boy?" Barlow asked. "You never did say."

"Girl. Falls Plenty. Bloody cute little thing." His voice was tight with worry. He hoped that the two-year-old was simply asleep, curled up under a tree.

Barlow knew what White Bear was thinking. It would not be past the Crows to have killed the child rather than drag her along if she had proved to be a problem.

They continued scanning the camp, trying to make out the number of Crows, as well as the number of pines around. There were two fires set among the trees. Clumps of ponies were interspersed with open areas and little thickets along a small river. To their left from the two men's vantage point, they could see a herd of horses grazing on the lush grass in a glade encircled by trees, heavily on the south and west, less so most of the rest of the way, and almost not at all along the river.

Soon, Barlow said, "I count eleven of them critters—eight warriors and three about the age of Derek or Little Leaf."

White Bear nodded. "I counted the same. The bloody young ones are probably on their first war trail." He paused a heartbeat. "And it's going to be their bloody last, too," he vowed.

Barlow didn't think that needed a response. The youths there were Crows and were in a camp holding two—and hopefully three—Shoshoni captives. They would have to suffer the consequences.

After ten more minutes of watching, the two heard a child's cry, quickly stifled. Since they could no longer see Lost Bird, they assumed that the woman had fed the child her breast. Barlow and White Bear looked at each other in relief.

"Appears like our medicine's gettin' strong again, hoss," Barlow said flatly.

"It's about bloody goddamn time," White Bear responded.

"Well, hoss, what do you want to do?" Barlow asked. "Go get the boys and hit 'em now? Or wait till dark, then try to slip in and get your people out of there? Or even wait till just before dawn and do it?"

White Bear continued staring down the hill while he thought that over. Each way had its good points. While he wanted to punish the Crows, getting Yellow Deer, Lost Bird, and Falls Plenty out of the camp alive was just as important. And he wanted his ponies back, if at all possible. Waiting until just after dark would probably be easiest for accomplishing the rescue and stealing back the horses, but in the dark, with two youths—one of whom had never been in such a situation—with them, it could be risky. They could wind up killing one of their own small group if chaos broke out. The same was true about waiting until just before dawn.

White Bear sucked in a big breath and then let it slowly out. "I suppose it's best that we move on those bloody bastards as soon as we can." He pointed to his left. "Little Leaf and Derek can come around that way and slip into the bloomin' camp, get the women and child, and get the hell out." He paused. "You and I can approach the bloody camp from the same direction, making our way through the trees, and take on those bloomin' bastards."

Barlow nodded, all seriousness. He did not question White Bear's idea of just the two of them attacking eleven Crows. They would do what they had to; it was that simple. Besides, they knew that Little Leaf, at the least, would join the battle as soon as he and Derek got the women and child to safety. In fact, he would tell Derek to stay with the rescued captives while Little Leaf came to help him and White Bear fight the Crows.

"Once we take care of those bloody Crows, we can get my stolen ponies—as well as any of theirs that're around."

"Reckon that suits this chile, hoss," Barlow said.

They scrabbled backward across the crest of the ridge, then turned and slinked downward a little. Soon they rose and strode down the rest of the way to where Derek and Little Leaf waited.

23

"YOU STAY HERE and watch the animals, Buffler," Barlow, who was kneeling, told the big dog, as he petted the Newfoundland's head. "We'll be back before long."

Derek would have thought his uncle was mad, except that he had seen the dog do some amazing things in the time he had been with Barlow. He was somewhat surprised, though, to see the dog cock his head, as if asking a question.

"We'll come back and get you before the doin's start, boy," Barlow said to the dog. He rose, still running a big hand over the canine's head, scratching behind the ears. He looked around, then said, "Let's go." He turned and headed back up the ridge, White Bear by his side and the two youths close behind.

Minutes later, all four were lying on the crest of the hill where Barlow and White Bear had lain not long ago. Barlow was on the left, with Derek to his right, then Little Leaf, and White Bear on the far right. They waited until White Bear spotted the captives again and pointed. Barlow nodded.

"You see the women, boys?" Barlow asked. When Derek and Little Leaf nodded, he said, "It's your task to get them out of the camp and back to where the horses are. Me'n White Bear'll attack the Crows and keep 'em occupied whilst you're rescuing the captives."

"But I want to be with you and Will when you two . . ." Little Leaf started.

White Bear spoke sharply—though briefly—to the youth in their own language.

"What'd White Bear say to Little Leaf, Uncle Will?" Derek asked, looking at Barlow.

"I told him he should bloody well shut up and listen to his betters," White Bear responded harshly, drawing Derek's attention, and glaring at the youth when he had it. He glanced over at Barlow. "Continue, old chap."

"Once you boys get the women and that li'l chile out of those critters' camp and back to our horses, Derek, you stay with 'em all and watch over 'em. Little Leaf, you can come on and join me and White Bear in our doin's against the Crows."

Little Leaf suddenly beamed.

Derek stared at his uncle, unsure of what he should be feeling. He wanted adventure, and here was some in the offing. But it was not what he expected. He wanted—or so he had always thought—a chance to fight hostile Indians. But he was glad in a way that he would not have to fight. On the other hand, he didn't want to be left out of the action. Still, the responsibility of watching over the rescued captives was not something to be taken lightly. He had no experience in fighting Indians, to be sure, so he could not expect to be trusted in the midst of battle. Yet to be trusted with the task he was given was still more than he really could have expected.

"You listenin', boy?" Barlow demanded, glaring at Derek.

With a pang of guilt, the young man nodded and tried to focus his attention on what his uncle was saying.

"You boys see where this ridge heads down over yonder?" Barlow said more than asked, while pointing to his left. He and White Bear had determined earlier that there was no one really guarding the horses, so that way would be clear for them. They were not surprised to have discovered that, considering that the Crows were deep in their own country and most likely figured that any Shoshoni pursuit that had been mounted would have long ago been called off.

"Me'n White Bear'll attack them from that way," Barlow continued. "You'll foller us from the same way, once we engage the Crows. We should be able to drive them devils away from you and the captives. You can grab the captives and get yourselves back the way you came, which'll be safest."

Derek and Little Leaf nodded solemnly. The former was more than a little worried, but he was determined to acquit himself well; the latter was eager.

The four lay there a few minutes longer, trying to fix the look of the camp in their minds. Then they slithered back down the hill to the horses and mule. Buffalo 2 stood there, tail whipping back and forth. Barlow patted the dog on the head.

Silently, they mounted their animals and took a few moments to check their weapons. Satisfied, they rode southwest along the bottom of the ridge as it tapered to almost nothing. They cut around it and into the trees, now heading northwest. The ridge rose to their right, angling away from them the more they worked their way through the trees.

They eased their way around the herd, not wanting to stir up any concern among the ponies, which would alert the Crows. As they moved past the herd, White Bear tossed coveting glances at the animals. He was determined to get back the ponies stolen from his village, as well as take those belonging to the Crows. He turned his head forward again. There was time for that later. First, the Crow warriors had to be driven off or eliminated.

Buffalo 2 stopped occasionally and sniffed the air, his nose working furiously. Then he would glance at Barlow, who continued riding, so the dog would trot after him.

A few yards farther on, the men stopped and dismounted. White Bear tapped Little Leaf, then Derek on the shoulder, and pointed in the direction of where they had last seen the captives. The two youths nodded and moved off, Little Leaf smoothly silent; Derek trying with all his might to move without making any noise.

White Bear looked at Barlow. "Well, are you ready, old chap?" he asked.

Barlow nodded once, then shook his head. He looked at his rifle, then decided it would be more of a nuisance than a help in the relatively tight confines in which he would be battling the Crows. He slid the rifle into the scabbard hanging from the saddle on Beelzebub. He nodded once again, sharply. "Now I'm ready, hoss," he said.

With Buffalo 2 between them, the two men moved off, slipping from tree to tree, heading toward where the two Crow campfires were. Within a minute they could hear the Crows talking, though it was yet another minute or so before they could make out words, even if they could not understand what was being said.

Barlow pulled a Colt Walker and, using the covering sound of a burst of laughter from the Crows, thumbed back the hammer. He glanced over at White Bear, who nodded. Barlow raised the pistol and fired, sending a .44-caliber lead ball smashing into the back of a Crow's head.

The other Crows froze for a moment, not sure exactly what had happened, and when they did, not knowing where the attack had come from.

Barlow fired again, just as the Crows began to move uncertainly. The pistol ball winged one of the warriors in the arm. Cursing, Barlow fired again, killing the wounded Crow.

The Crows scattered like leaves blowing in a high wind. White Bear burst out from behind the tree, charging after one fleeing enemy. Before the Crow could disappear into the cover of trees and brush, White Bear had caught up with him, grabbing the Crow by his hair, which flowed almost to his knees. He jerked the warrior's head back, and his knife flashed in the sunlight before slicing the enemy's throat, sending a fount of blood spurting into the air. To show his disdain for the Crows, White Bear knelt and within a few seconds, had made several precise cuts around the dead warrior's head and popped the scalp off with a loud sucking sound. He tossed it down, then cast his eyes around, looking for another Crow to attack.

Barlow was only a second behind his friend in charging out from behind his cover, with Buffalo 2 alongside— then swiftly ahead of—him. The dog pounced on a fleeing Crow's back, knocking the man down. The warrior tumbled on the grass, with the Newfoundland trying to latch his fangs onto him. The Crow managed to pull his knife and slashed at the dog. The canine darted back, unscathed, then bolted forward again, with the warrior flailing wildly with the knife, trying desperately to slash the dog.

Still running, Barlow glanced over and saw the Crow trying to kill Buffalo 2. He skidded to a stop, his feet almost sliding out from under him on the grass, and fired at the Indian. He missed the first shot, but managed to put the second ball through the man's face, forcing a bloody scream from the man. When Barlow saw Buffalo 2 dart in to finish the warrior off, Barlow spun and ran off again.

He had gotten only a few feet when he instinctively ducked. A Crow war club whooshed past his head, missing by a scant inch or two. Off balance from the maneuver, Barlow tumbled to the ground, grunting with the impact. He thrust himself over onto his back. Raising the pistol in his right hand, he swept back the hammer with the palm of his left. As the Crow leaped toward him, he fired.

The impact of the ball snapped the Indian backward, bent at the waist, and brought him to a halt. A moment later, he collapsed, blood still pouring from the hole in his chest and a bigger hole from the exit wound in his back.

Barlow scrambled up and shoved the pistol into his holster. He looked around, searching for the next enemy to fight. Through the trees, he could see White Bear pound the life out of a Crow with his tomahawk, then carve off the scalp. Barlow looked down at the warrior he had just killed, and for a moment considered taking the scalp. But he decided against it. He never had been one for doing such a thing, and he could see no reason to do so now.

He heard Buffalo 2 barking, then the rumble of horses beginning to run. "White Bear!" he bellowed. "The herd!" He charged off toward where the Crows had been keeping their horses.

When he got there, the horses were gone, and he could hear Buffalo 2 barking in their wake as the herd headed up the ridge to his left. He stopped for a moment, breathing heavily, checking the area around him. He saw no Crows.

White Bear puffed to a halt beside him. Barlow pointed to the hill. White Bear nodded, and the two men ran, racing around trees, leaping over downed logs and brush, until they were clear of the foliage. They continued racing up the hill, though they could see Buffalo 2 chasing the horse herd around the fall end of the ridge to his right.

One of White Bear's feet hit a loose rock and he fell hard, then rolled back to the bottom of the hill. Yelling British curses as well as what passed for swear words in Shoshoni, he got back up and started running again.

Barlow spared only a glance at his friend as he continued charging up the grass-covered, stony ridge. He reached the crest and stormed across it, then began plunging downward, his ankles and knees taking a terrific pounding. He took in the scene with a glance that was blurry and jumpy from his running.

Two Crows had managed to stop the horse herd and were trying to mount a couple of ponies. Buffalo 2, dashing back and forth after them, preventing them from doing so.

Two other enemy warriors—one of them a youth— were grappling with Little Leaf. An ashen-faced Derek was battling another Crow—an adult warrior—as he fiercely tried to protect the two women, who cowered on the ground behind him, one with a child in her arms.

Barlow wanted to help his nephew, but Little Leaf was closer and taking on two Crows instead of one. So Barlow continued running, and then barreled into all three of them, sending them all sprawling with arms and legs flailing wildly.

One of the Crows was up first, and kicked Barlow in the side as he tried to rise, knocking him over on his side. Barlow rolled a couple of times and came to his feet, reaching for the still-loaded Walker. But it was gone, lost in the wild tumble. Cursing, he started sliding out his tomahawk, but the Crow who had kicked him leaped at him, knife in hand.

Barlow blocked the thrust of the knife with his arm, but suffered a long, shallow slash in the doing. He swung his right forearm awkwardly, leaving the tomahawk still half stuck in his belt, and slammed the Crow across the forehead, knocking him back several steps.

Barlow went back to trying to yank out his tomahawk, but it was being contrary, having gotten partly turned and hung up in all the action. He finally gave up on it and pulled his knife instead, warily watching the Crow, who was regaining his equilibrium. He took two steps toward the warrior, and then with great surprise saw the Crow pitch forward toward him, a startled look in his suddenly dying eyes.

The Crow stumbled into the knife that Barlow had instinctively thrust out. The warrior released a final sigh, and then softly collapsed to the ground. Barlow watched him fall, then looked up.

"Thought you might need some bloody help, old chap," a panting White Bear said, squatting to wipe his knife blade clean in the back of the Crow's shirt.

Barlow nodded crisply, then spun, ready to charge off and help Derek.

But the youth did not need any help. Not with the warrior he had been battling at least. The Crow lay dead at his feet. Derek, smoking Colt Paterson in hand, stood there, his face sickly-looking. He glanced up and tried to grin, but failed. He looked as if he was ready to vomit.

Barlow turned back, but Little Leaf had killed the other Crow. Barlow began running after White Bear, who was racing toward the milling herd of horses. The last two Crows saw them coming, almost instantly joined by Little Leaf, and they give up their idea of trying to get the horse herd moving. They simply sprinted in different directions, splitting Buffalo 2's attention. One managed to mount a pony, then distracted the dog, while the other leaped on a horse. They whipped the animals into a run, galloping away from these wild men—and wilder dog—as fast as they could.

"Buffler, no!" Barlow bellowed at the Newfoundland, who had started racing after the fleeing Crows.

The Newfoundland stopped and trotted back, barking at the horses, preventing them from following the warriors.

Barlow, White Bear, and Little Leaf got to the herd, and despite being out of breath, they began moving among the horses—which had sometime during the melee been joined by Beelzebub, Derek's horse, and the two Shoshonis' ponies—trying to quiet them. Barlow headed toward his big mule first, and got the animal settled down, which helped soothe the horses.

It took more than half an hour, but they finally had the horses calm enough to where they thought they could leave the animals without worrying about them bolting off across the prairie. To be sure they didn't, though, Barlow said, "You watch over them horses, Buffler. Don't let 'em go wanderin' off."

Then he and the others headed toward Derek and the former captives. Barlow stopped in front of the former, while the two Shoshonis went to check on the latter.

Derek was sitting now, with his knees up, wrists resting on them, but he still held the pistol in his hand. His head sort of hung between his knees. He looked up as the others approached, and even managed what might have been called a slight smile.

"You done well, boy," Barlow said, squatting in front of him.

"I . . . I killed a man, Uncle Will," Derek said, his voice filled with wonder and sickness.

"He was a Crow, boy," Barlow said just a bit harshly, "and that means that in this case, he was an enemy. What he and his amigos did was bad doin's."

"I know, Uncle Will, but still . . ."

"Killin' a man ain't ever easy the first time, boy," Barlow said in a monotone.

"It gets easier?" Derek asked, eyes wide. He didn't know what to think of that notion.

"I reckon it does," Barlow said uncomfortably. "In some accounts anyways." He hesitated, then continued. "But that don't mean a man has to take a likin' to it. It just means a man gets more used to doin' what needs doin' is all."

Derek nodded, still unsure what to think. He was no longer certain, either, that he wanted more adventure. Not if it meant feeling this bad when it was over.

When Derek shifted his arm, Barlow noticed blood on his shirt. "You're hurt, boy," he said, surprised.

Derek looked at his side and shrugged. "It ain't much, Uncle Will," he said firmly. "I been hurt worse workin' on Pa's farm."

"I best take a look at it, though," Barlow said. He pushed Derek's arm out of the way, and with his fingers parted his shirt where it had been slit open by a knife. "You're right, boy, it ain't much," he pronounced. "It's hardly more'n a scratch." He paused, and offered his nephew a little grin. "You know, boy, when I said you done well, it weren't just because you rubbed out one of those damned Crows. It was 'cause you took on a responsible task—just as important a task as any of the rest of us—and did just fine with it. You helped rescue them women and that li'l chile there, and then you protected 'em from them hair-raisin' sons of bitches takin' 'em back. Not bad for a feller who ain't ever faced such hard doin's before."

"I did good then, Uncle Will?" Derek asked, his eyes brightening quite a bit.

"You did good, boy," Barlow affirmed. He rose and held out his hand. When Derek took it, he pulled the youth up. "Best clean your pistol, then reload it, boy," the man said. "Never can tell when you might have call to use it again." He winked at Derek.

Taking his own advice, Barlow wandered off to find his Colt Walkers. When he did, he cleaned and reloaded them.

While he sat there doing so, White Bear said, "I do believe there's a bloody good camp right over the hill, old chaps. I say we make use of it."

Barlow nodded. "Hey, Little Leaf," he said, "how's about you go on over there and drag them Crow bodies out of the way of the camp. Dump 'em in the river, if you have to."

Little Leaf nodded. Then with a grin he asked, "You want to help, Derek?"

Gulping, the white youth agreed, not wanting to seem squeamish in front of his new friend.

The two mounted their horses and galloped off, whooping wildly in their youthful exuberance.

Before long, the two were back. They all got the women on horses, and then the four men drove the herd around the hill and back to the pasture where they had been, and hobbled them. The women, who had accepted their captivity with a fair amount of stoicism, had for the most part sloughed off the ordeal already. They quickly and efficiently set about preparing a meal for the men who had rescued them.

24

AFTER EATING, WHITE Bear headed off to the herd, where he spent some time looking over the animals. Barlow preferred to stay where he was, at the fire, relaxing with a mug of coffee and a pipe of strong tobacco. And enjoying the view of the two women working around the camp. White Bear's sister, Yellow Deer, was a beautiful young woman with finely crafted features, full, desirable lips, and deep, dark eyes. Her simple buckskin dress was covered with dirt, grease, ash, and some blood, and it was worn through in spots. But that did not detract from her lovely, lithe figure.

It had been a week since he had been with Dora Lee Openshaw, and that week had been a hard one physically and mentally. He could do with a roll in the robes with her right now, but she was, of course, far away. Yellow Deer, on the other hand, was right here, and would make a delightful replacement, even if only temporary, he thought.

She caught him looking at him, and he smiled brazenly. She lowered her eyes quickly, but not before he noticed a spark of interest in her dark eyes.

Before Barlow could follow up on Yellow Deer's potential invitation, White Bear strolled back to the fire. "Derek," he intoned, seemingly all serious, "come with me."

Derek glanced at Barlow, suddenly looking quite nervous.

Barlow shrugged, and indicated with a jerk of his chin that his nephew should go with the Shoshoni.

Trying not to seem too frightened or uncertain, Derek rose and went with White Bear as he headed back toward the herd.

After a moment, Barlow and Little Leaf stood and followed them, wondering what was going to happen. Barlow knew it wouldn't be anything bad; he was just curious. Buffalo 2, lying on his side a few feet from the fire, raised his head, then plopped it back down again, ready for more sleep. There was nothing the humans were doing that interested him at the moment.

White Bear stopped and turned to face Derek, who halted beside him. "You were a bloody big help, old chap," White Bear said to the young man. "You never fought a bloomin' deadly battle before today, yet you risked your life for a couple of Shoshonis you never met. I'm bloody well honored to know you, old chap."

"I'm . . ." Derek started, embarrassed.

White Bear held up his hand, stopping the youth. "All that I've said is true. And to show my appreciation for your help, I think you should have one of these fine ponies." Before Derek could respond, White Bear pointed. "I think that reddish pinto over there would be a good choice, old chap. He seems to be well-broken and without a temper."

"I don't know what to say, White Bear," Derek stammered. "I . . ."

White Bear smiled and clapped the young man on the shoulder. "It's all right, old chap," he said. "Now, go pick out a pony." He grinned even more widely. "You, too, Little Leaf," he added. "Go pick out a pony, too. You deserve it, too."

Laughing a little, Barlow and White Bear headed back to the fire, leaving the two youths happily looking over the captured Crow horses, cheerfully debating each one's good points and bad.

The two men sat at the fire and took more coffee. As they sipped, Barlow said, "Yellow Deer seems to have some interest in this ol' chile. You mind if I approach her?"

"Why ask me, old chap?" White Bear countered.

"She's your sister."

White Bear shrugged. "She's old enough to make up her own bloody mind on such things, old chap. You should know that."

Barlow grinned. "Just wanted to make sure you weren't gonna go loco on me if she and I had a tumble in the robes."

"No bother at all, old chap." He paused, then grinned. "In fact, I was thinking of doing the same bloody thing with Lost Bird."

"I can see why," Barlow commented, reflecting on the woman's smooth, dusky skin, high-cheekboned face, and pleasant smile. He thought nothing of the fact that she was White Bear's wife's sister. Marrying a wife's sister was not all that uncommon, and this was not much different, all in all.

After some minutes of silence, Barlow said, "That was a nice thing you did for Derek, hoss."

White Bear shrugged. "As I told him, he bloody well deserved it. If it wasn't for him, that one bloomin' goddamn Crow would've likely killed Yellow Deer, Lost Bird, and Falls Plenty. Tell you the truth, old chap," he added with a sly grin, "one pony isn't enough."

Barlow laughed. "He'll be more'n satisfied with the one. Plus he'll have some real tales to tell when we get back to the wagon train. I reckon there's a few young ladies gonna take a fresh good look at that ol' hoss."

"He deserves that, too," White Bear said with a chuckle. "And, I suppose he'll handle those girls as well as he did that Crow, even though I suppose he has no more experience with women than he did with battling enemy warriors."

"I reckon you're right on that," Barlow agreed.

A few minutes later, White Bear rose and wandered off, leaving Barlow sitting there, half dozing. At one point, Barlow lifted lazy eyelids and spotted his friend talking with the two women. He went back to his rest.

When he returned and sat, White Bear said, "Yellow Deer will join you in the robes tonight, old chap."

"That what you were doin', hoss," Barlow asked, "talkin' them women into such doin's?"

"Of course."

It was not long before Barlow professed himself ready for his robes. As the boys had returned, still so excited that they showed little sign of going to sleep any time soon, Barlow and White Bear took their sleeping robes a little way off for privacy. No sooner had Barlow shucked his weapons belt and clothes and slid into the robes than Yellow Deer walked quietly up.

She bent and slipped off her moccasins and leggings. Done with that, she smiled warmly down at Barlow as she undid the ties to her dress at each shoulder and let the garment fall to the ground. She stood there unashamed in the fast-fading sunlight for a few moments to allow Barlow to enjoy a good long look at her.

"You shine, woman," he breathed in application. "Plumb shine." He stopped, then asked, "You speak or understand English?"

"Some," she acknowledged. "White Bear teach."

Barlow nodded, then held aside the thick buffalo robe he used for sleeping, inviting her in.

She smiled again and joined him, sliding her short, slender body alongside his. Before long, the soft, insistent music of their lovemaking mingled in the air over the camp with the similar sounds emitted by White Bear and Lost Bird.

Those songs were repeated three times during that evening before sleep overtook them.

"We best be on the move soon, hoss," Barlow said to White Bear over breakfast the next morning.

White Bear nodded, but Derek asked, "Why?"

"We're still deep in Crow country, boy," Barlow said. "Them two who got away yesterday just might get to some village and raise them a war party to come back here and raise our hair."

Derek suddenly looked concerned.

"Don't fret, boy. It'd likely take 'em a little while to do anything. But it ain't a good idea to loiter here."

After eating, the group swiftly broke camp and moved out, heading roughly due south. Barlow and Little Leaf rode out ahead, guiding the way and keeping an eye out for any sign of approaching Crows. The two women followed a little behind them, riding on recovered Shoshoni ponies. Lost Bird carried her child, Falls Plenty, on her back in the cradleboard. The horse herd came next, being driven and kept in line by White Bear and Derek. White Bear was not thrilled by having to ride at the end of the caravan, eating dust kicked up by the many hooves, but he and Barlow had decided that leaving the herding of the horses to the two youths would not be a wise idea, especially while still in Crow country.

They did not dally any, but they did not push too hard either, just moved at a strong, steady pace. Each afternoon, either Derek or Little Leaf would break off from the group, taking an extra horse with him, and go looking for fresh meat. With summer full upon them, and the grass still thick, finding game was no problem, and they ate well.

There were plenty of streams on their route, so their nightly camps were well-watered and had plenty of wood for cook fires. The women managed to find a plethora of ripe berries, as well as nuts, roots, and herbs to supplement and season the meat.

The days were hot under the unrelenting sun, but the nights were pleasant, especially for Barlow and White Bear, who enjoyed the company of the women.

Barlow was rather silent on the morning of the fifth day after they had left the Crow camp as he and the other males ate breakfast. Buffalo 2 had gotten up and wandered off, hunting for his own breakfast, Barlow figured.

"Something eating at you, old chap?" White Bear asked him, looking at his friend suspiciously, but with a touch of concern.

Barlow looked over at his nephew. "Go check on the animals, boy," he ordered.

"But, Uncle Will . . ."

"Just do what I say, boy," Barlow said, not harshly, but not all that kindly either. "And take Little Leaf with you."

The Shoshoni youth looked at White Bear, who shrugged and then nodded, indicating Little Leaf should do as he was told.

When the two youths had left, White Bear asked, "So, old chap, just what the bloody hell is going on?"

"Somethin' we were talkin' about the other day back in that Crow camp's been on my mind," Barlow said. He paused. "Remember when we was talkin' about Derek impressin' some of those young women when we get back?"

"Of course, old chap. You don't think he will?"

"Oh, I'm sure he will. But you brought up the fact that he has no experience with women. At least as far as I know, and I really doubt it." He paused again. "We pale-faces, by and large, ain't so free with sexual doin's as you red devils are."

"I learned that while I was being raised among you bloody white eyes, old chap," White Bear said dryly.

Barlow smiled a little. "Reckon you did."

"Why worry about him, old chap?" White Bear said. "Those bloomin' white-eyes girls won't know the difference." He smiled slyly.

"Reckon that's true, hoss," Barlow allowed. "But with

a wee bit of trainin', he can go round breakin' hearts from here to the Oregon country," he said, brightening a little.

"So what would you bloody well like to do about his situ . . . ?" White Bear stopped and looked over at Lost Bird and Yellow Deer. Then he looked back at Barlow, eyes wide. "Are you thinking . . . ?"

Barlow nodded, unsure of how he felt about it, and even more uncertain about how White Bear would take it.

The Shoshoni sat there for some seconds, mulling that over. Then, slowly, a grin began to spread across his face. "By Jove, old chap, I think you may have hit on something here," he said.

"You don't mind?" Barlow asked.

"Well, old chap, it's not as if I'm plannin' to marry him and one of those women off." He grinned lopsidedly. "Besides, I expect you figure to have Yellow Deer again before we get back to that bloody wagon train of yours."

"So you think Yellow Deer'd be better for him?" Barlow asked, beginning to have second thoughts.

White Bear shrugged. "Don't matter. He can have Lost Bird, if you'd rather. Just remember that I bloody well intend to have her again before we get back to the village."

Barlow liked that thought better, since it would leave Yellow Deer for him.

Then White Bear sighed and offered another lopsided grin. "Well, hell, old chap, since we're going to do this bloomin' thing, I suppose we should allow Little Leaf to get some experience, too. He probably has some already, but a man can never have enough of that kind of experience."

"Them're mighty true words, hoss," Barlow agreed.

"I'll arrange it," White Bear said, having second thoughts of his own now.

It was a strange night for Barlow, trying to sleep in his empty robes while hearing Derek being instructed in the art of lovemaking by Yellow Deer, and the accompanying sounds of Little Leaf and Lost Bird together.

So he was pretty grouchy when he sat at the fire the next morning and poured himself a mug of coffee. He glanced over the rim of his tin mug at White Bear, who looked to be in no better cheer than he did.

The two boys soon arrived, full of cheer, laughing and jostling each other, crowing and just plain being cocky kids in their teens impressed with their own prowess.

"Don't you boys go'n get too full of yourselves," Barlow growled. "Yellow Deer's goin' back to gracin' my sleepin' robes again tonight, and thereafter. I expect White Bear feels the same about Lost Bird."

Derek and Little Leaf went from joy to crestfallen in a blink.

"Don't be so bloody gloomy about it all, mates," White Bear said. "I'd say we're no more than a day or two from hooking up with that bloomin' wagon train again, which'll put an end to all this foolishness anyway."

With the resilience of youth, the two young men were soon happily joking with each other again.

White Bear's estimate was close, and midway through the afternoon of the following day, the small group stopped and waited when they spotted Tall Bull, who had a string of empty pack mules with him. The Shoshoni rode up to them and they exchanged greetings. They had cut the Oregon Trail several miles west, and were able to determine that the wagons had not passed there yet, so they began heading east.

White Bear and Tall Bull talked for a few minutes in Shoshoni, then White Bear told the others, "The wagons're a couple of miles behind. Tall Bull was just about to start the day's bloody hunting."

"How's about Little Leaf and Derek go with Tall Bull to help with the huntin' and bucherin', White Bear. Me and you can head back on up the trail with the horses and the women and find us a night spot. Maybe that place near where we cut the trail earlier today."

White Bear nodded, and Tall Bull and the two youths rode off, heading southwest. Barlow, White Bear, the two women and the child, plus Buffalo 2 and the horse herd, headed west, back the way they had come. A couple of hours later, they found the spot they'd thought would do, and began setting up a camp.

Before long, Tall Bull, Derek, and Little Leaf returned, the mules laden with buffalo meat. Not long after they had finished butchering the meat and dividing it into piles for distribution to the emigrants, Mattias Ohlmstead's wagon creaked into view, and then to a stop.

"Vell, I'll be," Ohlmstead said. "I vas beginning to t'ink maybe you vouldn't be coming back."

The return was cause for a grand celebration that night, with music and feasting and sessions of tall-tale-telling. Derek regaled his cousin with stories of his adventures, and then disappeared into the darkness with a girl about his age.

When it came time for bed, far later than most of the people were used to, Barlow was caught in something of a quandary. But Yellow Deer had vanished, so Barlow did not have to try to explain to Dora Lee Openshaw about the Indian woman. Barlow found out in the morning that White Bear had made sure that Yellow Deer was in the Shoshoni camp, somewhat outside the main camp of wagons.

Dora Lee was happy to see Barlow, and she showed him just how much once they had hit the sleeping robes. Barlow realized after their second round of lovemaking that night that he was pretty happy to be back with her, too.

The parting with White Bear and his Shoshonis was much harder for Barlow, and for Derek. But they had little time for long farewells, so they said what they had to say, and then the Shoshonis headed southwest. Barlow and

Derek, riding out to begin the day's guiding and hunting, accompanied the Indians for a short way, and then turned west, marking the trail for the wagons.

As Barlow stopped for a few moments to watch the Shoshonis riding away, he wondered if he would ever see White Bear again. And almost immediately realized how much he was going to miss his good friend. He shook his head and moved on. He had a job to do, and he was determined to see it through.

WILDGUN

THE HARD-DRIVING WESTERN SERIES
FROM THE CREATORS OF *LONGARM*

Jack Hanson

Oregon Trail	0-515-13470-8
Winter Hunt	0-515-13408-2
End of the Hunt	0-515-12998-4
War Scout	0-515-12930-5
Blood Trail	0-515-12870-8
Hostile Country	0-515-12788-4
Vengeance Trail	0-515-12732-9
Wildgun: The Novel	0-515-12656-X

Round 'em all up!

Available wherever books are sold or
to order call 1-800-788-6262

B061

PETER BRANDVOLD

series featuring Sheriff Ben Stillman